2.50
Firm

ALSO BY BORIS AKUNIN

The Winter Queen

Murder on the Leviathan

BORIS AKUNIN

TRANSLATED BY ANDREW BROMFIELD

Random House   New York

MURDER ON THE
LEVIATHAN

A Novel

Translation copyright © 2004 by Random House, Inc.

All rights reserved under International and Pan-American Copyright
Conventions. Published in the United States by Random House,
an imprint of The Random House Publishing Group, a division
of Random House, Inc., New York, and simultaneously in Canada by
Random House of Canada Limited, Toronto.

RANDOM HOUSE and colophon are registered trademarks
of Random House, Inc.

This work was originally published in Russian in 1998.
Copyright © 1998 by Boris Akunin.

Library of Congress Cataloging-in-Publication Data
Akunin, B. (Boris)
[Leviafan. English]
Murder on the Leviathan: a novel/Boris Akunin; translated by Andrew Bromfield.
p. cm.
ISBN 1-4000-6051-6
I. Bromfield, Andrew. II. Title.
PG3478.K78 L4813 2004
891.73'5—dc22 2003070379

Printed in the United States of America on acid-free paper
Random House website address: www.atrandom.com
2 4 6 8 9 7 5 3 1
First Edition

Murder on the Leviathan

*Record of an examination of the scene of the crime
carried out on the evening of March 15, 1878,
in the mansion of Lord Littleby on the Rue de Grenelle
(Seventh Arrondissement of the city of Paris)*

[*A brief extract*]

. . . For reasons unknown, the household staff were gathered in the pantry, which is located on the ground floor of the mansion to the left of the entrance hall (room 3 on diagram 1). The precise locations of the bodies are indicated on diagram 4, where:

No. 1—the body of the butler, Étienne Delarue, age 48,

No. 2—the body of the housekeeper, Laura Bernard, age 54,

No. 3—the body of the master's manservant, Marcel Prout, age 28,

No. 4—the body of the butler's son, Luc Delarue, age 11,

No. 5—the body of the maid, Arlette Foche, age 19,

No. 6—the body of the housekeeper's granddaughter, Anne-Marie Bernard, age 6,

No. 7—the position of the security guard Jean Lesage, age 42 years, who died in the Saint-Lazare hospital on the morning of March 16 without regaining consciousness,

No. 8—the body of the security guard Patrick Trois-Bras, age 29,

No. 9—the body of the porter, Jean Carpentier, age 40.

The bodies shown as Nos. 1–6 are in sitting positions around the large kitchen table. Nos. 1–3 have frozen with their heads lowered on their crossed arms; No. 4's cheek is lying on his hands; No. 5 is reclining against the back of her chair; No. 6 is in a kneeling position beside No. 2. The faces of Nos. 1–6 are calm, without any indication whatever of fear or suffering. On the other hand, Nos. 7–9, as the diagram shows, are lying at a distance from the table, and No. 7 is holding a whistle in his hand. However, none of the neighbors heard the sound of a whistle yesterday evening. The faces of Nos. 8 and 9 are set in expressions of horror, or at the very least of extreme astonishment (photographs will be provided tomorrow morning). There are no signs of a struggle. A rapid examination also failed to reveal any sign of injury to the bodies. The cause of death cannot be determined without a postmortem. From the degree of rigor mortis, the forensic medical specialist, Maître Bernhem, determined that death occurred at various times between ten o'clock in the evening (No. 6) and six o'clock in the morning, while No. 7, as stated above, died later in the hospital. Anticipating the results of the medical examination, I venture to surmise that all the victims were exposed to a potent and fast-acting poison inducing a narcotic effect, and the time at which their hearts stopped beating depended either on the dose of poison received or the physical strength of each victim.

The front door of the mansion was closed but not locked. However, the window of the conservatory (item 8 on diagram 1) bears clear indications of a forced entry: The glass is broken and in the narrow strip of loose cultivated soil below it is the indistinct imprint of a man's shoe with a sole 26 centimeters in length, a pointed toe, and a steel-shod heel (photographs will be provided). The felon probably gained entry to the house via the garden only after the servants had been poisoned and sank into slumber; otherwise they would certainly have heard the sound of breaking glass. It remains unclear, however, why, after the servants had been rendered harmless, the perpetrator found it necessary to enter the house through the garden when he could quite easily have walked through into the house from the pantry. In any event, the perpetrator made his way from the conservatory up to the second floor, where Lord Littleby's personal apartments are located (see diagram 2). As the diagram shows, the left-hand section of the second floor consists of only two rooms: a hall housing a collection of Indian curios and the master's bedroom, which communicates directly with the hall. Lord Littleby's body is indicated on diagram 2 as No. 10 (see also the outline drawing). His lordship was dressed in a smoking jacket and woollen pantaloons and his right foot was heavily bandaged. An initial examination of the body indicates that death occurred as a result of an extraordinarily powerful blow to the parietal region of the skull with a heavy oblong-shaped object. The blow was inflicted from the front. The carpet is spattered with blood and brain tissue to a distance of several meters from the body. Likewise spattered with blood is a broken glass display case that, according to its nameplate, previously contained a statuette of the Indian god Shiva (the inscription on the nameplate reads: "Bangalore, 2nd. half XVIII century, gold"). The missing sculpture was displayed against a background of painted Indian shawls, one of which is also missing.

FROM THE REPORT BY DR. BERNHEM ON THE RESULTS
OF PATHOLOGICAL AND ANATOMICAL EXAMINATION
OF THE BODIES REMOVED FROM THE RUE DE GRENELLE

. . . However, whereas the cause of Lord Littleby's death (body No. 10) is clear, the only aspect that may be regarded as unusual being the force of the blow, which shattered the cranium into seven fragments, in the case of Nos. 1–9 the picture was less obvious, requiring not only a postmortem, but also chemical analyses and laboratory investigation. The task was simplified to some extent by the fact that J. Lesage (No. 7) was still alive when he was initially examined. Certain typical indications (pinhole pupils, suppressed breathing, cold, clammy skin, rubefaction of the lips and earlobes) indicated a presumptive diagnosis of morphine poisoning. Unfortunately, during the initial examination at the scene of the crime we had proceeded on the apparently obvious assumption that the poison had been ingested perorally, and therefore only the victims' oral cavities and glottises were subjected to detailed scrutiny. Since no pathological indications were discovered, the forensic examination was unable to provide any conclusive answers. It was only during examination in the morgue that each of the nine deceased was discovered to possess a barely visible injection puncture on the inner flexion of the left elbow. Although it lies outside my sphere of competence, I can venture with reasonable certainty the hypothesis that the injections were administered by a person with considerable experience in such procedures: 1) the injections were administered with great skill and precision, and not one of the subjects bore any visible signs of hematoma; 2) since the normal interval before narcotic coma ensues is three minutes, all nine injections must have been administered within that period of time. Either there were several operatives involved (which is unlikely), or the single operative possessed truly remarkable skill—even if we are to assume he had prepared a loaded syringe for each victim in advance. Indeed, it is hard to imagine that a person in full possession of his faculties would offer his arm for an injection if he had just witnessed someone else lose consciousness as a result of the procedure. Admittedly, my assistant, Maître Jolie, believes that all these people could have been in a state of hypnotic trance, but in my many years in this line of work I have never encountered anything of the sort. Let me also draw the commissioner's attention to the fact that Nos. 7–9 were lying on the floor in poses clearly expressive of panic. I assume that these three were the last to receive the injection (or that they offered greater resistance to the narcotic) and that before they lost consciousness they realized something suspicious was happening to their companions. Laboratory analysis has demonstrated that each of the victims received a dose of morphine approximately three times in excess of the lethal threshold. Judging from the condition of the body of the little girl (No. 6), who must have been the first to die, the injections were administered between nine and ten o'clock on the evening of March 15.

TEN LIVES FOR A GOLDEN IDOL!
NIGHTMARE CRIME IN FASHIONABLE DISTRICT

Today, March 16, all Paris is talking of nothing but the spine-chilling crime that has shattered the decorous tranquillity of the aristocratic Rue de Grenelle. The Revue Parisienne's *correspondent was quick to arrive*

*at the scene of the crime and is prepared to satisfy the legitimate curiosity
of our readers.*

And so, as usual, shortly after seven o'clock this morning, postman
Jacques le Chien rang the doorbell of the elegant two-story mansion belonging to the well-known British collector, Lord Littleby.
M. Le Chien was surprised when the porter, Carpentier, who always
took in the post for his lordship in person, failed to open up, and,
noticing that the entrance door was slightly ajar, he stepped into
the hallway. A few moments later the seventy-year-old veteran of
the postal service ran back out into the street, howling wildly. Upon
being summoned to the house, the police discovered a scene from
the kingdom of Hades—seven servants and two children (the
eleven-year-old son of the butler and the six-year-old granddaughter of the housekeeper) lay in the embrace of eternal slumber. The
police ascended the stairs to the second floor, and there they discovered the master of the house, Lord Littleby, lying in a pool of
blood, murdered in the very repository that housed his celebrated
collection of oriental rarities. The fifty-five-year-old Englishman
was well known in the highest social circles of our capital. Despite
his reputation as an eccentric and unsociable individual, archeo-
logical scholars and orientalists respected Lord Littleby as a genuine connoisseur of Indian history and culture. Repeated attempts
by the directors of the Louvre to purchase items from the lord's di-
verse collection had been disdainfully rejected. The deceased prized
especially highly a golden statuette of Shiva, the value of which is
estimated by competent experts to be at least half a million francs.
A deeply mistrustful man, Lord Littleby was very much afraid of
thieves, and two armed guards were on duty in the repository day
and night.

It is not clear why the guards left their post and went down to
the ground floor. Nor is it clear what mysterious power the male-
factor was able to employ in order to subjugate all the inhabitants
of the house to his will without the slightest resistance (the police

suspect that use was made of some rapidly acting poison). It is clear, however, that he did not expect to find the master of the house himself at home, and his fiendish calculations were evidently thwarted. No doubt we should see in this the explanation for the bestial ferocity with which the venerable collector was slain. The murderer apparently fled the scene of the crime in panic, taking only the statuette and one of the painted shawls displayed in the same case. The shawl was evidently required to wrap the golden Shiva—otherwise the bright luster of the sculpture might have attracted the attention of some late-night passerby. Other valuables (of which the collection contains a goodly number) remained untouched. Your correspondent has ascertained that Lord Littleby was at home yesterday by chance, through a fatal confluence of circumstances. He had been due to depart that evening in order to take the waters, but a sudden attack of gout resulted in his trip being postponed—and condemned him to death.

The immense blasphemy and cynicism of the murders in the Rue de Grenelle defy the imagination. What contempt for human life! What monstrous cruelty! And for what? For a golden idol that it is now impossible to sell! If melted down, the Shiva will be transformed into an ordinary two-kilogram ingot of gold. A mere two hundred grams of yellow metal—such is the value placed by the criminal on each one of the ten souls who have perished. Well may we exclaim after Cicero: O tempora, o mores!

There is, however, reason to believe that this supremely heinous crime will not go unpunished. That most experienced of detectives at the Paris prefecture, M. Gustave Gauche, to whom the investigation has been entrusted, has confidentially informed your correspondent that the police are in possession of a certain important piece of evidence. The commissioner is absolutely certain that retribution will be swift. When asked whether the crime was committed by a member of the professional fraternity of thieves, M. Gauche smiled slyly into his gray mustache and enigmatically replied: "Oh, no, young man, the thread here leads into good society." Your humble servant was unable to extract so much as another word from him.

J. DU ROI

WHAT A CATCH!

THE GOLDEN SHIVA IS FOUND!

WAS THE "CRIME OF THE CENTURY"

IN THE RUE DE GRENELLE

THE WORK OF A MADMAN?

Yesterday, March 17, between five o'clock and six o'clock in the afternoon, thirteen-year-old Pierre B. was fishing by the Pont des Invalides when his hook became snagged so firmly at the bottom of the river that he was obliged to wade into the cold water. ("I'm not so stupid as to just throw away a genuine English hook!" the young fisherman told our reporter.) Pierre's valor was richly rewarded: The hook had not caught on some common tree root but on a weighty object half buried in the silt. Once extracted from the water, the object shone with an unearthly splendor, blinding the eyes of the astonished fisherman. Pierre's father, a retired army sergeant and veteran of the Battle of Sedan, guessed that it must be the famous golden Shiva for which ten people had been killed only two days earlier, and he handed in the find at the prefecture.

What are we to make of this? For some reason a criminal who did not baulk at the cold-blooded and deliberate murder of so many people has chosen not to profit from the spoils of his monstrous initiative! Police investigators and the public alike have been left guessing in the dark. The public appears inclined to believe that belated pangs of conscience must have led the murderer, aghast at the horror of his awful deed, to cast the golden idol into the river. Many go so far as to surmise that the miserable wretch also drowned himself somewhere nearby. The police, however, are less romantically inclined and discern clear indications of insanity in the inconsistency of the criminal's actions.

Shall we ever learn the true story behind this nightmarish and unfathomable case?

A BEVY
OF PARISIAN
BEAUTIES

A series of twenty photocards forwarded cash on delivery for a price of 3 fr. 99 cent., including the cost of postage. A unique offer! Hurry—this is a limited edition! Paris, Rue Cuypel, Patoux et Fils printing house.

PART ONE

PORT SAID
TO ADEN

Commissioner Gauche

AT PORT SAID another passenger boarded the *Leviathan,* occupying stateroom number eighteen, the last first-class cabin still vacant, and Gustave Gauche's mood immediately improved. The newcomer looked highly promising: that self-assured and unhurried way of carrying himself, that inscrutable expression on the handsome face. At first glance he seemed quite young, but when he removed his bowler hat, the hair on his temples was unexpectedly gray. A curious specimen, the commissioner decided. It was clear straight off that he had character and what they call "a past." All in all, definitely a client for papa Gauche.

The passenger walked up the gangway, swinging his shoulder bag, while the porters sweated as they struggled under the weight of his ample baggage: expensive suitcases that squeaked, high-quality pigskin traveling bags, huge bundles of books, and even a folding tricycle (one large wheel, two small ones, and an array of gleaming metal tubes). Bringing up the rear came two poor devils lugging an imposing set of gymnastic weights.

Gauche's heart, the heart of an old sleuth (as the commissioner himself was fond of testifying), had thrilled to the lure of the hunt when the newcomer proved to have no golden badge—neither on the silk lapel of his dandified summer coat, nor on his jacket, nor on his watch chain. Warmer now, very warm, thought Gauche, vigilantly scrutinizing the fop from beneath his bushy brows and puffing on his favorite clay pipe. But of course, why had he, old fool that he was, assumed the murderer would board the steamship at Southampton? The crime was committed on the fifteenth of March, and today was already the first of April. It would have been perfectly easy to reach Port Said while the *Leviathan* was rounding the western rim of Europe. And there you had it, everything fitted: the right kind of character for a client, plus a first-class ticket, plus the most important thing—no golden whale.

For some time Gauche's dreams had been haunted by that accursed badge with the abbreviated title of the Jasper-Artaud Partnership steamship company, and without exception his dreams had been uncommonly bad. Take the latest, for instance.

The commissioner was out boating with Mme. Gauche in the Bois de Boulogne. The sun was shining high in the sky and the birds were twittering in the trees. Suddenly a gigantic golden face with inanely goggling eyes loomed up over the treetops, opened cavernous jaws that could have accommodated the Arc de Triomphe with ease, and began sucking in the pond. Gauche broke into a sweat and laid on the oars. Meanwhile it transpired that events were not taking place in the park at all, but in the middle of a boundless ocean. The oars buckled like straws, Mme. Gauche was jabbing him painfully in the back with her umbrella, and an immense gleaming carcass blotted out the entire horizon. When it spouted a fountain that eclipsed half the sky, the commissioner woke up and began fumbling around on his bedside table with trembling fingers—where were his pipe and those matches?

Gauche had first laid eyes on the golden whale at the Rue de Grenelle, when he was examining Lord Littleby's earthly remains. The Englishman lay there with his mouth open in a soundless scream—his false teeth had come halfway out and his forehead was a bloody soufflé. Gauche squatted down: He thought he had caught a glimpse of gold glinting between the corpse's fingers. Taking a closer look, he chortled in delight. Here was a stroke of uncommonly good luck, the kind that occurred only in crime novels. The helpful corpse had literally handed the investigation an important clue—and not even on a plate, but in the palm of its hand. There you are, Gustave, take it. And may you die of shame if you dare let the person who smashed my head open get away, you old numskull.

The golden emblem (at first, of course, Gauche had not known that it was an emblem; he had thought it was a bracelet charm or a monogrammed hairpin) could only have belonged to the murderer. Naturally, just to be sure, the commissioner had shown the whale to the junior manservant (what a lucky lad—the fifteenth of March was his day off, and that had saved his life!), but the manservant had never seen his lordship with the trinket before.

After that the entire ponderous mechanism of the police system had whirred into action, flywheels twirling and pinions spinning, as the minister and the prefect threw their very finest forces into solving "the crime of the century." By the evening of the following day Gauche already knew that the three letters on the golden whale were not the initials of some prodigal hopelessly mired in debt, but the insignia of a newly established Franco-British shipping consortium. The whale proved to be the emblem of the miracle ship *Leviathan,* newly off the slipway at Bristol and currently being readied for its maiden voyage to India.

The newspapers had been trumpeting the praises of the gigantic steamship for more than a month. Now it transpired that on the eve of the *Leviathan*'s first sailing the London Mint had produced gold and silver commemorative badges: gold for the first-class passengers and senior officers of the ship, silver for second-class passengers and subalterns. Aboard this luxurious vessel, where the achievements of modern science were combined with an unprecedented degree of comfort, no provision at all was made for third class. The company guaranteed travelers a comprehensive service, making it unnecessary to take servants along on the voyage. "The shipping line's attentive valets and tactful maids are on hand to ensure that you feel entirely at home on the *Leviathan*," promised the advertisement printed in newspapers right across Europe. Those fortunate individuals who had booked a cabin for the first cruise from Southampton to Calcutta received a gold or silver whale with their ticket, according to their class—and a ticket could be booked in any major European port, from London to Constantinople.

Very well, then, having the emblem of the *Leviathan* was less useful than having the initials of its owner, but this only complicated matters slightly, the commissioner had reasoned. There was a strictly limited number of gold badges. All he had to do was to wait until the nineteenth of March (that was the day appointed for the triumphant first sailing), go to Southampton, board the steamer, and see which of the first-class passengers was missing a golden whale. Or else (this was more likely), which of the passengers who had laid out the money for a ticket failed to turn up for boarding. That would be papa Gauche's client. Simple as potato soup.

Gauche thoroughly disliked traveling, but this time he couldn't resist. He badly wanted to solve the Crime of the Century himself. Who could tell, they might just make him a superintendent at long last. He had only three years left to retirement. A third-class pension was one thing; a second-class pension was different altogether. The difference was one and a half thousand francs a year, and that kind of money didn't grow on trees.

So he had taken the job on. He thought he would just nip across to Southampton and then, at worst, sail as far as Le Havre (the first stop), where there would be gendarmes and reporters lined up on the quayside. A big headline in the *Revue Parisienne:* "Crime of the Century Solved: Our Police Rise to the Occasion." Or better yet: "Old Sleuth Gauche Pulls It Off!"

But ha! The first unpleasant surprise had been waiting for the commissioner at the shipping line office in Southampton, where he discovered that the infernally huge steamship had a hundred first-class cabins and ten senior officers. All the tickets had been sold: all hundred and thirty-two of them. And a gold badge had been issued with each one. Yes—a total of a hundred and forty-two suspects. But then, only one of them would have no badge, Gauche had reassured himself.

On the morning of the nineteenth of March, the commissioner, wrapped up against the damp wind in a warm woollen muffler, had been standing close to the gangway beside the captain, Mr. Josiah Cliff, and the first lieutenant, M. Charles Renier. They were greeting the passengers. The brass band played English and French marching tunes in turn, the crowd on the pier generated an excited buzz, and Gauche puffed away in a rising fury, biting down hard on his wholly blameless pipe. For, alas, due to the cold weather all the passengers were wearing raincoats, overcoats, greatcoats, or capotes. Just try figuring out who has a badge and who doesn't! That was unpleasant surprise number two.

Everyone due to board the steamship in Southampton had arrived, indicating that the criminal must have shown up for the sailing despite the loss of the badge. Evidently he must think policemen were total idiots. Or was he hoping to lose himself in the immense crowd? Or perhaps he simply had no other choice?

In any case, one thing was clear: Gauche would have to go as far as Le Havre. He had been allocated the cabin reserved for honored guests of the shipping line.

Immediately after the ship had sailed a banquet was held in the first-class grand salon, an event the commissioner had especially high hopes for, since the invitations bore the instruction "Admission on presentation of a gold badge or first-class ticket." Why would anyone bother to carry a ticket around when it was so much simpler to pin on your little gold leviathan?

At the banquet Gauche let his imagination run wild as he mentally frisked everyone present. He was even obliged to stick his nose into some ladies' décolletés to check whether they had anything dangling in there on a gold chain, perhaps a whale, perhaps simply a pendant. How could he not check?

Everyone was drinking champagne, nibbling on various savory delicacies from silver trays, and dancing, but Gauche was hard at work, eliminating from his list those who had their badge in place. The men caused him the biggest problems. Many of the swine had attached the whale to their watch chains or even stuck it in their waistcoat pockets, and the commissioner was obliged to inquire after the exact time on eleven occasions.

Surprise number three was that all the officers had their badges in place, but no less than four passengers were wearing no emblem, including two of the female sex! The blow that had cracked open Lord Littleby's skull like a nutshell was so powerful it could surely have been struck only by a man, and a man of exceptional strength at that. On the other hand, as a highly experienced specialist in criminal matters, the commissioner was well aware that in a fit of passion or hysterical excitement even the weakest of ladies was capable of performing genuine miracles. He had no need to look far for examples. Why, only last year a milliner from Neuilly, a frail little chit of a thing, had thrown her unfaithful lover out a fourth-floor window—and he had been a well-nourished rentier twice as fat and half as tall again as herself. So it would not do at all to eliminate women who happened to have no badge from the list of suspects. Although who had ever heard of a woman, especially a woman of good society, mastering the knack of administering injections like that?

With one thing and another, the investigation on board the *Leviathan* threatened to drag on, and so the commissioner had set about dealing with things in his customary thorough fashion. Captain Josiah Cliff was the only officer of the steamship who had been made privy to the secret investigation, and he had instructions from the management of the shipping company to afford the French guardian of the law every possible assistance. Gauche exploited this privilege quite unceremoniously by demanding that all individuals of interest to him be assigned to the same salon.

It should be explained at this point that, out of considerations of privacy and comfort (after all, the ship's advertisement had claimed: "On board, you will discover the atmosphere of a fine old English country estate"), those individuals traveling first-class were not expected to take their meals in the vast dining hall along with the six hundred bearers of democratic silver whales, but were assigned to their own comfortable "salons," each of which bore its own aristocratic title and looked like a high-class hotel: crystal chandeliers, stained oak and mahogany, velvet-upholstered chairs, gleaming silver tableware, prim waiters, and officious stewards. For his own purposes Commissioner Gauche had singled out the Windsor Salon, located on the upper deck in the very bow of the ship: Its three walls of continuous window afforded a magnificent view, so that even on overcast days there was no need to switch on the lamps. The velvet upholstery here was a fine shade of golden brown and the linen table napkins were adorned with the Windsor coat of arms.

Set around the oval table with its legs bolted to the floor (a precaution against any likelihood of severe pitching and rolling) were ten chairs with their tall backs carved in designs incorporating a motley assortment of gothic decorative flourishes. The commissioner liked the idea of everyone sitting around the same table, and he had ordered the steward not to set out the nameplates at random, but with strategic intent: He had seated the four passengers without badges directly opposite himself so that he could keep a close eye on those particular birds. It had not proved possible to seat the captain himself at the head of the table, as Gauche had planned. Mr. Josiah

Cliff did not wish (as he himself had expressed it) "to have any part in this charade," and had chosen to base himself in the York Salon, where the new viceroy of India was taking his meals with his wife and two generals of the Indian army. York was located in the prestigious stern, as far removed as possible from plague-stricken Windsor, where the head of the table was taken by first mate Charles Renier. The commissioner had taken an instant dislike to Renier, with that face bronzed by the sun and the wind, that honey-eyed way of speaking, that head of dark hair gleaming with brilliantine, that dyed mustache with its two spruce little curls. He was a buffoon, not a sailor.

In the course of the twelve days that elapsed since they had sailed, the commissioner had subjected his salon mates to close scrutiny, absorbed the rudiments of society manners (that is, he had learned not to smoke during a meal and not to mop up his gravy with a crust of bread), more or less mastered the complex geography of this floating city, and grown accustomed to the ship's pitching, but he had still made no progress toward his goal.

The situation was now as follows:

Initially his list of suspects had been headed by Sir Reginald Milford-Stokes, an emaciated ginger-haired gentleman with unkempt sideburns. He looked about twenty-eight or thirty years old and behaved oddly, either gazing aimlessly into the distance with those wide green eyes of his and not responding to questions, or suddenly becoming animated and prattling on about the island of Tahiti, coral reefs, emerald lagoons, and huts with roofs made of palm leaves. Clearly some kind of mental case. Why else would a baronet, the scion of a wealthy family, go traveling to some godforsaken Oceania? What did he think he would find there? And note, too, that twice the damned aristocrat had ignored a question about his missing badge. He either stared straight through the commissioner or, when he did happen to glance at him, he seemed to be scrutinizing some insignificant insect. A rotten snob. Back in Le Havre (where they had stood for four hours) Gauche had made a dash to the telegraph office and sent off an inquiry about Milford-Stokes to Scotland Yard: Who was he, did he have any record of violent behavior, had he ever dabbled in the study of medicine? The reply that had arrived just before they sailed contained nothing of great interest, but it had explained the strange mannerisms. Even so, the ginger gentleman did not have a golden whale, which meant it was still too early for Gauche to remove him from his list of potential clients.

The second suspect was M. Gintaro Aono, a "Japanese nobleman" (or so it said in the passenger register). He was a typical oriental, short and skinny. With that thin mustache and those narrow, piercing eyes, he could be almost any age. He remained silent most of the time at table. When asked what he did, he mumbled, embarrassed: "An officer in the Imperial Army." When asked about his badge, he became even more embarrassed, cast a glance of searing hatred at the commissioner, excused himself, and left the room without even finishing his soup. Decidedly suspicious! An absolute savage. He fanned himself in the salon with a bright-colored paper contraption, like some pederast from one of those dens of dubious delight behind the Rue de Rivoli, and he strolled about the deck in his wooden slippers and cotton robe without any pants at all. Of course, Gustave Gauche was all in favor of liberty, equality, and fraternity, but a popinjay like that really ought not to have been allowed into first class.

And then there were the women.

Mme. Renate Kleber. Young, barely twenty perhaps. The wife of an employee of a Swiss bank, traveling to join her husband in Calcutta. She could hardly be described as a beauty, with that pointed nose, but she was lively and talkative. She informed him she was pregnant the very moment they were introduced. All her thoughts and feelings were governed by this single circumstance. A sweet and ingenuous woman, but absolutely unbearable. In twelve days she had succeeded in boring the commissioner to death by chattering about her precious health, embroidering nightcaps, and other such nonsense. Nothing but a belly on legs, although she was not very far along yet and the belly was only just beginning to show. Gauche, naturally, had chosen his moment and asked where her emblem was. The Swiss lady had blinked her bright little eyes and complained that she was always losing things. Which seemed very likely to be true. For Renate Kleber the commissioner felt a mixture of irritation and protectiveness, but he did not take her seriously as a client.

When it came to the second lady, Mlle. Clarissa Stamp, the worldly-wise detective felt a far keener interest. There was something about her that seemed not quite right. She appeared to be a typical Englishwoman, nothing out of the ordinary. No longer young, with dull, colorless hair and rather sedate manners, but just occasionally those watery eyes would give a flash of devilment. He'd seen her type before. What was it the English said about still waters? There were a few other small details worthy of note—mere trifles really, no one else would have paid any attention to that kind of thing, but nothing escaped Gauche, the old dog. Miss Stamp's dresses and her wardrobe in general were expensive and brand-new, everything in the latest Parisian style. Her handbag was genuine tortoiseshell (he'd seen one like it in a shop window on the Champs Elysées—three hundred fifty francs), but the notebook she took out of it was old and cheaply made. On one occasion she had sat on the deck wearing a shawl (it was windy at the time), and it was exactly like one that Mme. Gauche had, made of dog's hair. Warm, but not at all the thing for an English lady. And it was curious that absolutely all of Clarissa Stamp's new things were expensive, while her older ones were shoddy and of the very lowest quality. This was a clear discrepancy. One day just before five o'clock tea Gauche had asked her: "Why is it, my dear lady, that you never put on your golden whale? Do you not like it? It seems to me a very stylish trinket." And what was her response? She had blushed an even deeper color than the "Japanese nobleman" and said she had worn it already but he simply hadn't noticed. That was a lie. Gauche would have noticed all right. The commissioner had a certain subtle ploy in mind, but he would have to choose exactly the right psychological moment. Then he would see how she would react, this Clarissa.

Since there were ten places at the table and only four passengers without emblems, Gauche had decided to make up the complement with other specimens who were also noteworthy in their own way, even though they possessed badges. It would widen his field of inquiry: In any case, the places were there.

First of all he had demanded that the captain assign the ship's chief physician, M. Truffo, to Windsor. Josiah Cliff had muttered a little but eventually gave way. The reason for Gauche's interest in the physician was clear enough—skilled in the art of administering injections, he was the only medic on board the *Leviathan* whose status entitled him to a golden whale. The doctor turned out to be a rather short, plump Italian with an olive complexion, a high forehead, and a bald patch with a few sparse strands of hair combed backward across it. It was simply impossible to imagine this comical specimen in the role of a ruthless killer. In addition to the doctor, another place had to be allocated to his wife. Having married only two weeks previously, the physician had decided to combine duty and pleasure by making this voyage his honeymoon. The chair occupied by the new Mme. Truffo was completely wasted. The dreary, unsmiling English-woman who had found favor with the shipboard Aesculapius appeared twice as old as her twenty years and inspired in Gauche a deadly ennui— as, indeed, did the majority of her female compatriots. He immediately dubbed her "the sheep" because of her white eyelashes and bleating voice. As it happened, she rarely opened her mouth, since she did not know French and for the most part conversations in the salon were, thank God, conducted in that most noble of tongues. Mme. Truffo had no badge of any kind, but that was only natural, since she was neither an officer nor a paying passenger.

The commissioner had also spotted in the register of passengers a certain specialist in Indian archeology, one Anthony F. Sweetchild, and decided that an Indologist might just come in handy. After all, the deceased Lord Littleby had also been something of the kind. Mr. Sweetchild, a lanky beanpole with round-rimmed spectacles and a goatee, had himself struck up a conversation about India at the very first dinner. After the meal Gauche had taken the professor aside and cautiously steered the conversation around to the subject of Lord Littleby's collection. The Indian specialist had contemptuously dismissed his late lordship as a dilettante and his collection as a "cabinet of curiosities" assembled without the benefit of scholarship. He claimed that the only item of genuine value in it was the golden Shiva and said it was a good thing the Shiva had turned up on its own, because everybody knew the French police were good for nothing but taking bribes. This grossly unjust remark set Gauche coughing furiously, but Sweetchild merely advised him to smoke less. The scholar went on to remark condescendingly that Littleby had, admittedly, acquired a fairly decent collection of decorative fabrics and shawls, which happened to include some extremely curious items, but their significance lay in the area of Indian arts and crafts. The sixteenth-century sandalwood chest from Lahore with carvings on a theme from the *Mahabharata* was not too bad, either—and then he had launched into a diatribe that soon had the commissioner nodding off.

Gauche had selected his final salon mate by eye, as they say. Quite literally so. The commissioner had only recently finished reading a most diverting volume translated from the Italian. One Cesare Lombroso, a professor of forensic medicine in the Italian city of Turin, had developed an entire theory of criminalistics, according to which congenital criminals were not responsible for their antisocial behavior. In accordance with Dr. Darwin's theory of evolution, mankind passed through a series of distinct stages in its development, gradually approaching perfection. But a criminal was an evolutionary reject, a random throwback to a previous stage. It was therefore a very simple matter to identify the potential robber and murderer: He resembled the monkey from whom we are all descended. The commissioner had pondered long and hard about what he had read. On the one hand, by no means had every one of the varied crew of thieves and murderers with whom he had dealt in the course of thirty years of police work resembled gorillas; some of them had been such sweet angels that a single glance at them brought a tender tear to one's eye. On the other hand, there had been plenty of anthropoid types, too. As a convinced anticlerical, old Gauche did not believe in Adam and Eve. Darwin's theory appeared rather more sound to him. And then he had come across a certain individual among the first-class passengers, a type who might have sat for a picture entitled "The Typical Killer": low forehead, prominent ridges above small eyes, flat nose, and crooked chin. And so the commissioner had requested that this Etienne Boileau, a tea trader, be assigned to the Windsor Salon. He had turned out to be an absolutely charming fellow—ready wit, father of eleven children, and confirmed philanthropist.

It had looked as though papa Gauche's voyage was unlikely to terminate even in Port Said, the next stop after Le Havre. The investigation was dragging on. Moreover, the keen intuition developed by the commissioner over the years was already hinting to him that he had drawn a blank, that there was no serious candidate among the company he had assembled. He was beginning to discern the sickening prospect of cruising the entire confounded length of the route to Port Said and Aden and Bombay and

Calcutta—and then hanging himself from the first palm tree he saw in Calcutta. He couldn't go running back to Paris with his tail between his legs! His colleagues would make him a laughingstock; his superiors would carp about the small matter of a first-class voyage at the treasury's expense. They might even kick him out on early retirement.

At Port Said, since the voyage was turning out to be a long one, with an aching heart Gauche bankrupted himself buying some more shirts, stocked up on Egyptian tobacco, and, for lack of anything else to fill his time, spent two francs on a cab ride along the famous waterfront. In fact, there was nothing exceptional about it. An enormous lighthouse; a couple of piers as long as your arm. The town itself made a strange impression, neither Asia nor Europe. A glance at the residence of the governor-general of the Suez Canal, and it seemed like Europe. The streets in the city center were crowded with European faces; there were ladies strolling about with white parasols and wealthy gentlemen in panama hats and straw boaters plodding along, large paunches to the fore. But once the carriage turned into the native quarter, a fetid stench filled the air and everywhere there were flies, rotting refuse, and grubby little Arab urchins pestering people for small change. Why did these rich idlers bother to go traveling? It was the same everywhere: Some grew fat from gorging on delicacies while others' bellies were swollen by hunger.

Exhausted by these pessimistic observations and the heat, the commissioner returned to the ship feeling dejected. But then it happened: He had a new client. And he looked like a promising one.

THE COMMISSIONER PAID the captain a visit and made some inquiries. It turned out that his name was Erast P. Fandorin and he was a Russian subject. For some reason this Russian subject had not given his age. A diplomat by profession, he had arrived from Constantinople, was traveling to Calcutta, and from there going on to Japan to take up his post. From Constantinople? Aha! He must have been involved in the peace negotiations that had concluded the recent Russo-Turkish War. Gauche punctiliously copied all the details on a sheet of paper and stowed it away in the special calico-bound file in which he kept all the materials having to do with the case; he never let it out of his sight. He leafed through it and reread the reports and newspaper clippings, and in pensive moments he drew little fishes and houses in the margins of the papers. It was the secret dream of his heart breaking through to the surface: the dream of how he would become a divisional commissioner, earn a decent pension, buy a nice little house somewhere in Normandy, and live out his days there with Mme. Gauche. The retired Paris *flic* would go fishing and press his own cider. What was wrong with that? But if only he had a little bit of capital to add to his pension—he needed twenty thousand at least . . .

He was obliged to make another visit to the port—luckily the ship was delayed waiting for its turn to enter the Suez Canal—and dash off a brief telegram to the prefecture, asking whether the Russian diplomat Erast P. Fandorin was known in Paris and whether he had entered the territory of the Republic of France at any time in the recent past.

The reply arrived quickly, after only two and a half hours. It turned out that the fellow had crossed into French territory not once, but twice. The first time in the summer of 1876 (all right, we can let that go) and the second time in December 1877, just three months earlier. His arrival from London had been recorded at the passport and customs control point in Pas-de-Calais. It was not known how much time he had spent in France. He could quite possibly still have been in Paris on the fifteenth of March. He could even have dropped round to the Rue de Grenelle with a syringe in his hand—stranger things had happened.

It now seemed that one of the places at the table would have to be freed up. The best thing, of course, would be to get rid of the doctor's wife, but he could hardly encroach on the sacred institution of marriage. After some thought, Gauche decided to pack the tea trader off to a different salon, since the theoretical hopes he had inspired had proved to be unfounded and he was the least promising of all the candidates. The steward could reassign him, tell him there was a place with more important gentlemen or prettier ladies. After all, stewards were there to arrange such things.

The appearance of a new personality in the salon caused a minor sensation. In the course of the journey they had all become thoroughly bored with one another, and now here was a fresh gentleman, and such a superior individual at that. Nobody bothered to inquire after poor M. Boileau, that representative of a previous stage of evolution. The commissioner noted that the person who evinced the liveliest reaction was Miss Clarissa Stamp, the old maid, who started babbling about artists, the theater, and literature. Gauche himself was fond of passing his leisure hours in an armchair with a good book, preferring Victor Hugo to all other authors. Hugo was at once so true to life, so high-minded, that he could always bring a tear to the eye. Besides, he was marvelous for dozing off over. But of course Gauche had never even heard of these Russian writers with those hissing sibilants in their names, so he was unable to join in the conversation. Anyway, the old English trout was wasting her time; "M. Fandorine" was far too young for her.

Renate Kleber was not slow off the mark, either. She made an attempt to press the new arrival into service as one of her minions, whom she bullied mercilessly into bringing her shawl or her parasol or a glass of water. Five minutes after dinner began, Mme. Kleber had already initiated the Russian into the detailed history of her delicate condition, complained of a migraine, and asked him to fetch Dr. Truffo, who for some reason was late that day. However, the diplomat seemed to have realized immediately who he was dealing with and politely objected that he did not know the doctor by sight. The ever-obliging Lieutenant Renier, the pregnant banker's wife's most devoted nursemaid, volunteered and went racing off to perform the errand.

The initial impression made by Erast Fandorin was that he was taciturn, reserved, and polite. But he was a bit too neat and polished for Gauche's taste: the starched collar sticking up like alabaster, the jeweled pin in the necktie, the red carnation (how very suave) in the buttonhole, the perfectly parted hair with not a strand out of place, the carefully manicured nails, the thin black mustache that seemed to have been drawn on with charcoal.

It was possible to tell a great deal about a man from his mustache. If it was like Gauche's, a walrus drooping at the corners of the mouth, it meant the man was a down-to-earth fellow who knew his own worth, not some gull easily to be taken in. If it was curled up at the ends, especially into points, he was a lady's man and bon vivant. If it merged into his sideburns, he was a man of ambition with dreams of becoming a general, statesman, or banker. And when it was like "M. Fandorine's," it meant he entertained romantic notions about himself.

What else could he say about the Russian? He spoke decent enough French, even though he stammered. There was no sign of his badge. The diplomat showed most interest in the Japanese, asking him all sorts of tiresome questions about his country, but the samurai answered guardedly, as if anticipating some kind of trick. The point was that the new passenger had not explained to the company where he was going and why; he had simply given his name and said that he was Russian. The commissioner, though, could understand the Russian's inquisitiveness, since he knew he was going to live in Japan. Gauche pictured to himself a country in which every single person was the same as M. Aono; everybody lived in doll's houses with bowed roofs and disemboweled themselves at the drop of a hat. No, the Russian was not to be envied.

After dinner, when Fandorin took a seat to one side in order to smoke a cigar, the commissioner settled into an armchair beside him and began puffing away at his pipe. Gauche had previously introduced himself to his new acquaintance as a Parisian rentier who was making the journey east out of curiosity (that was the cover he was using). But now he turned the conversation to the matter at hand, approaching it obliquely and with due caution. Fiddling with the golden whale on his lapel (the very same one retrieved from the Rue de Grenelle), he said casually, as though he were simply striking up a conversation, "A beautiful little bauble. Don't you agree?"

The Russian glanced sideways at his lapel but said nothing.

"Pure gold. So stylish!" said Gauche admiringly.

Another pregnant silence followed, but a perfectly civil one. The man was simply waiting for what would come next. His blue eyes were alert. The diplomat had clear skin, as smooth as a peach, with a bloom on his cheeks like a young girl's. But he was no mama's boy; that much was obvious immediately.

The commissioner decided to try a different tack.

"Do you travel much?"

A noncommittal shrug.

"I believe you're in the diplomatic line?"

Fandorin inclined his head politely in assent, extracted a long cigar from his pocket, and cut off the tip with a little silver knife.

"And have you ever been in France?"

Again an affirmative nod of the head. *Monsieur le Russe is no great conversationalist*, thought Gauche, but he had no intention of backing down.

"More than anything I love Paris in the early spring, in March," the detective mused out loud. "The very best time of the year!"

He cast a keen glance at the other man, wondering what he would say.

Fandorin nodded twice, though it wasn't clear if he was simply acknowledging the remark or agreeing with it. Beginning to feel irritated, Gauche furrowed his brows in an antagonistic scowl.

"So you don't like your badge, then?"

His pipe sputtered and went out.

The Russian gave a short sigh, put his hand into his waistcoat pocket, extracted a golden whale from it with his finger and thumb, and finally condescended to open his mouth: "I observe, monsieur, that you are interested in my b-badge. Here it is, if you please. I do not wear it because I do not wish to resemble a janitor with a name tag, not even a golden one. That is one. You do not much resemble a rentier, M. Gauche—your eyes are too probing. And why would a Parisian rentier lug a civil-service file around with him? That is two. Since you are aware of my professional orientation, you would appear to have access to the ship's documents. I assume therefore that you are a detective. That is three. Which brings us to number four. If there is something you want to find out from me, please do not beat about the bush. Ask directly."

You try having a conversation with someone like that.

Gauche had to think quickly. He whispered confidentially to the excessively perspicacious diplomat that he was the ship's house detective, whose job it was to see to the passengers' safety, but secretly and with the greatest possible delicacy, in order not to avoid offending the refined sensibilities of his public. It was not clear whether Fandorin believed him, but at least he did not ask any questions.

Every cloud has a silver lining. The commissioner now had, if not an intellectual ally, then at least an interlocutor, and someone who possessed remarkable powers of observation and quite exceptional knowledge on matters of criminology.

They often sat together on the deck, glancing now and then at the gently sloping bank of the canal as they smoked (Gauche his pipe, the Russian his cigar), and discussed various intriguing subjects—for instance, the very latest methods for the identification and conviction of criminals.

"The Paris police conducts its work in accordance with the very latest advances in scientific method," Gauche once boasted. "The prefecture there has a special identification unit headed by a young genius, Alphonse Bertillon. He has developed a complete system for classifying and recording criminal elements."

"I met with Dr. Bertillon during my last visit to Paris," Fandorin said unexpectedly. "He told me about his anthropometric method. Bertillonage is a clever theory, very clever. Have you already begun to apply it in practise? What have the results been?"

"There haven't been any yet," the commissioner said with a shrug. "First, one has to apply bertillonage to all the recidivists, and that will take years. It's bedlam in Alphonse's department: They bring in the prisoners in shackles, measure them up from every angle like horses at a fair, and jot down the data on little cards. But then pretty soon it will make police work as easy as falling off a log. Let's say you find the print of a left hand at the scene of a burglary. You measure it and go to the card index. Aha, middle finger eighty-nine millimeters long, look in section number three. And there you find records of seventeen burglars with a finger of the right length. After that, the whole thing is as easy as pie: Check where each of them was on the day of the robbery and nab the one who has no alibi."

"You mean criminals are divided up into categories according to the length of the middle finger?" the Russian asked with lively interest.

Gauche chuckled condescendingly into his mustache.

"There is a whole system involved, my young friend. Bertillon divides all people into three groups according to the length of the skull. Each of *those* three groups is divided into three subgroups according to the width of the skull. That makes nine subgroups in all. Each subgroup is in turn divided into three sections according to the size of the middle finger of the left hand. Twenty-seven sections. But that's not all. There are three divisions in each section according to the size of the right ear. So how many divisions does that make? That's right, eighty-one. Subsequent classification takes into account the height, the length of the arms, the height when seated, the size of the foot, and the length of the elbow joint. A total of 18,683 categories! A criminal who has undergone full bertillonage and been included in our card index will never be able to escape justice again. They used to have it so easy—just give a false name when you're arrested and you could avoid any responsibility for anything you did before."

"That is remarkable," the diplomat mused. "However, bertillonage does not offer much help with the solution of a particular crime if an individual has not previously been arrested."

Gauche spread his arms helplessly.

"Well, that is a problem science cannot solve. As long as there are criminals, people will not be able to manage without us professional sleuths."

"Have you ever heard of fingerprints?" Fandorin asked, presenting to the commissioner a narrow but extremely firm hand with polished nails and a diamond ring.

Glancing enviously at the ring (a commissioner's annual salary at the very least), Gauche laughed.

"Some kind of gypsy palmistry?"

"Not at all. It has been known since ancient times that the raised pattern of papillary lines on the tips of the fingers is unique to every individual. In China, coolies seal their contracts of hire with the imprint of their thumb dipped in ink."

"Well now, if only every murderer were so obliging as to dip his thumb into ink and leave an imprint at the scene of the crime." The commissioner laughed good-naturedly.

The diplomat, however, was not in the mood for joking.

"Monsieur ship's detective, allow me to inform you that modern science has established with certainty that an imprint is left when a finger comes into contact with any dry, firm surface. If a criminal has so much as touched a door in passing, or the murder weapon, or a windowpane, he has left a trace that allows the p-perpetrator to be identified and unmasked."

Gauche was about to retort ironically that there were twenty thousand criminals in France, that between them they had two hundred thousand fingers and thumbs and you would go blind staring at all of them through your magnifying glass, but he hesitated, recalling the shattered display case in the mansion on the Rue de Grenelle. There had been fingerprints left all over the broken glass. But it had never entered anyone's head to copy them, and the shards had been thrown out with the garbage.

My, what an amazing thing progress was! Just think what it meant. All crimes were committed with hands, were they not? And now it seemed that hands could inform every bit as well as paid informants! Just imagine—if you were to copy the fingers of every bandit and petty thief, they wouldn't dare turn their filthy hands to any more dirty work! It would be the end of crime itself.

The very prospect was enough to set a man's head spinning.

Reginald Milford-Stokes

2 April 1878
18 hours, 34½ minutes, Greenwich Mean Time

My precious Emily,

Today we entered the Suez Canal. In yesterday's letter I described the history and topography of Port Said to you in detail, and now I simply cannot resist the temptation of relating to you certain curious and instructive facts concerning the Great Canal, this truly colossal monument to human endeavor, which next year celebrates its tenth anniversary. Are you aware, my adorable little wife, that the present canal is actually the fourth to have existed and that the first was excavated as long ago as the fourteenth century before Christ, during the reign of the great Pharaoh Rameses? When Egypt fell into decline, the desert winds choked up the channel with sand, but under the Persian king Darius, five hundred years before Christ, slaves dug out another canal at the cost of 120,000 human lives. Herodotus tells us that the voyage along it took four days and that two triremes traveling in opposite directions could easily pass each other without their oars touching. Several ships from Cleopatra's shattered fleet fled to the Red Sea by this route and so escaped the fearful wrath of the vengeful Octavian.

Following the fall of the Roman Empire, time again separated the Atlantic and Indian Oceans with a barrier of shifting sand a hundred miles wide, but no sooner was a powerful state established in these barren lands by the followers of the prophet Mohammed than people took up their mattocks and pickaxes once again. As I sail through these dead salt meadows and endless sand dunes, I marvel unceasingly at the stubborn courage and antlike diligence of humankind in waging its never-ending struggle, doomed to inevitable defeat, against all-powerful Chronos. Vessels laden with grain plied the Arabian canal for two hundred years, and then the earth erased this pitiful wrinkle from its forehead and the desert was plunged into sleep for a thousand years.

Regrettably the father of the new Suez was not a Briton, but the Frenchman Lesseps, a representative of a nation which, my darling Emily, I quite justifiably hold in the most profound contempt. This crafty diplomat persuaded the Egyptian governor to issue a *firman* for the establishment of "The Universal Company of the Suez Maritime Canal." The company was granted a ninety-nine-year lease on the future waterway, and the Egyptian government was allotted only fifteen percent of the net revenue! And these villainous French dare to label us British pillagers of the backward peoples! At least we win our privileges with the sword, not by striking grubby bargains with greedy local bureaucrats.

Every day one thousand six hundred camels delivered drinking water to the workers digging the Great Canal, but still the poor devils died in the thousands from thirst, intense heat, and infectious diseases. Our *Leviathan* is sailing over corpses, and I seem to see the yellow teeth of fleshless, eyeless skulls grinning out at me from beneath the sand. It took ten years and fifteen million pounds sterling to complete this gargantuan construction job. But now a ship can sail from England to India in almost half the time it used to take. A mere twenty-five days or so and you arrive in Bombay. It is quite incredible! And the scale of it! The canal is more than a hundred feet deep, so that even our gigantic ark can sail fearlessly here, with no risk of running aground.

Today at lunch I was overcome by a quite irresistible fit of laughter; I choked on a crust of bread, began coughing, and simply could not calm myself. The pathetic coxcomb Renier (I wrote to you about him, he is the *Leviathan*'s first lieutenant) inquired with feigned interest what was the cause of my merriment, and I was seized by an even stronger paroxysm, for I certainly could not tell him about the thought that had set me laughing: that the French had built the canal, but the fruits had fallen to us, the English. Three years ago Her Majesty's government bought a controlling block of shares from the Egyptian khedive, and now we British are the masters of Suez. And incidentally, a single share in the canal, which was once sold for fifteen pounds, is now worth three thousand! How's that! How could I help but laugh?

But I fear I must have wearied you with these boring details. Do not blame me, my dear Emily, for I have no other recreation apart from writing long letters. While I am scraping my pen across the vellum paper, it is as though you are here beside me and I am making leisurely conversation with you. You know, thanks to the hot climate here I am feeling very much better. I can no longer recall the terrible dreams that haunt me in the night. But they have not gone away. In the morning when I wake up, the pillow-case is still soaked with tears and sometimes gnawed to shreds.

But that is all nonsense. Every new day and every mile of the journey bring me closer to a new life. There, under the soothing sun of the equator, this dreadful separation that is tearing my very soul apart will finally come to an end. How I wish it could be sooner! How impatient I am to see your tender, radiant glance once again, my dear friend.

What else can I entertain you with? Perhaps at least with a description of our *Leviathan*, a more than worthy theme. In my earlier letters I have written too much about my own feelings and dreams and I have still not presented you with a full picture of this great triumph of British engineering.

The *Leviathan* is the largest passenger ship in the history of the world, with the single exception of the colossal *Great Eastern*, which has been furrowing the waters of the Atlantic Ocean for the last twenty years. When Jules Verne described the *Great Eastern* in his book *The Floating City*, he had not seen our *Leviathan*—otherwise he would have renamed the old *G.E.* "The Floating Village." That vessel now does nothing but lay telegraph cables on the ocean floor, but *Leviathan* can transport a thousand people and ten thousand tons of cargo in addition. This fire-breathing monster is more than six hundred feet long and eighty feet across at its widest. Do you know, my dear Emily, how a ship is built? First they "lay it out in the molding loft," that is to say, they make a full-scale drawing of the vessel directly on the smoothly planed floor of a special building. The drawing of the *Leviathan* was so huge that they had to build a shed the size of Buckingham Palace!

This miracle of a ship has two steam engines, two powerful paddle wheels on its sides, and in addition a gigantic propeller on its stern. Its six masts, fitted with a full set of rigging, tower up to the very sky and with a fair wind and engines running full ahead the ship can make a speed of sixteen knots! All the very latest advances in shipbuilding have been used in her. These include a double metal hull, which ensures the vessel's safety even if it should strike a rock; special side keels to reduce pitching and rolling; electric lighting throughout; waterproof compartments; immense coolers for the spent steam—it is impossible to list everything. The entire experience of centuries of effort by the indefatigably inventive human mind has been concentrated in this proud vessel cleaving fearlessly through the ocean waves. Yesterday, following my old habit, I opened the Holy Scriptures at the first page that came to hand and I was astonished when my eyes fell upon the lines about Leviathan, the fearsome monster of the deep from the Book of Job. I began trembling at the sudden realization that this was no description of a sea serpent, as the ancients believed it to be, nor of a sperm whale, as our modern-day rationalists claim—no, the biblical text clearly refers to the very same Leviathan that has undertaken to deliver me out of darkness and terror into happiness and light. Judge for yourself: "He maketh the deep to boil like a pot: he maketh the sea like a pot of ointment. He maketh a path to shine after him: one would think the deep to be hoary. Upon earth there is not his like, who is made without fear. He beholdeth all high things: he is king over the children of pride."

The pot—that is the steam boiler; the pot of ointment—that is the fuel oil; the shining path—that is the wake at the stern. It is all so obvious!

And I felt afraid, my darling Emily. For these lines contain a terrible warning, either to me personally or to the passengers on the *Leviathan*, or to the whole of mankind. From the biblical point of view, pride is surely a bad thing? And if Man with his technological playthings "beholdeth all high things," is this not fraught with some catastrophic consequences? Have we not become too proud of the keenness of our intellect and the skill of our hands? Where is this king of pride taking us? What lies in store for us?

And so I opened my prayerbook to pray—the first time for a long, long time. And there I read: "It is in their thoughts that their houses are eternal and their dwellings are from generation to generation, and they call their lands after their own names. But man shall not abide in honor; he shall be likened unto the beasts who die. This path of theirs is their folly, though those that come after them do commend their opinion."

But when, in a paroxysm of mystical feeling, I opened the Book once again with a trembling hand, my feverish gaze fell on the boring passage in Numbers where the sacrifices made by the tribes of the Israelites are itemized with a bookkeeper's tedious precision. And I calmed down, rang my silver bell, and told the steward to bring me some hot chocolate.

The level of comfort prevailing in the section of the ship assigned to the respectable public is absolutely staggering. In this respect the *Leviathan* is truly without equal. The times are gone when people traveling to India or China were cooped up in dark, cramped little cubbyholes and piled one on top of another. You know, my dearest wife, how keenly I suffer from claustrophobia, but on board the *Leviathan* I feel as though I were in the wide open spaces of the Thames embankment. Here there is everything required to combat boredom: a dance hall, a musical salon for concerts of classical music, even a rather decent library. The decor in a first-class cabin is in no way inferior to a room in the finest London hotel, and the ship has a hundred such cabins. In addition, there are two hundred and fifty second-class cabins with six hundred berths (I have not looked into them—I cannot endure the sight of squalor) and they say there are also capacious cargo holds. The *Leviathan*'s service personnel alone, not counting sailors and officers, numbers more than two hundred—stewards, chefs, valets, musicians, chambermaids. Just imagine—I do not regret in the least not bringing Jeremy with me. The idle loafer was always sticking his nose into matters that did not concern him, and here at precisely eleven o'clock the maid comes and cleans the room and carries out any other errands I may have for her. This is both rational and convenient. If I wish I can ring for a valet and have him help me dress, but I regard that as excessive—I dress and undress myself. It is most strictly forbidden for any servant to enter the cabin in my absence, and on leaving it I set a hair across the crack of the door. I am afraid of spies. Believe me, my sweet Emily, this is not a ship, but a veritable city, and it has its share of riffraff.

For the most part my information concerning the ship has been garnered from the explanations of Lieutenant Renier, who is a great patriot of his own vessel. He is, however, not a very likeable individual and the object of serious suspicion on my part. He tries his hardest to play the gentleman, but I am not so easily duped. I have a keen nose for low breeding. Wishing to produce a good impression, this fellow invited me to visit his cabin. I did call, but less out of curiosity than from a desire to assess the seriousness of the threat that might be posed by this swarthy gentleman (concerning his appearance, see my letter of the twentieth of March). The meagerness of the decor was rendered even more glaringly obvious by his tasteless attempts at *bon ton* (Chinese vases, Indian incense burners, a dreadful seascape on the wall, and so forth). Standing on the table among the maps and navigational instruments was a large photographic portrait of a woman dressed in black, with an inscription in French: "Seven feet under the keel, my darling! Françoise B." I inquired whether it was his wife. It turned out to be his mother. Touching, but it does not allay my suspicions. I am as determined as ever to take independent readings of our course every three hours, even though it means that I have to get up twice during the night. Of course, while we are sailing through the Suez Canal this might seem a little excessive, but I do not wish to lose my proficiency in handling a sextant.

I have more than enough time at my disposal and apart from the writing of letters my leisure hours are filled by observing the Vanity Fair that surrounds me on all sides. Among this gallery of human types there are some who are most amusing. I have already written to you about the others, but yesterday a new face appeared in our salon. He is Russian—can you imagine that? His name is Erast Fandorin. You are aware, Emily, of my feelings regarding Russia, that misshapen excrescence that has extended over half of Europe and a third of Asia. Russia seeks to disseminate its own parody of the Christian religion and its own barbarous customs throughout the entire world, and Albion stands as the only barrier in the path of these new Huns. If not for the resolute position adopted by Her Majesty's government in the current eastern crisis, Tsar Alexander would have raked in the Balkans with his bear's claws, and . . .

But I have already written to you about that and I do not wish to repeat myself. And in any case, thinking about politics has rather a bad effect on my nerves. It is now four minutes to eight. As I have already informed you, life on the *Leviathan* is conducted according to British time as far as Aden, so that it is already dark here at eight o'clock. I shall go and take readings of the longitude and latitude, then have dinner and continue with my letter.

Sixteen minutes after ten—

I see that I did not finish writing about Mr. Fandorin. I do believe I like him, despite his nationality. Good manners, reticent, knows how to listen. He must be a member of that estate referred to in Russia by the Italian word *intelligenzia*, which I believe denotes the educated European class. You must admit, dear Emily, that a society in which the European class is separated into a distinct stratum of the population and also referred to by a foreign word can hardly be ranked among the civilized nations. I can imagine what a gulf separates a civilized human being like Mr. Fandorin from some bearded *kossack* or *muzhik*, who make up ninety percent of the population of that Tartarian-Byzantine empire. On the other hand, a distance of such magnitude must elevate and ennoble an educated and thinking man to an exceptional degree, a point that I shall have to ponder at greater length.

I liked the elegant way in which Mr. Fandorin (by the way, it seems he is a diplomat, which explains a great deal) put down that intolerable yokel Gauche, who claims to be a rentier, although it is clear from a mile away that the fellow is involved in some grubby little business or other. I should not be surprised if he is on his way to the East to purchase opium and exotic dancers for Parisian dens of vice. [The last phrase has been scratched out.] I know, my darling Emily, that you are a real lady and will not attempt to read what has been crossed out here. I got a little carried away and wrote something unworthy for your chaste eyes to read.

And so, back to today's dinner. The French bourgeois, who just recently has grown bold and become quite terribly talkative, began discoursing with a self-satisfied air on the advantages of age over youth. "I am older than anyone else here," he said condescendingly, à la Socrates. "Gray-haired, bloated, and decidedly not good-looking, but you needn't go thinking, ladies and gentlemen, that papa Gauche would agree to change places with you. When I see the arrogance of youth, flaunting its beauty and strength, its health, in the face of age, I do not feel envious in the least. Why, I think, that is no great trick; I was like that myself once. But you, my fine fellow, still do not know if you will live to my sixty-two years. I am twice as happy as you are at thirty, because I have been fortunate enough to live in this world for twice as long." And he sipped at his wine, very proud of the originality of his thought and his seemingly unimpeachable logic. Then Mr. Fandorin, who had so far not said a word, suddenly remarked with a very serious air, "That is undoubtedly the case, M. Gauche, if one takes the oriental viewpoint on life, as existence at a single point of reality in an eternal present. But there is also another way of reasoning that regards a man's life as a unified work that can only be judged when its final page has been read. Moreover, this work may be as long as a tetralogy or as short as a novella. And yet who would undertake to assert that a fat, vulgar novel is necessarily of greater value than a short, beautiful poem?" The funniest thing of all was that our rentier, who is indeed both fat and vulgar, did not even understand the reference to himself. Even when Miss Stamp (by no means stupid, but a strange creature) giggled and I gave a rather loud snort, the Frenchie failed to catch on and stuck with his own opinion, and all credit to him for that.

It is true, however, that in the conversation that followed over dessert, Mr. Gauche demonstrated a degree of common sense that quite amazed me. There are, after all, certain advantages in not having a regular education: A mind unfettered by authorities is sometimes capable of making interesting and accurate observations.

Judge for yourself. The amoeba-like Mrs. Truffo, the wife of our muttonhead of a doctor, started up again with her mindless prattle about the joy and delight Mme. Kleber will bring to her banker with her "tiny tot" and "little angel." Since Mrs. Truffo does not speak French, the task of translating her sickly sentiments on the subject of family happiness being inconceivable without "baby babble" fell to her unfortunate husband. Gauche huffed and puffed and then suddenly declared: "I cannot agree with you, madam. A genuinely happy married couple has no need whatsoever of children, since husband and wife are perfectly sufficient for each other. Man and woman are like two uneven surfaces, each with bumps and indentations. If the surfaces do not fit tightly against each other, then glue is required, otherwise the structure—in other words, the family—cannot be preserved. Children are that selfsame glue. If, however, the surfaces form a perfect fit, bump to indentation, then no glue is required. Take me and my Blanche, if you like. Thirty-three years we've lived in perfect harmony. Why would we want children? Life is splendid without them." I am sure you can imagine, dear Emily, the tidal wave of righteous indignation that came crashing down on the head of this subverter of eternal values. The most zealous accuser of all was Mme. Kleber, who is carrying the little Swiss in her womb. The sight of her neat little belly so carefully exhibited at every opportunity sets me writhing. I can just see the miniature banker nestled inside with his curly mustache and puffy little cheeks. In time the Klebers will no doubt produce an entire battalion of Swiss Guards.

I must confess to you, my tenderly adored Emily, that the sight of pregnant women makes me feel sick. They are repulsive! That inane bovine smile, that disgusting manner of constantly listening to their own entrails. I try to keep as far away from Mme. Kleber as possible. Swear to me, my darling, that we shall never have children. The fat bourgeois is right a thousand times over! Why do we need children when we are already boundlessly happy without them? All we need to do is survive this forced separation.

But it is already two minutes to eleven. Time to take a reading.

Damnation! I have turned the whole cabin upside down. My sextant has disappeared. This is no delusion! It was lying in the trunk together with the chronometer and the compass, and now it is not there! I am afraid, Emily! Oh, I had a premonition of this. My worst suspicions have been confirmed!

Why? What have I done? They are prepared to commit any vileness in order to prevent our reunion! How can I check now that the ship is following the right course? It is that Renier, I know! I caught the expression in his eyes when he saw me handling the sextant on deck last night! The scoundrel!

I shall go to the captain and demand retribution. But what if they are in it together? My God, my God, have pity on me!

I had to pause for a while. I was so agitated that I was obliged to take the drops prescribed for me by Dr. Jenkinson. And I did as he told me, and started thinking of pleasant things. Of how you and I will sit on a white veranda and gaze into the distance, trying to guess where the sea ends and the sky begins. You will smile and say: "Darling Reggie, here we are together at last." Then we will get into a cabriolet and go for a drive along the seashore.

Lord, what nonsense is this! What cabriolet?

I am a monster, and there can be no forgiveness for me.

Renate Kleber

SHE WOKE UP in an excellent mood, smiled affably at the spot of sunlight that had crept onto her round cheek where it was creased by the pillow, and listened to her belly. The baby was quiet, but she felt terribly hungry. There was still an entire fifty minutes until breakfast, but Renate had no lack of patience, and she simply did not know the meaning of boredom. In the morning, sleep released her as swiftly as it embraced her at night, when she simply sandwiched her hands together and laid her head on them, and a second later she was immersed in sweet dreams.

As Renate performed her morning toilet, she purred a frivolous little song about poor Georgette who fell in love with a chimney sweep. She wiped her fresh little face with an infusion of lavender and then styled her hair quickly and deftly, fluffing up the bangs over her forehead, drawing her thick chestnut tresses into a smooth bun, and arranging two long ringlets over her temples. The effect was precisely what was required—demure and sweet. She glanced out the porthole. Still the same view: the regular border of the canal, the yellow sand, the white mud-daub houses of some wretched little hamlet. It was going to be hot. That meant the white lace dress, the straw hat with the red ribbon, and she mustn't forget her parasol—a stroll after breakfast was de rigueur. Only she couldn't be bothered to drag her parasol around with her. Never mind; someone would fetch it.

Renate twirled in front of the mirror with evident satisfaction, stood sideways, and pulled her dress taut over her belly. Although, to tell the truth, there was not much to look at as yet.

Renate asserted her rights as a pregnant woman by arriving ahead of time for breakfast, when the waiters were still laying the table. She immediately ordered them to bring her orange juice, tea, croissants with butter, and everything else. By the time the first of her tablemates arrived—it was the fat M. Gauche, another early bird—the mother-to-be had already dealt with three croissants and was preparing to set about a mushroom omelette. The breakfast served on the *Leviathan* was not some trifling continental affair, but the genuine full English variety: with roast beef, exquisite egg dishes, blood pudding, and porridge. The French part of the consortium provided nothing but the croissants. At lunch and dinner, however, the menu was dominated by French cuisine. Well, one could hardly serve kidneys and beans in the Windsor salon!

The first mate appeared, as always at precisely nine o'clock. He inquired solicitously as to how Mme. Kleber was feeling. Renate lied and said she had slept badly and felt absolutely shattered, and it was all because the porthole didn't open properly and it was too stuffy in the cabin. Alarmed, Lieutenant Renier promised he would make enquiries in person and have the fault rectified. He did not eat eggs or roast beef—he was a devotee of some peculiar diet, sustaining himself largely on fresh greens. Renate pitied him for that.

Gradually the others also appeared. The conversation over breakfast was usually listless—the older passengers had not yet recovered from a wretched night, while the younger were still not fully awake. It was rather amusing to observe the repulsive Clarissa Stamp attempting to coax a response out of the stammering Russian diplomat. Renate shook her head in disbelief: How could she make such a fool of herself? After all, dearie, he could be your son, despite those impressive streaks of gray. Surely the handsome boy was too tough a morsel for this aging, insipid creature?

The very last to arrive was the Ginger Lunatic (Renate's private name for the English baronet). Tousled hair sticking out in all directions, red eyes, a twitch at the corner of his mouth—he was a terrible mess. But Mme. Kleber was not in the least bit afraid of him, and, given the chance, she never missed the opportunity to have a bit of fun at his expense. This time she passed the milk jug to the Lunatic with a warm, guileless smile. As she had anticipated, Milford-Stokes (what a silly name!) squeamishly set his cup to one side. Renate knew from experience that now he would not even touch the milk jug, and would drink his coffee black.

"Why do you draw back like that, sir?" she babbled in a quavering voice. "Don't be afraid; pregnancy is not infectious." Then she concluded, no longer quavering: "At least not for men."

The Lunatic cast her a glance of withering scorn that broke against the serenely radiant glance opposed to it. Lieutenant Renier concealed a smile behind his hand; the rentier chuckled. Even the Japanese half smiled at Renate's prank. Of course, this M. Aono was always smiling, even when there was absolutely no reason for it. Perhaps for the Japanese a smile was not an expression of merriment at all; perhaps it indicated something quite different—boredom, perhaps, or repugnance.

When he had finished smiling, M. Aono disgusted his neighbors at table by playing his usual trick: He took a paper napkin out of his pocket, blew his nose into it loudly, crumpled it up, and deposited it neatly on the edge of his dirty plate. A fine ikebana arrangement for them to contemplate. Renate had read about ikebana in one of Pierre Loti's novels, and now recalled the mellifluous-sounding word. It was an interesting idea—composing bouquets of flowers not simply to look nice, but with a philosophical meaning. She would have to try it sometime.

"What are your favorite flowers?" she asked Dr. Truffo.

He translated the question for his horse-faced Englishwoman, then replied:

"Pansies."

Then he translated his reply into English as well.

"I just adore flowers!" exclaimed Miss Stamp (what an impossible ingénue). "But only live ones. I love to walk across a flowering meadow! My heart simply breaks when I see poor cut flowers wither and drop their petals! That's why I never allow anyone to give me bouquets." And she cast a languid glance at the handsome young Russian.

What a shame, otherwise absolutely everyone would be tossing bouquets at you, thought Renate, but aloud she said: "I believe that flowers are the crowning glories of God's creation and I think trampling a meadow in bloom is a crime."

"In the parks of Paris it is indeed considered a crime," M. Gauche pronounced solemnly. "The penalty is ten francs. And if the ladies will permit an old boor to light up his pipe, I will tell you an amusing little story on the subject."

"Oh, ladies, pray do indulge us!" cried the owlish Indologist Sweetchild, wagging his beard à la Disraeli. "M. Gauche is such a wonderful raconteur!"

Everyone turned to look at the pregnant Renate, on whom the decision depended, and she rubbed her temple as a hint. Of course, she did not have the slightest trace of a headache—she was simply savoring the sweetness of the moment. However, she too was curious to hear this "little story," and so she nodded her head with a pained expression and said: "Very well, smoke. But then someone must fan me."

Since repulsive Clarissa, the owner of a luxurious ostrich-feather fan, pretended this remark did not apply to her, the Japanese had to fill the breach. Gintaro Aono seated himself beside Renate and set to work, flapping his bright fan with the butterfly design in front of the long-suffering woman's nose so zealously that the bright kaleidoscope rapidly made her feel genuinely dizzy. The Japanese received a reprimand for his excessive fervor.

Meanwhile the rentier drew on his pipe with relish, puffed out a cloud of aromatic smoke, and embarked on his tale.

"Believe it or not as you wish, but this is a true story. There was once a gardener who worked in the Luxembourg Gardens—little papa Picard. For forty years he had watered the flowers and pruned the shrubs, and now he had only three years to go until he retired and drew his pension. Then, one morning, when little papa Picard went out with his watering can, he saw a swell dolled up in a white shirt and tails sprawled in the tulip bed. He was stretched out full-length, basking in the morning sunshine, obviously recovering from his nocturnal revels—after carousing until dawn, he had fallen asleep on his way home." Gauche screwed up his eyes and surveyed his audience with a sly glance. "Picard, of course, was furious—his tulips were crushed—and he said: 'Get up, monsieur, in our park lying in the flower beds is not allowed! We fine people for it, ten francs.' The reveler opened one eye and took a gold coin out of his pocket. 'There you are, old man,' he said, 'now leave me be. I haven't had such a wonderful rest in ages.' Well, the gardener took the coin but did not go away. 'You have paid the fine, but I have no right to leave you here, monsieur. Be so good as to rise.' At this the gentleman in the tails opened both eyes, but he seemed in no haste to rise. 'How much do I have to pay you to get out of my sun? I'll pay any amount you like if you'll just stop pestering me and let me doze for an hour.' Old papa Picard scratched his head and moved his lips while figuring something out. 'Well then, sir,' he said eventually, 'if you wish to purchase an hour's rest lying in a flower bed in the Luxembourg Gardens, it will cost you eighty-four thousand francs and not a single sou less.' " Gauche chuckled merrily into his gray mustache and shook his head, as if in admiration of the gardener's impudence. " 'And not a single sou less,' he said, so there! And let me tell you that this tipsy gentleman was no ordinary man, but the banker Laffite himself, the richest man in the whole of Paris. Laffitte was not in the habit of making idle promises; he had said 'any amount,' and now he was stuck with it. It would have been shameful for him to back down and break his word as a banker. Of course, he wasn't happy about simply giving away that kind of money to the first rascal he met. But what could he do about it?" Gauche shrugged, mimicking a state of total perplexity. "Then suddenly Laffitte ups and says: 'Right, you old scoundrel, you'll get your eighty-four thousand, but only on one condition: You have to prove to me that lying for an hour in your rotten flower bed is really worth the money. If you can't prove it, I'll get up this very moment and give you a good drubbing with my cane, and that bit of mischief will cost me a forty-franc administrative fine.' " Crazy Milford-Stokes laughed loudly and ruffled up his ginger mane in approval, but Gauche raised a yellow-stained finger as if to say: Don't be so hasty with your laughter; it's not the end yet. "And what do you think, ladies and gentlemen? Old papa Picard, not batting an eye, began adding up the balance: 'In half an hour, at precisely eight o'clock, monsieur the park director will arrive, see you in the flower bed, and start yelling at me to get you out of there. I shall not be able to do that, because you will have paid for a full hour, not half an hour. I shall get into an argument with monsieur the director, and he will kick me out of my job with no pension and no severance pay. I still have three years to go before I retire and take the pension due to me, which is set at one thousand two hundred francs a year. I intend to live at my ease for twenty years, so altogether that makes twenty-four thousand francs already. Now for the matter of accommodation. They will throw me and my wife out of our municipal apartment. And then the question is— where are we going to live? We shall have to buy a house. Any modest little house somewhere in the Loire region will run to twenty thousand at least. Now, sir, consider my reputation. Forty years I've slaved away loyally in this park, and anyone will tell you that old papa Picard is an honest man. Then suddenly an incident like this brings shame on my old gray head. This is bribery, this is graft! I think a thousand francs for each year of irreproachable service would hardly be too much by way of moral compensation. So altogether it comes to exactly eighty-four thousand.' Laffitte laughed, stretched himself out a bit more comfortably in the flower bed, and closed his eyes again. 'Come back in an hour, you old rogue,' he said, 'and you'll be paid.' And that is my wonderful little story, ladies and gentlemen."

"So a year of faultless conduct went for a thousand f-francs?" the Russian diplomat said with a laugh. "Not so very expensive. Evidently with a discount for wholesale."

The company began a lively discussion of the story, expressing the most contradictory opinions, but Renate Kleber gazed curiously at M. Gauche as he opened his black file with a self-satisfied air and began rummaging through his papers. He was an intriguing specimen, this old grandpa, no doubt about it. And what secrets was he keeping in there? Why was he shielding the file with his elbow?

That question had been nagging at Renate for a long time. Once or twice she had tried to exploit her position as a mother-to-be by glancing over Gauche's shoulder as he conjured with that precious file of his, but the mustachioed boor had impudently slammed the file shut in the lady's face and even wagged his finger at her, as much as to say: Now that's not allowed.

Today, however, something remarkable happened. When M. Gauche, as usual, rose from the table ahead of the others, a sheet of paper slid silently out of his mysterious file and floated to the floor. Engrossed in some gloomy thoughts of his own, the rentier failed to notice it and left the salon. The door had scarcely closed behind him before Renate adroitly raised her body with its slightly thickened waist out of her chair. But she was not the only one to have been so observant. The well-brought-up Miss Stamp (such a nimble creature!) was the first to reach the scrap of paper.

"Ah, I think M. Gauche has dropped something!" she exclaimed, deftly grabbing up the scrap and fastening her beady eyes upon it. "I'll catch up to him and return it."

But Mme. Kleber was already clutching the edge of the paper in her tenacious fingers and had no intention of letting go.

"What is it?" she asked. "A newspaper clipping? How interesting!"

The next moment everyone in the room had gathered around the two ladies, except for the Japanese blockhead, who was still pumping the air with his fan, and Mrs. Truffo, who observed this flagrant invasion of privacy with a reproachful expression on her face.

The clipping read as follows:

"THE CRIME OF THE CENTURY":
A NEW ANGLE?

The fiendish murder of ten people that took place the day before yesterday in the Rue de Grenelle continues to exercise the imagination of Parisians. Of the possible explanations proposed thus far, the two most prevalent are a maniacal doctor and a fanatical sect of bloodthirsty Hindu devotees of the god Shiva. However, in the course of conducting our own independent investigation, we at Le Soir have uncovered a circumstance that could possibly open up a new angle on the case. It would appear that in recent weeks the late Lord Littleby was seen at least twice in the company of the international adventuress Marie Sanfon, well known to the police forces of many countries. The Baron de M., a close friend of the murdered man, has informed us that his lordship was infatuated with a certain lady, and on the evening of the fifteenth of March had intended to set out for Spa for some kind of romantic rendezvous. Could this rendezvous, which was prevented by the most untimely attack of gout suffered by the unfortunate collector, possibly have been arranged with Mlle. Sanfon? The editors would not make so bold as to propose our own version of events, but we regard it as our duty to draw the attention of Commissioner Gauche to this noteworthy circumstance. You may expect further reports from us on this subject.

CHOLERA EPIDEMIC ON THE WANE

The municipal health authorities inform us that the foci of the cholera infection they have been combating energetically since the summer have finally been isolated. The vigorous prophylactic measures taken by the physicians of Paris have yielded positive results, and we may now hope that the epidemic of this dangerous disease, which began in July, is beg—

"What could that be about?" Renate asked, wrinkling up her brow in puzzlement. "Something about a murder, and cholera or something of the kind."

"Well, the cholera obviously has nothing to do with the matter," said Professor Sweetchild. "It's simply the way the page has been cut. The important thing, of course, is the murder in the Rue de Grenelle. Surely you must have heard about it? A sensational case—the newspapers were all full of it."

"I do not read the newspapers," Mme. Kleber replied with dignity. "In my condition it places too much strain on the nerves. And in any case I have no desire to learn about all sorts of unpleasant goings-on."

"Commissioner Gauche?" said Lieutenant Renier, peering at the clipping and running his eyes over the article once again. "Could that be our own M. Gauche?"

Miss Stamp gasped: "Oh, it couldn't be!"

At this point even the doctor's wife joined them. This was a genuine sensation and everyone started talking at once.

"The police, the French police, are involved in this!" Sir Reginald exclaimed excitedly.

Renier muttered: "So that's why the captain keeps asking me about the Windsor salon . . ."

M. Truffo translated as usual for his spouse, while the Russian took possession of the clipping and scrutinized it closely.

"That bit about the Indian fanatics is absolute nonsense," declared Sweetchild. "I made my opinion on that clear from the very beginning. In the first place, there is no bloodthirsty sect of followers of Shiva. And in the second place, everyone knows the statuette was recovered. Would a religious fanatic be likely to throw it into the Seine?"

"Yes, the business of the golden Shiva is a genuine riddle," said Miss Stamp with a nod. "They wrote that it was the jewel of Lord Littleby's collection. Is that correct, professor?"

The Indologist shrugged condescendingly.

"What can I say, madam? Lord Littleby only started collecting relatively recently, about twenty years ago. In such a short period, it is difficult to assemble a truly outstanding collection. They do say that the deceased did rather well out of the suppression of the Sepoy Mutiny of 1857. The notorious Shiva, for instance, was presented to the lord by a certain maharajah who was threatened with court-martial for intriguing with the insurgents. Littleby served for many years in the Indian military prosecutor's office, you know. Undoubtedly his collection includes quite a few valuable items, but the selection is rather chaotic."

"But do tell me, at least, why this lord of yours was killed," Renate demanded. "Look, M. Aono doesn't know anything about it, either, do you?" she asked, appealing for support to the Japanese, who was standing slightly apart from the others.

The Japanese smiled, moving only his lips, and bowed, and the Russian mock-applauded.

"Bravo, Mme. Kleber. You have quite c-correctly identified the most important question here. I have been following this case in the press. And in my opinion the reason behind the c-crime is more vital than anything else. That is where the key to the riddle lies. Precisely in the question of why. For what purpose were ten people killed?"

"Ah, but that is very simple!" said Miss Stamp, shrugging. "The plan was to steal everything that was most valuable from the collection. But the thief lost his head when he came face-to-face with the owner. After all, it had been assumed his lordship was not at home. It must be one thing to inject someone with a syringe, but quite another to smash a man's head open. Then again, I wouldn't know; I have never tried it." She twitched her shoulders. "The villain's nerves gave out and he left the job half finished. But as for the abandoned Shiva . . ." Miss Stamp pondered. "Perhaps *that* is the heavy object with which poor Littleby's brains were beaten out. It is quite possible that a criminal also has normal human feelings, and he found it repugnant or even simply frightening to hold the bloody murder weapon in his hand. So he walked as far as the embankment and threw it in the Seine."

"Concerning the murder weapon, that seems very probable," the diplomat agreed. "I th-think the same."

The old maid flushed brightly with pleasure and was clearly embarrassed when she caught Renate's mocking glance.

"You are saying quite outrageous things," the doctor's wife rebuked Clarissa Stamp. "Shouldn't we find a more suitable subject for table talk?"

But the colorless creature's appeal fell on deaf ears.

"In my opinion, the greatest mystery here is the death of the servants," said the lanky Indologist, keen to contribute to the analysis of the crime. "How did they come to allow themselves to be injected with such abominable muck? Not at pistol point, surely! After all, two of them were guards, and they were both carrying revolvers in holsters on their belts. That's where the mystery lies!"

"I have a hypothesis of my own," Renier announced with a solemn expression. "And I am prepared to defend it against any objections. The crime in the Rue de Grenelle was committed by a person who possesses exceptional mesmeric powers. The servants were in a state of mesmeric trance—that is the only possible explanation! Animal magnetism is a terrifying force. An experienced manipulator can do whatever he chooses with you. Yes, yes, madam," the lieutenant said, turning toward Mrs. Truffo, who had twisted her face into a doubtful grimace, "absolutely anything at all."

"Not if he is dealing with a lady," she replied primly.

Tired of playing the role of interpreter, Dr. Truffo wiped the sweat from his gleaming forehead with his handkerchief and rushed to the defense of the scientific worldview.

"I am afraid I must disagree with you," he started jabbering in his strongly accented French. "Mr. Mesmer's teaching has been exposed as having no scientific basis. The power of mesmerism or, as it is now known, hypnotism, has been greatly exaggerated. The honorable Mr. James Braid has proved conclusively that only psychologically suggestible individuals are subject to hypnotic influence, and then only if they have complete trust in the hypnotist and have agreed to allow themselves to be hypnotized."

"It is quite obvious, my dear doctor, that you have not traveled in the East!" said Renier, flashing his white teeth in a smile. "At any Indian bazaar, a fakir will show you miracles of mesmeric art that would make the most hardened skeptic gape in wonder. But those are merely tricks for showing off! Once in Kandahar I observed the public punishment of a thief. Under Muslim law, theft is punished by the amputation of the right hand, a procedure so intensely painful that those subjected to it frequently die from the shock. On this occasion the accused was a mere child, but since he had been caught for the second time, there was nothing else the judge could do; he had to sentence the thief to the penalty prescribed under Shariah law. The judge, however, was a merciful man. He sent for a dervish who was well known for his miraculous powers. The dervish took the convicted prisoner's head in his hands, looked into his eyes, and whispered something—and the boy became calm and stopped trembling. A strange smile appeared on his face, and did not leave it even when the executioner's ax severed his arm up to the very elbow! And I saw all this with my own eyes, I swear to you."

Renate grew angry. "Ugh—how horrible! You and your Orient, Charles. I am beginning to feel faint!"

"Forgive me, Mme. Kleber," said the lieutenant, taking fright. "I only wished to demonstrate that in comparison with that a few injections are child's play."

"Once again, I am afraid that I cannot agree with you—" The stubborn doctor was preparing to defend his point of view, but just at that moment the door of the salon swung open and in came either a rentier or a policeman—in short, M. Gauche.

Everybody turned toward him in consternation, as if they had been engaged in some action that was not entirely decent.

Gauche ran a keen gaze over their faces and spotted the ill-starred clipping in the hands of the diplomat. His face darkened.

"So that's where it is . . . I was afraid of that."

Renate went over to this old man with the gray mustache, looked his massive figure over mistrustfully up and down, and blurted out: "M. Gauche, are you really a policeman?"

"The same c-commissioner Gauche who was leading the investigation into the Crime of the Century?" asked Fandorin. (Yes, that was the Russian diplomat's name, Renate recalled.) "In that case, how are we to account for your masquerade, and in general for your p-presence on board?"

Gauche breathed hard for a few moments, raised his eyebrows, lowered them again, and reached for his pipe. He was obviously racking his brains in an effort to decide what to do.

"Please, sit down, ladies and gentlemen," said Gauche in an unfamiliar, imposing bass, and turned the key to lock the door behind him. "Since this is the way things have turned out, I shall have to be frank with you. Be seated, be seated, or else somebody's legs might just give way under them."

"What kind of joke is this, M. Gauche?" the lieutenant asked, annoyed. "By what right do you presume to command here, and in the presence of the captain's first mate?"

"That, my young man, is something the captain himself will explain to you," Gauche replied with a hostile sideways glance at Renier. "He knows what is going on here."

Renier dropped the matter and, following the others' example, took his place at the table.

The talkative, good-humored grumbler for whom Renate had taken the Parisian rentier was behaving differently now. A certain dignity had appeared in the broad set of his shoulders, his gestures had become imperious, his eyes had acquired a new, harder gleam. The mere fact that he could maintain a prolonged pause with such calm confidence said a great deal. The strange rentier's piercing gaze paused in turn on each person present in the room, and Renate saw some of them flinch under its weight. To be honest, even she was a little disturbed by it, but then she immediately felt ashamed of herself and tossed her head nonchalantly. He may be a police commissioner, but what of that? He was still an obese, short-winded old duffer and nothing more.

"Please do not keep us guessing any longer, M. Gauche," she said sarcastically. "Excitement is dangerous for me."

"There is probably only one person here who has cause for excitement," Gauche replied mysteriously. "But I shall come back to that. First, allow me to introduce myself to the honorable company once again. Yes, my name is Gustave Gauche, but I am not a rentier—alas, I have no investments from which to draw income. I am, ladies and gentlemen, a commissioner in the criminal police of the city of Paris, and I work in the department that deals with particularly serious and complicated crimes. The post I hold is entitled Investigator for Especially Important Cases." The commissioner pronounced the title with distinct emphasis.

The deadly silence in the salon was broken only by the hasty whispering of Dr. Truffo.

"What a scandal!" squeaked the doctor's wife.

"I was obliged to embark on this voyage, and to travel incognito because . . ." Gauche began puffing his cheeks in and out energetically in an effort to revive his half-extinguished pipe. ". . . because the Paris police have strong grounds for believing that the person who committed the crime in the Rue de Grenelle is on board the *Leviathan*."

"Ah!" The sigh rustled quietly round the salon.

"I presume you have already discussed the case, which is a mysterious one in many respects." The commissioner jerked his double chin in the direction of the newspaper clipping, which was still in Fandorin's hands. "And that is not all, mesdames et messieurs. I know for a fact that the murderer is traveling first-class . . ." (another collective sigh) ". . . and moreover, happens to be present in this salon at this very moment," Gauche concluded. He then seated himself in a satin-upholstered armchair by the window and folded his arms expectantly just below his silver watch chain.

"Impossible!" cried Renate, clutching involuntarily at her belly.

Lieutenant Renier leapt to his feet.

The ginger baronet began chortling and applauding demonstratively.

Professor Sweetchild gulped convulsively and removed his glasses.

Clarissa Stamp froze with her fingers pressed against the agate brooch on her soft collar.

Not a single muscle twitched in the face of the Japanese, but the polite smile instantly disappeared.

The doctor grabbed his wife by the elbow, forgetting to translate the most important thing of all, but to judge by the frightened expression in her staring eyes, Mrs. Truffo had guessed it for herself.

The Russian diplomat asked quietly, "What reasons do you have?"

"My presence here," the commissioner replied imperturbably, "is explanation enough. There are other considerations, but there is no need for you to know about them . . . Well, then"—there was a clear note of disappointment in the policeman's voice—"I see no one is about to swoon and cry out: 'Arrest me, I killed them!' But, of course, I was not really counting on that. So listen to me." He raised a stubby finger in warning. "None of the other passengers must be told about this. And it is not in your interests to tell them—the rumor would spread instantly, and people would start treating you like lepers. Do not attempt to transfer to a different salon— that will merely increase my suspicion. And you would not be able to do it; I have an arrangement with the captain."

Renate began babbling in a trembling voice.

"Dear M. Gauche, can you not at least spare me this nightmare? I am afraid to sit at the same table as a murderer. What if he sprinkles poison in my food? I shan't be able to swallow a single morsel now. You know, it's dangerous for me to be worried. I won't tell anyone, anyone at all, honestly!"

"My regrets, Mme. Kleber," the sleuth replied coolly, "but there can be no exceptions. I have grounds to suspect every person here, and not least of all you."

Renate threw herself against the back of her chair with a weak moan and Lieutenant Renier stamped his foot angrily: "You take too many liberties, monsieur . . . Investigator for Especially Important Cases! I shall report everything to Captain Cliff immediately."

"Go right ahead," said Gauche indifferently. "But not just at this moment; a bit later. I haven't quite finished my little speech yet. So as yet I do not know for certain which of you is my client, but I am close, very close, to my goal."

Renate expected these words to be followed by an eloquent glance, and she strained her entire body forward in anticipation. But no—the policeman was looking at his stupid pipe. He was probably lying and didn't have his eye on anyone in particular.

"You suspect a woman, it's obvious!" exclaimed Miss Stamp with a nervous flutter of her hands. "Otherwise why would you be carrying around a newspaper article about some Marie Sanfon? Who is this Marie Sanfon? And anyway, it doesn't matter who she is. It's plain stupid to suspect a woman! How could a woman ever be capable of such brutality?"

Mrs. Truffo rose abruptly to her feet, ready to rally to the banner of female solidarity.

"We shall speak of Mlle. Sanfon on some other occasion," the detective replied, giving Clarissa Stamp a mysterious look. "I have plenty of these little articles, and each of them contains its own version of events." He opened his file and rustled the newspaper clippings; there must have been several dozen of them. "Very well, mesdames et messieurs, I ask you please not to interrupt me anymore!" The policeman's voice had turned to iron. "Yes, there is a dangerous criminal among us. Possibly a psychopath." (Renate noticed the professor quietly shift his chair away from Sir Reginald.) "Therefore, I ask you all to be careful. If you notice something out of the ordinary, even the very slightest thing, come to me immediately. And it would be best, of course, if the murderer were to make a full and frank confession; there is no escape from here in any case. That is all I have to say."

Mrs. Truffo put her hand up like a pupil in school: "In fact I *did* see something extraordinary, only yesterday! A charcoal black face, definitely not human, looked in at me from outside while I was in our cabin! I was so scared!" She turned to her other half and jabbed him with her elbow: "I told you, but you paid no attention!"

"Oh," said Renate with a start, "and yesterday a mirror in a genuine tortoiseshell frame disappeared from my toiletry set."

Monsieur the Lunatic apparently also had something to report, but before he had a chance the commissioner slammed his file shut.

"Do not try to make a fool of me! I am an old bloodhound! You won't throw Gustave Gauche off the scent! If necessary, I shall have every one of you put ashore and we will deal with each of you separately! Ten people have been killed; this is not a joke. Think, mesdames et messieurs, think!"

He left the salon, slamming the door loudly behind him.

"Gentlemen, I am not feeling well," Renate declared in a weak voice. "I shall go to my cabin."

"I shall accompany you, Mme. Kleber," said Charles Renier, immediately leaping to her side. "This is simply intolerable! Such incredible insolence!"

Renate pushed him away.

"No thank you. I shall manage quite well on my own."

She walked unsteadily across the room and leaned against the wall by the door for a moment. In the corridor, which was empty, her stride quickened. Renate opened her cabin and went inside, took a travel bag out from under the bed, and thrust a trembling hand in under its silk lining. Her face was pale but determined. In an instant her fingers had located a small metal box.

Inside the box, glittering with cold glass and steel, lay a syringe.

Clarissa Stamp

THINGS HAD BEGUN to go wrong first thing in the morning, when Clarissa quite distinctly spotted two new wrinkles in the mirror—two fine, barely visible lines running from the corners of her eyes toward her temples. It was all the sun's fault. It was so bright here that no parasol or hat could save you. Clarissa spent a long time inspecting herself in that pitiless polished surface and stretching her skin with her fingers, hoping it might be the way she'd slept and that the wrinkles would smooth out. Just as she finished her inspection, she turned her neck and spotted a gray hair behind her ear. That really made her feel glum. Might it perhaps be the sun's fault too? Did hairs fade? Oh no, Miss Stamp, no point in deceiving yourself. As the poet said:

> *November's chill breath trimmed her braids with silver,*
> *Whispering that youth and love were lost forever.*

She took greater pains than usual with her appearance. The gray hair was mercilessly plucked out. It was stupid, of course. Wasn't it John Donne who said the secret of female happiness was knowing when to make the transition from one age to the next, and there were three ages of woman: daughter, wife, and mother? But how could she progress from the second state to the third when she had never been married?

The best cure for thoughts like that was a walk in the fresh air, and Clarissa set out to take a turn round the deck. Huge as *Leviathan* was, it had long since been measured out by her leisurely, even paces—at least the upper deck, which was intended for the first-class passengers. The distance round the perimeter was three hundred fifty-five paces. Seven and a half minutes, if she didn't pause to admire the sea or chat with casual acquaintances.

At this early hour none of her acquaintances were on deck, and Clarissa completed her promenade along the starboard side of the ship unhindered all the way to the stern. The ship was ploughing a smooth path through the brownish surface of the Red Sea and a lazy gray furrow extended from its powerful propeller right out to the horizon. Oh, but it was hot!

Clarissa looked enviously at the sailors polishing the copper fittings one level below. Lucky beasts, in nothing but their linen trousers—no bodice, no bloomers, no stockings with tight garters, no long dress. You couldn't help envying that outrageous Mr. Aono, swanning about the ship in his Japanese dressing gown, and no one in the least bit surprised, because he was an oriental.

She imagined herself lying in a canvas deck chair with absolutely nothing on. No, she could be in a light tunic, like a woman in ancient Greece. And it was perfectly normal. In a hundred years or so, when the human race finally rid itself of prejudice, it would be absolutely natural.

There was Mr. Fandorin riding toward her, the rubber tires on his American tricycle squeaking. They did say that kind of exercise was excellent for developing the elasticity of the muscles and strengthening the heart. The diplomat was dressed in a light sporting outfit: checked pantaloons, gutta-percha shoes with gaiters, a short jacket, and a white shirt with its collar unbuttoned. His bronzed face lit up in a friendly smile of greeting. Mr. Fandorin politely raised his cork helmet and went rustling by. He did not stop.

Clarissa sighed. The idea of a stroll had been a failure; all she had succeeded in doing was soak her underclothes with perspiration. She had to go back to her cabin and change.

Breakfast had been spoiled for Clarissa by that *poseuse* Mme. Kleber. What an incredible ability to transform her own weakness into a means of exploiting others! At the precise moment when the coffee in Clarissa's cup had cooled to the required temperature, that unbearable Swiss woman had complained that she felt stifled and asked for someone to loosen her bodice. Clarissa usually pretended not to hear Renate Kleber's whining and some male volunteer was always found for her, but a man was clearly not suitable for such a delicate task, and as luck would have it Mrs. Truffo was not there—she was helping her husband attend to some lady who had fallen ill. Apparently the tedious creature had previously worked as a nurse. What remarkable social climbing—straight up to the wife of the senior doctor and dining in first-class! And she tried to act like a real British lady, but somewhat overdid it.

Anyway, Clarissa had been forced to fuss with Mme. Kleber's laces, and in the meantime her coffee had gone completely cold. It was a trivial matter, of course, but it was that Kleber woman through and through.

After breakfast she went out for a walk, did ten circuits, and began feeling tired. Taking advantage of the fact that there was no one nearby, she peeped carefully in at the window of cabin number eighteen. Mr. Fandorin was sitting at the secretary, wearing a white shirt with red, white, and blue suspenders, a cigar clenched in the corner of his mouth. He was tapping noisily with his fingers on a bizarre black apparatus made of iron, with a round roller and a large number of keys. Clarissa was so intrigued that she let her guard down and was caught red-handed. The diplomat jumped to his feet, bowed, threw on his jacket, and came across to the open window.

"It's a Remington t-typewriter," he explained. "The very latest model, only just on sale. A most c-convenient device, Miss Stamp, and quite light. Two porters can carry it without any difficulty. Quite indispensable on a journey. You see, I am p-practising my stenography by copying out a piece of Hobbes."

Still red with embarrassment, Clarissa nodded slightly and walked away, then sat down under a striped awning close by. There was a fresh breeze blowing. She opened *The Charterhouse of Parma* and began reading about the selfless love of the beautiful but aging Duchess Sanseverina for the youthful Fabrice del Dongo. Moved to shed a sentimental tear, she wiped it away with her handkerchief, and, as if by design at that moment, Mr. Fandorin emerged on the deck, wearing a white suit with a broad-brimmed panama hat and carrying a cane. And looking exceptionally handsome.

Clarissa called to him. He approached, bowed, and sat down beside her. Glancing at the cover of her book, he said: "I am willing to b-bet that you skipped the description of the Battle of Waterloo. A pity—it is the finest passage in the whole of Stendhal. I have never read a more accurate description of war."

Strangely enough, Clarissa was indeed reading *The Charterhouse of Parma* for the second time, and both times she had simply leafed through the battle scene.

"How could you tell?" she asked curiously. "Are you a mind reader?"

"Women always skip battle scenes," said Fandorin with a shrug. "At least women of your temperament."

"And just what is my temperament?" Clarissa asked in a wheedling voice, feeling she cut a poor figure playing the coquette.

"An inclination to view yourself skeptically and the world around you romantically." He looked at her, his head inclined slightly to one side. "And specifically concerning yourself, I can say that recently there has been some kind of sudden change for the b-better in your life and that you have suffered some k-kind of shock."

Clarissa started and glanced at her companion with frank alarm.

"Don't be frightened," the astonishing diplomat reassured her. "I know absolutely nothing about you. It is simply that I have developed my powers of observation and analysis with the help of special exercises. Usually a single insignificant detail is enough for me to recreate the entire p-picture. Show me a charming button like that"—he pointed delicately to a large ornamental pink button on her jacket—"and I will tell you immediately who lost it—a very big pig or a very small elephant."

Clarissa smiled and asked: "And can you see right through absolutely everybody?"

"Not right through, but I do see a lot. For instance, what can you tell me about that gentleman over there?"

Fandorin pointed to a thickset man with a large mustache observing the shoreline through a pair of binoculars.

"That's Mr. Babble, he's—"

"Stop!" said Fandorin, interrupting her. "I'll try to guess myself."

He looked at Mr. Babble for about thirty seconds, then said: "He is traveling to the east for the first time. He married recently. A factory owner. Business is not going well; there is a whiff of imminent bankruptcy about the gentleman. He spends almost all his time in the billiard room, but he plays badly."

Clarissa had always prided herself on being observant, and she began inspecting Mr. Babble, the Manchester industrialist, more closely.

A factory owner? Well, that was possible to guess. If he was traveling first-class, he must be rich. It was clear from his face that he was no aristocrat. And he didn't look like a businessman, either, in that baggy frock coat, and his features lacked animation. All right, then.

Recently married? Well, that was simple enough—the ring on his third finger gleamed so brightly that it was obviously brand new.

Plays billiards a lot? Why was that? Aha, his jacket was smeared with chalk.

"What makes you think Mr. Babble is traveling to the East for the first time?" she asked. "Why is there a whiff of bankruptcy about him? And what is the basis for your assertion that he is a poor billiards player? Perhaps you have been there and seen him play?"

"No, I have not been in the b-billiard room, because I cannot stand pastimes that involve gambling, and I have never laid eyes on this gentleman before," Fandorin replied. "It is evident that he is traveling this way for the first time from the stubborn persistence with which he is studying the empty shoreline. Otherwise Mr. Babble would be aware that he will not see anything of interest on that side until we reach the Strait of Mandeb. That is one. This gentleman's business affairs must be going very badly, otherwise he would never have embarked on such a long journey, especially so soon after his wedding. A badger like that might leave his set if the end of the world is nigh, but certainly not before. That is two."

"What if he is taking a honeymoon voyage together with his wife?" asked Clarissa, knowing that Mr. Babble was traveling alone.

"And lingering forlornly on the deck like that, and loitering in the billiard room? And he plays quite incredibly badly—his jacket is all white at the front. Only absolutely hopeless players scrape their bellies along the edge of the table like that. That is three."

"Oh, all right, but what will you say about that lady over there?"

Clarissa, now completely engrossed in the game, pointed to Mrs. Blackpool, who was proceeding majestically along the deck, arm-in-arm with her female companion.

Fandorin scanned the estimable lady in question with a disinterested glance.

"With that one everything is written on the face. She is on her way back from England to join her husband. She has been to visit their grown-up children. Her husband is a military man. A colonel."

Mr. Blackpool was indeed a colonel in command of a garrison in some city or other in northern India. This was simply too much.

"Explain!" Clarissa demanded.

"Ladies of that kind do not travel to India on their own b-business, only to the places where their husbands are serving. She is not of the age to have embarked on a journey like this for the first time—so she must be returning. Why could she have traveled to England? Only in order to see her children. I am assuming her parents have already passed away. It is clear from her determined and domineering expression that she is a woman used to command. That is the look of the first lady of a garrison or a regiment. They are usually regarded as a level of command senior to the commanding officer himself. Perhaps you would like to know why she must be a colonel's wife? Well, because if she were a general's wife, she would be traveling first-class, and this lady, as you can see, has a silver badge. But let us not waste any more time on trifles." Fandorin leaned closer and whispered: "Let me tell you about that orangutan over there. A curious specimen."

The monkey-like gentleman who had halted beside Mr. Babble was M. Boileau, the former Windsor habitué who had forsaken the ill-fated salon in time and so slipped through Commissioner Gauche's net.

Speaking in a low voice directly into Clarissa's ear, the diplomat told her: "The man you see there is a criminal and a villain. Most probably a dealer in opium. He lives in Hong Kong and is married to a Chinese woman."

Clarissa burst into laughter.

"Well, you're really wide off the mark this time! That is M. Boileau from Lyon, a philanthropist and the father of eleven entirely French children. And he deals in tea, not opium."

"I rather think not," Fandorin replied calmly. "Look closely. His cuff is bent up and you can see the blue circle of a tattoo on his wrist. I have seen one like that before in a book about China. It is the mark of one of the Hong Kong triads, secret criminal societies. Any European who becomes a member of a triad must be a master criminal operating on a truly grand scale. And of course, he has to marry a Chinese woman. A single look at the face of this 'philanthropist' should make everything clear to you."

Clarissa didn't know whether to believe him or not, but Fandorin continued with a serious expression: "And that is by no means all, Miss Stamp. I can tell a lot about a person even if I am b-blindfolded—from the sounds that he makes and his smell. Why not test me for yourself?"

And, so saying, he untied his white satin necktie and handed it to Clarissa.

She fingered the fabric—it was dense and opaque—and then blindfolded the diplomat with it. As though by accident, she touched his cheek—it was smooth and hot.

The ideal candidate soon put in an appearance from the direction of the stern—the well-known suffragette Lady Campbell, making her way to India in order to collect signatures for her petition for married women to be given the vote. Mannish and massive, with cropped hair, she lumbered along the deck like a cart horse. He would never guess it was a lady and not a boatswain.

"Right, who is this coming our way?" Clarissa asked, choking in anticipatory laughter.

Alas, her merriment was short-lived.

Fandorin wrinkled up his brow and began tossing out staccato phrases.

"A skirt hem rustling. A woman. A heavy stride. A strong c-character. Elderly. Plain. Smokes tobacco. Short-cropped hair."

"Why does she have short-cropped hair?" Clarissa squealed, covering her eyes and listening carefully to the suffragette's elephantine footfall. How, how did he do it?

"If a woman smokes, she must have bobbed hair and be progressive in her views," Fandorin declared in a firm voice. "And this one also despises fashion and wears a kind of shapeless robe, bright green with a scarlet belt."

Clarissa was dumbstruck. It was absolutely incredible! She took her hands away from her eyes in superstitious terror and saw that Fandorin had already removed the necktie and even retied it in an elegant knot. The diplomat's blue eyes were sparkling merrily.

It was all very pleasant, but then the conversation ended badly. When she stopped laughing, Clarissa very delicately broached the subject of the Crimean War and what a tragedy it had been both for Europe and Russia. She cautiously recalled her own memories of the time, remembering them as somewhat more infantile than they were in reality. She was anticipating reciprocal confidences, and hoping to learn exactly how old Fandorin really was. Her worst fears were confirmed.

"I was not b-born yet then," he confessed, artlessly clipping Clarissa's wings.

After that everything went from bad to worse. Clarissa had tried to turn the conversation to painting, but she got everything so mixed up that she couldn't even explain properly why the pre-Raphaelites had called themselves pre-Raphaelites. He must have thought her an absolute idiot. Ah, but what difference did it make now?

AS SHE WAS making her way back to her cabin, feeling sad, something terrifying happened.

She saw a gigantic black shadow quivering in a dark corner of the corridor. Clutching at her heart, Clarissa let out an immodest squeal and made a dash for her own door. Once she was in her cabin, it was a long time before she could calm her wildly beating heart. What was that thing? Neither man nor beast. Some concretion of evil, destructive energy. Her guilty conscience. The phantom of her Paris nightmare.

No more, she told herself, she had put all that behind her. It was nothing. It was delirium, a delusion, nothing more. She had sworn she would not torment herself with remorse. This was a new life, bright and happy— "And may your mansion be illumined by the lamp of bliss."

To soothe her nerves, she put on her most expensive day dress, the one she had not even tried on yet (white Chinese silk with a pale green bow at the back of the waist) and put her emerald necklace around her neck. She admired the gleam of the stones.

Very well, so she wasn't young. Or beautiful, either. But she was far from stupid, and she had money. And that was much better than being an ugly, aging fool without a penny to her name.

Clarissa entered the salon at precisely two o'clock, but the entire company was already assembled. Strangely enough, rather than fragmenting the Windsor contingent, the commissioner's astounding announcement of the previous day had brought them all closer together. A common secret that cannot be shared with anyone else binds people to one another more tightly than a common cause or a common interest. Clarissa noticed that her fellow diners now gathered around the table in advance of the times set for breakfast, lunch, five o'clock tea, and dinner, and lingered on afterward, something that had hardly ever happened before. Even the captain's first mate, who was only indirectly involved in the whole affair, spent a lot of time sitting on in the Windsor salon with the others rather than hurrying off about his official business (but then, of course, the lieutenant might possibly be acting on the captain's orders). It was as though the Windsorites had joined some elite club that was closed to the uninitiated. Several times Clarissa caught swift, stealthy glances being cast in her direction. Glances that could mean one of two things: "Are you the murderer?" or "Have you guessed I am the murderer?" Every time it happened, she felt a sweet trembling sensation welling up from somewhere deep inside, from the very depths of her, a pungent cocktail of fear and excitement. The image of the Rue de Grenelle rose up clearly before her eyes, the way it looked in the evening: beguilingly quiet and deserted, with the bare branches of the black chestnut trees swaying against the sky. God forbid the commissioner should somehow find out about the Ambassador Hotel. The very thought of it terrified Clarissa, and she cast a furtive glance in the policeman's direction.

Gauche presided at the table like the high priest of a secret sect. They were all constantly aware of his presence and followed the expression on his face out of the corner of their eyes, but Gauche appeared not to notice that at all. He assumed the role of a genial philosopher happy to relate his "little stories" while the others listened tensely.

By unspoken agreement, *that* was discussed only in the salon, and only in the commissioner's presence. If two Windsorites chanced to meet somewhere in neutral territory—in the music salon, on the deck, in the reading hall—they did not discuss *that* under any circumstances. And not even in the salon did they return to the tantalizing subject on every occasion. It usually happened spontaneously, following some entirely chance remark.

Today at breakfast, for instance, a general conversation had completely failed to materialize, but now as Clarissa took her seat the discussion was in full swing. She began studying the menu with a bored expression on her face, as though she had forgotten what she had ordered for lunch, but she could already feel that familiar tingle of excitement.

"The thing that bothers me about the crime," Dr. Truffo was saying, "is the complete pointlessness of it. Apparently all those people were killed for absolutely nothing. The golden Shiva ended up in the Seine, and the killer was left empty-handed."

Fandorin rarely participated in these discussions, preferring to remain silent most of the time, but for once even he felt compelled to express an opinion.

"That is not quite true. The p-perpetrator was left with the shawl."

"What shawl?" asked the doctor, confused.

"The painted Indian shawl. In which, if we are to believe the newspapers, the killer wrapped the stolen Shiva."

This joke was greeted with rather nervous laughter.

The doctor gestured expressively.

"But a mere shawl . . ."

Sweetchild gave a sudden start and raised his spectacles from his nose, a gesture of his that indicated intense agitation.

"No, don't laugh! I made enquiries as to exactly which shawl was stolen. And it is, gentlemen, an extremely unusual piece of material with a story of its own. Have you ever heard of the Emerald Rajah?"

"Wasn't he some kind of legendary Indian nabob?" asked Clarissa.

"Not legendary, but quite real, madam. It was the name given to Bagdassar, the ruler of the principality of Brahmapur. The principality is located in a large, fertile valley, surrounded on all sides by mountains. The rajahs trace their line of descent from the great Babur and are adherents of Islam, but that did not prevent them from reigning in peace for three hundred years over a little country in which the majority of the population are Hindus. Despite the difference in religion between the ruling caste and their subjects, the principality never suffered a single rebellion or feud. The rajahs prospered and grew rich, and by Bagdassar's time the house of Brahmapur was regarded as the wealthiest in the whole of India after the nizams of Hyderabad, whose wealth, as you are no doubt aware, eclipses that of every monarch in the world, including Queen Victoria and the Russian emperor Alexander."

"The greatness of our queen does not consist in the extent of her personal fortune, but in the prosperity of her subjects," Clarissa remarked primly, stung by the professor's remark.

"Undoubtedly," agreed Sweetchild, who was already in full swing and not to be halted. "However, the wealth of the rajahs of Brahmapur was of a very special kind. They did not hoard gold; they did not stuff trunks to overflowing with silver; they did not build palaces of pink marble. No, for three hundred years these rulers knew only one passion—precious stones. Do you know what the Brahmapur Standard is?"

"Isn't it a style of faceting diamonds?" Dr. Truffo asked uncertainly.

"The Brahmapur Standard is a jewelers' term referring to a diamond, sapphire, ruby, or emerald that is faceted in a particular manner and is the size of a walnut, which corresponds to one hundred and sixty *tandool*s; in other words, it is eighty carats in weight."

"But that is very large," Renier exclaimed in amazement. "Stones as large as that are very rare. If my memory does not deceive me, even the Regent diamond, the glory of the French state jewels, is not very much larger."

"No, lieutenant, the Pitt diamond, also known as the Regent, is almost twice as large," the professor corrected him with an air of authority, "but eighty carats is still a considerable size, especially if one is dealing with stones of the first water. But can you believe, ladies and gentlemen, that Bagdasssar had five hundred and twelve such stones, and all of absolutely irreproachable quality!"

"That's impossible!" exclaimed Sir Reginald.

Fandorin asked: "Why exactly five hundred and t-twelve?"

"Because of the sacred number eight," Sweetchild gladly explained. "Five hundred and twelve is eight times eight times eight, that is, eight to the power of three or eight cubed, the so called 'ideal number.' There is here, undoubtedly, some influence from Buddhism, in which the number eight is regarded with particular reverence. In the northeastern part of India, where Brahmapur lies, religions are intertwined in the most bizarre fashion imaginable. But the most interesting thing of all is where this treasure was kept, and how."

"And where was it kept?" Renate Kleber inquired curiously.

"In a simple clay casket without any adornment whatever. In 1852 I visited Brahmapur as a young archeologist and met the rajah Bagdassar. An ancient temple had been discovered in the jungle within the principality, and the rajah invited me to assess the significance of the find. I carried out the necessary research, and what do you think I discovered? The temple turned out to have been built in the time of King Chandragupta, when—"

"Stop, stop, stop!" the commissioner interrupted. "You can tell us about archeology some other time. Let's get back to the rajah."

"Ah, yes indeed," said the professor, fluttering his eyelashes. "That really would be best. Well then, the rajah was pleased with me and as a token of his favor he showed me his legendary casket. Oh, I shall never forget the sight!" Sweetchild narrowed his eyes as he continued: "Imagine a dark dungeon with only a single torch burning in a bronze bracket beside the door. The rajah and I were alone; his retainers remained outside the massive door, which was protected by a dozen guards. I got no clear impression of the interior of this treasure house, since my eyes had no time to adjust to the semidarkness. I only heard the locks clanging as his highness opened them. Then Bagdassar turned to me and in his hands I saw a cube that was the color of earth and appeared to be very heavy. It was the size of . . ." Sweetchild opened his eyes and looked around. Everyone was sitting and listening with bated breath, and Renate Kleber had even parted her lips like a child. "Oh, I don't know. I suppose about the size of Miss Stamp's hat, if one were to place that piece of headgear in a square box." As though on command, everyone turned and began staring curiously at the diminutive Tyrolean hat decorated with a pheasant feather. Clarissa endured this public scrutiny with a dignified smile, in the manner she had been taught as a child. "This cube resembled most closely one of the ordinary clay bricks they use for building in those parts. His highness later explained to me that the coarse, dull uniformity of the clay surface made a far better foil than gold or ivory for the magnificent glimmering light of the stones. Indeed, I was able to see that for myself when Bagdassar slowly raised a hand studded with rings to the lid of the casket, then opened it with a rapid movement and . . . I was blinded, ladies and gentlemen!" The professor's voice quavered. "It . . . it is impossible to express it in words! Picture to yourselves a mysterious, multicolored, lambent radiance spilling out of that dark cube and painting the gloomy vaults of that dungeon with shimmering patches of rainbow-colored light! The round stones were arranged in eight layers, and in each layer were sixty-four faceted sources of quite unbearable brilliance! And the effect was certainly enhanced by the flickering flame of the solitary torch. I can still see Rajah Bagdassar's face bathed from below in that magical light . . ."

The professor closed his eyes again and fell silent.

"And how much, for instance, are these glass baubles worth?" the commissioner's rasping voice inquired.

"Yes, indeed, how much?" Mme. Kleber repeated enthusiastically. "Say, in your English pounds?"

Clarissa heard Mrs. Truffo whisper rather loudly to her husband: "She's so vulgar!" But even so she pushed her mousy curls back off her ear in order not to miss a single word.

"You know," Sweetchild said with a genial smile, "I've often wondered about that. It's not an easy question to answer, since the value of precious stones fluctuates according to the market, but as things stand today—"

"Yes, please, as things stand today, not in the time of King Chandragupta," Gauche put in gruffly.

"Hmm . . . I don't know exactly how many diamonds, how many sapphires, and how many rubies the rajah had. But I do know that he valued emeralds most of all, which was how he acquired his popular name. In the course of his reign seven emeralds were acquired from Brazil and four from the Urals, and for each of them Bagdassar gave one diamond and some additional payment. You see, each of his ancestors had a favorite type of stone he preferred to all others and tried to acquire in greater numbers. The magical number of five hundred and twelve stones had already been reached in the time of Bagdassar's grandfather, and since then the ruler's primary goal had not been to increase the number of stones, but to improve their quality. Stones that fell even slightly short of perfection or that the current ruler did not favor for some reason, were sold—hence the fame of the Brahmapur Standard, which gradually spread around the world. Their place in the casket was taken by other, more valuable stones. Bagdassar's ancestors carried their obsession with the Brahmapur Standard to quite insane lengths. One of them purchased a yellow sapphire weighing three hundred *tandool*s from the Persian shah Abbas the Great, paying ten caravans of ivory for this marvel, but the stone was larger than the standard size and the rajah had his jewelers cut away all the excess!"

"That is terrible, of course," said the commissioner, "but let us get back to the question of the stones' value."

This time, however, it proved less easy to direct the flow of the Indologist's speech into the required channel.

"The question of value can wait for a moment!" he said, peremptorily dismissing the detective's request. "Is it really so important? When one considers a noble stone of such size and quality, the first thing that comes to mind is not money but the magical properties that have been attributed to it since ancient times. The diamond, for instance, is considered a symbol of purity. Our ancestors used to test their wives' fidelity by placing a diamond under their sleeping spouse's pillow. If she was faithful, she would immediately, without waking, turn to her husband and embrace him. If she was unfaithful, she would toss and turn and attempt to throw the diamond to the floor. And the diamond is also reputed to guarantee its owner's invincibility. The ancient Arabs used to believe that in battle the general who owned the larger diamond would be victorious."

"Ancient Arab mistaken," said Gintaro Aono, interrupting the inspired speaker in full flow.

Everyone stared in astonishment at the Japanese, who very rarely joined in the general conversation and never interrupted anyone. The oriental continued hastily in that odd accent of his.

"In the Academy of St. Cyr we were taught that the duke of Burgundy Charles the Bold speciarry took the huge Sancy diamond with him into battle against the Swiss, but it did not save him from defeat."

Clarissa felt sorry for the poor devil—making a rare attempt to show off his knowledge at such an inopportune moment.

The Japanese gentleman's remark was greeted with deadly silence, and Aono blushed in painful embarrassment.

"Yes, indeed, Charles the Bold," the professor said with a sharp nod of dissatisfaction, and he concluded without his former ardor. "The sapphire symbolizes devotion and constancy; the emerald confers improved sharpness of vision and foresight; the ruby protects against illness and the evil eye . . . But you were asking about the value of Bagdassar's treasures?"

"I realize it must be an incredibly large sum, but could you at least give us an approximate idea of how many zeros, at least?" Mme. Kleber enunciated clearly, as if she were addressing a dull-witted pupil, demonstrating yet again that once a banker's wife, always a banker's wife.

Clarissa would have enjoyed listening to more on the subject of the magical properties of precious stones and would have preferred to avoid talk of money. Apart from anything else, it was so vulgar.

"Very well, then, let me just add it up." Sweetchild took a pencil out of his pocket and poised himself to write on a paper napkin. "Formerly the diamond was considered the most expensive stone, but since the discovery of the South African fields it has fallen significantly in value. Large sapphires are found more often than other precious stones, and so on average they are only worth a quarter as much as diamonds, but that does not apply to yellow and star sapphires, and they made up the majority of Bagdassar's collection. Pure rubies and emeralds of great size are also rare and have a higher value than diamonds of the same weight . . . Very well, for simplicity's sake, let us assume all five hundred and twelve stones are diamonds, and all of the same value. Each of them, as I have already said, weighs eighty carats. According to Tavernier's formula, which is used by jewelers all over the world, the value of a single stone is calculated by taking the market value of a one-carat diamond and multiplying it by the square of the number of carats in the stone concerned. That would give us . . . a one-carat diamond costs about fifteen pounds on the Antwerp exchange. Eighty squared is six thousand four hundred. Multiply by fifteen . . . mmm . . . ninety-six thousand pounds sterling—so that is the value of an average stone from the Brahmapur casket. Multiply by five hundred and twelve . . . about fifty million pounds sterling. And in actual fact even more, because, as I have already explained, colored stones of such a great size are more valuable than diamonds," Sweetchild concluded triumphantly.

"Fifty million pounds? As much as that?" Renier asked in a voice suddenly hoarse. "But that's a billion and a half francs!"

Clarissa caught her breath, all thoughts of the romantic properties of precious stones driven out of her head by astonishment at this astronomical figure.

"Fifty million! But that's half the annual budget of the entire British Empire!" she gasped.

"That's three Suez Canals!" mumbled the redheaded Milford-Stokes. "Or even more!"

The commissioner also took a napkin and became absorbed in some calculations of his own.

"It is my salary for three hundred thousand years," he announced in dismay. "Are you not exaggerating, Professor? The idea of some petty native princeling possessing such immense wealth!"

Sweetchild replied as proudly as if all the treasure of India belonged to him personally.

"Why, that's nothing! The jewels of the nizam of Hyderabad are estimated to be worth three hundred million, but of course you couldn't get them all into one little casket. In terms of compactness, certainly, Bagdassar's treasure had no equal."

Fandorin touched the Indologist's sleeve discreetly.

"Nonetheless, I p-presume this sum is rather abstract in nature. Surely no one would be able to sell such a huge number of gigantic p-precious stones all at once? It would bring down the market price."

"You are mistaken to think so, monsieur diplomat," the scholar replied with animation. "The prestige of the Brahmapur Standard is so great that there would be no shortage of buyers. I am certain that at least half the stones would not even leave India—they would be bought by the local princes, in the first instance by the nizam, whom I have already mentioned. The remaining stones would be fought over by the banking houses of Europe and America, and the monarchs of Europe would not let slip the chance to add the masterpieces of Brahmapur to their treasuries. Oho, if he had wished, Bagdassar could have sold the contents of his casket in a matter of weeks."

"You keep referring to this man in the p-past tense," remarked Fandorin. "Is he dead? And, if so, what happened to the casket?"

"Alas, that is something nobody knows. Bagdassar's own end was tragic. During the Sepoy Mutiny the rajah was incautious enough to enter into secret dealings with the rebels, and the vice-regent declared Brahmapur enemy territory. There was malicious talk of Britannia simply wishing to get its hands on Bagdassar's treasure, but of course it was untrue. That is not the way we English go about things."

"Oh, yes," nodded Renier with a dark smile, exchanging glances with the commissioner.

Clarissa stole a cautious glance at Fandorin—surely he could not also be infected with the bacillus of Anglophobia? The Russian diplomat, however, sat there with an air of absolute equanimity.

"A squadron of dragoons was dispatched to Bagdassar's palace. The rajah attempted to escape by fleeing to Afghanistan, but the cavalry overtook him at the Ganges crossing. Bagdassar considered it beneath his dignity to submit to arrest and he took poison. The casket was not found on him; in fact, he had with him nothing but a small bundle containing a note in English. In the note, which was addressed to the British authorities, the rajah swore that he was innocent and requested them to forward the bundle to his only son. The boy was studying in a boarding school somewhere in Europe—it's the thing among Indian grandees of the new breed. I should mention that Bagdassar was no stranger to the spirit of civilization; he visited London and Paris several times. He even married a Frenchwoman."

"Oh, how unusual!" Clarissa exclaimed. "To be an Indian rajah's wife! What became of her?"

"Never mind the damned wife, tell us about the bundle," the commissioner said impatiently. "What was in it?"

"Absolutely nothing of any interest," said the professor with a regretful shrug of his shoulders. "A volume of the Koran. But the casket disappeared without a trace, although it was looked for everywhere."

"And was it a perfectly ordinary Koran?" asked Fandorin.

"It could hardly have been more ordinary: printed by a press in Bombay, with devout comments in the deceased's own hand in the margins. The squadron commander decided that the Koran could be forwarded as requested, and for himself he took only the shawl in which it was wrapped as a souvenir of the expedition. The shawl was later acquired by Lord Littleby for his collection of Indian paintings on silk."

To clarify the point, the commissioner asked: "So that is the same shawl in which the murderer wrapped the Shiva?"

"The very same. It is genuinely unusual. Made of the very finest silk, almost weightless. The painting is rather trivial—an image of the bird of paradise, the sweet-voiced Kalavinka. But it possesses two unique features that I have never encountered in any other Indian shawl. First, where Kalavinka's eye should be is a hole, the edges of which have been sewn up very carefully with brocade thread. Second, the shawl itself is an interesting shape—not rectangular, but tapering. A sort of irregular triangle, with two crooked sides and one absolutely straight."

"Is the shawl of any g-great value?" asked Fandorin.

"All this talk about the shawl is boring," complained Mme. Kleber, sticking out her lower lip capriciously. "Tell us more about the jewels! They ought to have searched a bit more thoroughly."

Sweetchild laughed.

"Oh, madam, you cannot even imagine how thoroughly the new rajah searched for them. He was one of the local *zamindar*s who had rendered us invaluable service during the Sepoy Mutiny and received the throne of Brahmapur as a reward. But greed unhinged the poor man's mind. Some wit whispered to him that Bagdassar had hidden the casket in the wall of one of the buildings. And since in size and appearance the casket looked exactly like an ordinary clay brick, the new rajah ordered all buildings constructed of that material to be taken apart. The houses were demolished one after another and each brick was smashed under the personal supervision of the new ruler. Bearing in mind that in Brahmapur ninety percent of all structures are built of clay bricks, in a few months a flourishing city was transformed into a heap of ruins. The insane rajah was poisoned by his own retainers, who feared a popular revolt even more fierce than the Sepoy Mutiny."

"Serve him right, the Judas," Renier declared with feeling. "Nothing is more abominable than treachery."

Fandorin patiently repeated his question: "But nonetheless, Professor, is the shawl of any g-great value?"

"I think not. It is more of a rarity, a curiosity."

"But why are things always b-being wrapped in it—first the Koran, and then the Shiva? Could this piece of silk perhaps have some ritual significance?"

"I've never heard of anything of the sort. It is simply a coincidence."

Commissioner Gauche got to his feet with a grunt and straightened his numbed shoulders.

"Mm, yes, an entertaining story, but unfortunately it has nothing to contribute to our investigation. The murderer is unlikely to be keeping this piece of cloth as a sentimental souvenir. It would be handy if he was, though," he mused. "One of you, my dear suspects, simply takes out a silk shawl with a picture of the bird of paradise—out of sheer absent-mindedness—and blows his nose into it. Old papa Gauche would know what to do then, all right."

The detective laughed, clearly in the belief that his joke was very witty. Clarissa gave the vulgar lout a disapproving look.

Catching her glance, the commissioner narrowed his eyes.

"By the way, Mademoiselle Stamp, about your wonderful hat. A very stylish item, the latest Parisian chic. Is it long since your last visit to Paris?"

Clarissa braced herself and replied in an icy tone, "The hat was bought in London, commissioner. And I have never been to Paris."

What was Mr. Fandorin staring at so intensely? Clarissa followed the line of his gaze and turned pale.

The diplomat was studying her ostrich-feather fan, and the words inscribed in gold on its ivory handle: *Meilleurs souvenirs! Hotel AMBAS-SADEUR. Rue de Grenelle, Paris.*

What an appalling blunder!

Gintaro Aono

⸺⧼⧽⸺

The fifth day of the fourth month,
in sight of the Eritrean coast

Below—the green stripe of the sea,
Between—the yellow stripe of sand,
Above—the blue stripe of the sky.
Such are the colors
Of Africa's flag.

This trivial pentastich is the fruit of my hour-and-a-half-long efforts to attain a state of inner harmony—the confounded harmony that has stubbornly refused to be restored.

I have been sitting alone on the stern, watching the dreary coastline of Africa and feeling my infinite isolation more acutely than ever. I can at least be thankful that the noble habit of keeping a diary was instilled in me from childhood. Seven years ago, as I set out to study in the remote country of Furansu, I dreamed in secret that one day the diary of my travels would be published as a book and bring fame to me and the entire clan of Aono. But alas, my intellect is too imperfect and my feelings are far too ordinary for these pitiful pages ever to rival the great diaristic literature of former times.

And yet if not for these daily entries I should certainly have gone insane long ago.

Even here, on board a ship traveling to East Asia, there are only two representatives of the yellow race—myself and a Chinese eunuch, a court

official of the eleventh rank who has visited Paris to obtain the latest per-
fumes and cosmetics products for the Empress Dowager Tz'u Hsi. For
the sake of economy he is traveling second-class, of which he is greatly
ashamed, and our conversation was broken off the moment it emerged that
I am traveling first-class. What a disgrace for China! In the court official's
place I should certainly have died of humiliation, for on this European vessel each of us is the representative of a great Asian power. I understand
courtier Chan's state of mind, but it is nonetheless a pity that he feels too
ashamed even to leave his cramped cabin—there are things we could have
talked about. That is, although we could not talk about them, we could
communicate with the aid of ink, brush, and paper, for while we speak different languages, we use the same hieroglyphs.

Never mind, I tell myself, hold on. The difficulties remaining are mere
trifles. In a month or so you will see the lights of Nagasaki, and from there
it is a mere stone's throw to your hometown of Kagoshima. And what do I
care that my return promises me only humiliation and disgrace, that I shall
be the laughingstock of all my friends? For I shall be home once again, and,
after all, no one will dare to express his contempt for me openly, since
everyone knows that I was carrying out my father's will, and that orders
are not a matter for discussion. I have done what I had to do, what my duty
obliged me to do. My life may be ruined, but if that is what the welfare of
Japan requires . . . But enough, no more of that!

And yet who could have imagined that returning to my homeland, the
final stage of my seven-year ordeal, would prove so hard? In France at least
I could take my food alone, I could delight in solitary walks and com-
muning with nature. But here on the ship I feel like a grain of rice that has
fallen by accident into a bowl of noodles. Seven years of life among the
red-haired barbarians have failed to inure me to some of their disgusting
habits. When I see the fastidious Kleber-san cut a bloody beefsteak with
her knife and then lick her red-stained lips with her pink tongue, it turns
my stomach. And these English washbasins in which you have to plug the
drain and wash your face in contaminated water! And those appalling
clothes, the invention of some perverted mind! They make you feel like a
carp wrapped in greased paper, being roasted over hot coals. Most of all I
hate the starched collars that leave a red rash on your chin and the leather

shoes, a genuine instrument of torture. Exploiting my position as an "oriental savage," I take the liberty of strolling around the deck in a light *yukata,* while my unfortunate dining companions stew in their clothes from morning till night. My sensitive nostrils suffer greatly from the smell of European sweat, so harsh, greasy, and fleshy. Equally terrible is the round-eyes' habit of blowing their noses into handkerchiefs and then putting them back into their pockets, together with the mucus, then taking them out and blowing heir noses into them again. They will simply not believe it at home; they will think I have made it all up. But then, seven years is a long time. Perhaps by now our ladies are also wearing those ridiculous bustles on their hindquarters and tottering along on high heels. It would be interesting to see how Kyoko-san would look in a costume like that. After all, she is quite grown up now—thirteen years old already. In another year or two they will marry us. Or perhaps it will happen even sooner. Oh, to be home soon!

Today I found it especially difficult to attain inner harmony because:

1. I discovered that my finest instrument, capable of easily cutting through the very thickest muscle, has been stolen from my travel bag. What does this strange theft mean?

2. At lunch I once again found myself in a position of humiliation—far worse than the incident with Charles the Bold (see my entry for yesterday). Fandorin-san, who continues as before to be very curious concerning Japan, began questioning me about Bushido and samurai traditions. The conversation moved on to my family and my ancestors. Since I had introduced myself as an officer, the Russian began to question me about the weapons, uniforms, and service regulations of the Imperial Army. It was terrible! When it emerged that I had never even heard of the Berdan rifle, Fandorin-san looked at me very strangely. He must have thought the Japanese army is staffed with absolute ignoramuses. In my shame I completely forgot my manners and ran out of the salon, which of course only rendered the incident even more embarrassing.

It was a long time before I was able to settle my nerves. First I went up onto the boat deck, which is deserted because the sun is at its fiercest there. I stripped to my loincloth and for half an hour practiced the kicking technique of *mawashi-geri.* When I had reached the right condition and the sun began to look pink, I seated myself in the *ʒa-ʒen* pose and attempted to meditate for forty minutes. And only after that did I dress myself and go to the stern to compose a *tanka*.

All of these exercises were helpful. Now I know how to save face. At dinner I shall tell Fandorin-san that we are forbidden to talk to strangers about the Imperial Army and that I ran out of the salon in such haste because I am suffering from terrible diarrhea. I think that will sound convincing and in the eyes of my neighbors at table I shall not appear to be an ill-mannered savage.

The evening of the same day

So much for harmony! Something quite catastrophic has happened. My hands are trembling in shame, but I must immediately note down all the details. It will help me to concentrate and make the correct decision. To begin with, only the facts; conclusions later.

And so.

Dinner in the Windsor salon began as usual at eight o'clock. Although during the afternoon I had ordered red-beet salad, the waiter brought me bloody, half-raw beef. Apparently he thought I had said "red beef." I prodded the slaughtered animal's flesh, still oozing blood, and observed with secret envy the captain's first mate, who was eating a most appetizing vegetable stew with lean chicken.

What else happened?

Nothing out of the ordinary. Kleber-san, as always, was complaining of a migraine but eating with a voracious appetite. She looks the very picture of health, a classic example of an easy pregnancy. I am sure that when her time comes the child will pop out of her like a cork out of sparkling French wine.

There was talk of the heat, of tomorrow's arrival in Aden, of precious stones. Fandorin-san and I discussed the relative advantages of Japanese and English gymnastics. I found myself in a position to be condescending, since in this sphere the superiority of the East over the West is self-evident. The difference, of course, is that for them physical exercise is sport, a game, but for us it is the path to spiritual self-improvement. It is spiritual improvement that is important—physical perfection is of no importance, it is automatically dragged along behind, as carriages follow a steam locomotive. I should mention that the Russian is very interested in sport and has even heard something of the martial-arts schools of Japan and China. This morning I was meditating on the boat deck earlier than usual and I saw Fandorin-san there. We merely bowed to each other and did not enter into conversation, because each of us was occupied with his own business: I was bathing my soul in the light of the new day, while he, dressed in gymnast's tights, was performing squats and push-ups with each arm in turn and lifting weights that appeared to be very heavy.

Our common interest in gymnastics rendered our evening conversation unforced, and I felt more relaxed than usual. I told the Russian about jujitsu. He listened with unflagging interest.

At about half past eight (I did not notice the precise time), Kleber-san, having drunk her tea and eaten two cakes, complained of feeling dizzy. I told her that this happens to pregnant women when they eat too much. For some reason she evidently took offence at my words and I realized that I had spoken out of turn. How many times have I sworn not to do so? After all, I was taught by wise teachers: When you find yourself in strange company, sit, listen, smile pleasantly, and from time to time nod your head— you will acquire the reputation of being a well-bred individual, and at the very least you will not say anything stupid. It is not the place of an "officer" to be giving medical advice!

Renier-san immediately leapt to his feet and volunteered to accompany the lady to her cabin. He is in general a most considerate man, and especially with Kleber-san. He is the only one who is not yet sick of her interminable caprices. He stands up for the honor of his uniform; I applaud him.

When they left, the men moved to the armchairs and began smoking. The ship's Italian doctor and his English wife went to visit a patient and I attempted to impress upon the waiter that they should not put either bacon or ham in my omelette for breakfast. After so many days, they should have grown used to the idea by now.

Perhaps about two minutes later we suddenly heard a woman's high-pitched scream.

First, I did not immediately realize it was Kleber-san screaming. Second, I did not understand that her bloodcurdling scream of "Oscure! Oscure!" meant *"Au secours! Au secours!"* But that does not excuse my behavior. I acted disgracefully, quite disgracefully. I am unworthy of the title of samurai!

But everything in order.

The first to reach the door was Fandorin-san, followed by the commissioner of police, then Milford-Stokes-san and Sweetchild-sensei, and I was still glued to the spot. They have all decided, of course, that the Japanese army is staffed by pitiful cowards. In actual fact, I simply did not understand immediately what was happening.

When I did understand, it was too late—I was the last to come running up to the scene of the incident. I was even behind Stamp-san.

Kleber-san's cabin is very close to the salon, the fifth door on the right along the corridor. Peering over the shoulders of those who had reached the spot before me, I saw a quite incredible sight. The door of the cabin was wide open. Kleber-san was lying on the floor and moaning pitifully, with some immense, heavy, shiny black mass slumped across her. I did not immediately realize that it was a Negro of immense stature. He was wearing white canvas trousers. The handle of a sailor's dirk was protruding from the back of his neck. From the position of his body, I knew immediately that the Negro was dead. A blow like that, struck to the base of the skull, requires great strength and precision, but it kills instantly and surely.

Kleber-san was floundering in a vain effort to wriggle out from under the heavy carcass that was pinning her down. Lieutenant Renier was bustling about beside her. His face was whiter than the collar of his shirt. The scabbard hanging at his side was empty. The lieutenant was completely flustered, torn between dragging this unsavory deadweight off the pregnant woman and turning to us and launching into an incoherent explanation of what had happened to the commissioner.

Fandorin-san was the only one who remained calm and composed. Without any visible effort, he lifted up the heavy corpse and dragged it off to one side (I remembered his exercises with the weights), then helped Kleber-san into an armchair and gave her some water. I came to my senses and checked quickly to make sure she was not wounded or bruised. She did not seem to be. Whether there is any internal damage will become clear later. Everyone was so agitated that they were not surprised when I examined her. White people are convinced that all orientals are part shaman and know the art of healing. Kleber-san's pulse was ninety-five, which is perfectly understandable.

Interrupting each other as they spoke, Renier-san and Kleber-san told us the following story.

The lieutenant:

He saw Kleber-san to her cabin, wished her a pleasant evening, and took his leave. However, he had scarcely taken two steps away from her door when he heard her desperate scream.

Kleber-san:

She went into her cabin, switched on the electric light, and saw a gigantic black man standing by her dressing table with her coral beads in his hands (I actually saw these beads on the floor afterward). The Negro threw himself on her without speaking, tossed her to the floor, and grabbed hold of her throat with his massive hands. She screamed.

The lieutenant:

He burst into the cabin, saw the appalling (he said "fantastic") scene, and for a moment was at a loss. He grabbed the Negro by the shoulders, but was unable to shift the giant by even an inch. Then he kicked him in the head, but again without the slightest effect. It was only then, fearing for the life of Kleber-san and her child, that he grabbed his dirk out of its sheath and struck a single blow.

It occurred to me that the lieutenant must have spent a turbulent youth in taverns and bordellos, where skill in handling a knife determines who will sober up the following morning and who will be carried off to the cemetery.

Captain Cliff and Dr. Truffo ran in. The cabin became crowded. No one could understand how the African had come to be on board the *Leviathan*. Fandorin-san carefully inspected a tattoo covering the dead man's chest and said he had seen one like it before. Apparently during the recent Balkan conflict he was held prisoner by the Turks, and there he saw black slaves with precisely the same zigzag lines in concentric circles around the nipples. They are the ritual markings of the Ndanga tribe, recently discovered by Arab slave traders in the very heart of equatorial Africa. Ndanga men are in great demand at markets throughout the East.

It seemed to me that Fandorin-san said all this with a rather strange expression on his face, as though he were puzzled by something. However, I could be mistaken, since the facial expressions of Europeans are freakish and do not correspond at all to ours.

Commissioner Gauche listened to the diplomat carefully. He said there were two questions that interested him as a representative of the law: How the Negro had managed to get on the ship and why he had attacked Mme. Kleber.

Then it emerged that things had begun disappearing in a mysterious fashion from the cabins of several of the people present. I remembered the item that had disappeared from my cabin, but naturally I said nothing. It was also established that people had seen a massive black shadow (Miss Stamp) or a black face peeping in at their window (Mrs. Truffo). It is clear now that these were not hallucinations and not the fruit of morbid imaginings.

Everyone turned on the captain. Apparently the passengers had been in mortal danger all the time they had been on board and the ship's command had not even been aware of it. Cliff-san was scarlet with shame. And it must be admitted that a terrible blow has been struck to his prestige. I tactfully turned away so that he would suffer less from his loss of face.

Then the captain asked the witnesses to the incident to move into the Windsor salon and addressed us with a speech of great power and dignity. Above all he apologized for what had happened. He asked us not to tell anyone about this "regrettable occurrence," since it might cause mass psychosis on board the ship. He promised that his sailors would immediately comb all the holds, the 'tween-decks, the wine cellar, the storerooms, and even the coal bins. He gave us his guarantee that there would not be any more black burglars on board his ship.

The captain is a good man, a genuine old sea dog. He speaks awkwardly, in short, clipped phrases, but it is clear that he is strong in spirit and he performs his job with sober diligence. I once heard Truffo-sensei telling the commissioner that Captain Cliff is a widower and dotes on his only daughter, who is being educated in a boarding school somewhere. I find that very touching.

Now I seem to be gradually recovering my composure. The lines of writing are more even and my hand is no longer shaking. I can go on to the most unpalatable moment of all.

During my superficial examination of Kleber-san, I noticed that she was not bruised. There were also several other observations that ought to be shared with the captain and the commissioner. But I wished above all to reassure a pregnant woman who was struggling to recover her wits after a shock—who seemed intent, in fact, on plunging into hysterics.

I said to her in a most soothing tone of voice: "Perhaps this black man had no intention of killing you, madam. You entered so unexpectedly and switched on the light and he was simply frightened. After all, he—"

Kleber-san interrupted before I could finish.

"He was frightened?" she hissed with sudden venom. "Or perhaps it was you who were frightened, my dear Asian monsieur? Do you think I didn't notice your nasty little yellow face peeping out from behind other people's backs?"

No one has ever insulted me so outrageously. The worst thing of all was that I could not pretend these were the foolish words of an hysterical woman and shield myself from them with a smile of disdain. Kleber-san's thrust had found my most vulnerable spot!

There was nothing I could say in reply; I was badly hurt, and the grimace on her tear-stained face when she looked at me was humiliating. If at that moment I could have fallen through the floor into the famous Christian hell, I would certainly have pressed the lever of the trapdoor myself. Worst of all, my sight was veiled by the red mist of rage, and that is the condition I fear most. It is in this state of frenzy that a samurai commits those deeds that are disastrous for his karma. Then afterward he must spend the rest of his life seeking to expiate the guilt of that single moment of lost self-control. He can do things for which even *seppuku* will not be sufficient atonement.

I left the salon, afraid I would not be able to restrain myself and do something terrible to a pregnant woman. I am not sure that I could have controlled myself if a man had said something like that to me.

I locked myself in my cabin and took out the sack of Egyptian gourds I bought at the bazaar in Port Said. They are small, about the size of a human head, and very hard. I bought fifty of them.

In order to disperse the scarlet mist in front of my eyes, I set about improving my straight chop with the edge of the hand. Because of my extreme agitation, I delivered the blow poorly: Instead of two equal halves, the gourds split into seven or eight pieces.

It is hard.

PART TWO

ADEN TO BOMBAY

Gintaro Aono

The seventh day of the fourth month, in Aden

The Russian diplomat is a man of profound, almost Japanese intellect. Fandorin-san possesses the most un-European ability to see a phenomenon in all its fullness, without losing his way in the maze of petty details and technicalities. The Europeans are unsurpassed masters of everything that concerns *doing;* they have superlative understanding of *how.* But true wisdom belongs to us orientals, since we understand *why.* For the hairy ones, the fact of movement is more important than the final goal, but we never lower our gaze from the guiding star twinkling in the distance, and therefore we often neglect to pay due attention to what lies closer to hand. This is why time and again the white peoples are the victors in petty skirmishes, but the yellow race maintains its unshakable equanimity, in the certain knowledge that such trivial matters are unworthy of serious attention. In all that is truly important, in the genuinely essential matters, victory will be ours.

Our emperor has embarked on a great experiment: to combine the wisdom of the East with the intellect of the West. Yet while we Japanese strive meekly to master the European lesson of routine daily conquest, we do not lose sight of the ultimate end of human life—death and the higher form of existence that follows it. The red-hairs are too individualistic, their precious ego obscures their vision, distorting their picture of the world around them and making it impossible for them to see a problem from different points of view. The soul of the European is fastened tightly to his body with rivets of steel; it cannot soar aloft.

But if Fandorin-san is capable of illumination, he owes it to the semi-Asiatic character of his homeland. In many ways Russia is like Japan: the same reaching out by the East for the West. Except that, unlike us, the Russians forget about the star by which the ship maintains its heading and spend too much time gazing idly around them. To emphasize one's individual "I" or to dissolve it in the might of the collective "we"—therein lies the antithesis between Europe and Asia. I believe the chances are good that Russia will turn off the first road on to the second.

However, I have become carried away by my philosophizing. I must move on to Fandorin-san and the clarity of mind he has demonstrated. I shall describe events as they happened.

The *Leviathan* arrived in Aden before dawn. Concerning this port, my guidebook says the following: "The port of Aden, this Gibraltar of the Orient, serves England as her link with the East Indies. Here steamships take on coal and replenish their reserves of fresh water. Aden's importance has increased immeasurably since the opening of the Suez Canal. The town itself, however, is not large. It has extensive dockside warehouses and shipyards, and a number of trading stations, shipping offices, and hotels. The streets are laid out in a distinctively regular pattern. The dryness of the local soil is compensated by thirty ancient reservoirs that collect the rainwater that runs down from the mountains. Aden has a population of 34,000, consisting primarily of Indian Moslems." For the time being I must be content with this scanty description, since the gangway has not been lowered and no one is being allowed ashore. The alleged reason is quarantine for medical reasons, but we vassals of the principality of Windsor know the true reason for the turmoil and confusion: Sailors and police from ashore are combing the gigantic vessel from stem to stern in search of Negroes.

After breakfast we stayed on in the salon to wait for the results of the manhunt. It was then that an important conversation took place between the commissioner and the Russian diplomat in the presence of our entire company (even for me it has already become "ours").

At first people spoke about the death of the Negro, then as usual the conversation turned to the murders in Paris. Although I took no part in the discussion on that topic, I listened very attentively, and at first it seemed to me that they were trying yet again to catch a green monkey in a thicket of bamboo or a black cat in a dark room.

Stamp-san said: "So we have nothing but riddles. We don't know how the black man managed to get on board, and we don't know why he wanted to kill Mme. Kleber. It's just like the Rue de Grenelle. More mystery."

But then Fandorin-san said: "There is no mystery there at all. It is true that we still haven't cleared up the business with the Negro, but I think we have a fairly clear picture of what happened in the Rue de Grenelle."

Everyone stared at him in bewilderment, and the commissioner smiled scornfully and said: "Is that so? Well, then, out with it; this should be interesting."

Fandorin-san: "I think what happened was this. That evening someone arrived at the door of the mansion on the Rue de Grenelle . . ."

The commissioner (in mock admiration): "Oh, bravo! A brilliant deduction!"

Someone laughed, but most of us continued listening attentively, for the diplomat is not a man to indulge in idle talk.

Fandorin-san (continuing imperturbably): ". . . someone whose appearance completely failed to arouse the servants' suspicions. It was a physician, possibly wearing a white coat and certainly carrying a doctor's bag. This unexpected visitor requested everyone in the house to gather immediately in one room, because the municipal authorities had instructed that all Parisians were to receive a prophylactic vaccination."

The commissioner (starting to get angry): "What idiotic fantasy is this? What vaccination? Why should the servants take the word of a total stranger?"

Fandorin-san (sharply): "If you do not take care, M. Gauche, you may find yourself demoted from Investigator for Especially Important Cases to Investigator for Rather Unimportant Cases. You do not pay sufficient attention to studying your own materials, and that is unforgivable. Take another look at the article from *Le Soir* that mentions Lord Littleby's connection with the international adventuress Marie Sanfon."

The detective rummaged in his black file, took out the article in question, and glanced over it.

The commissioner (with a shrug): "Well, what of it?"

Fandorin-san (pointing): "Down here, at the bottom. Do you see the headline of the next article—CHOLERA EPIDEMIC ON THE WANE? And what it says about 'the vigorous prophylactic measures taken by the physicians of Paris'?"

Truffo-sensei: "Why, yes indeed, gentlemen, Paris has been plagued by outbreaks of cholera all winter. They even set up a medical checkpoint in the Louvre for the boats arriving from Calais."

Fandorin-san: "That is why the sudden appearance of a physician did not make the servants suspicious. No doubt their visitor acted confidently and spoke very convincingly. He could have told them it was late and that he still had several more houses to visit, or something of the kind. The servants evidently decided not to bother the master of the house, since he was suffering from an attack of gout, but of course they called the security guards down from the second floor. And it only takes a moment to give an injection."

I was delighted by the diplomat's perspicacity and the ease with which he had solved this difficult riddle. His words even set Commissioner Gauche thinking.

"Very well, then," the latter said reluctantly. "But how do you explain the fact that after poisoning the servants this medico of yours didn't simply walk up the stairs to the second floor, but went outside, climbed over the fence, and broke into the house through a window in the conservatory?"

Fandorin-san: "I've thought about that. Did it not occur to you that two culprits might have been involved? That one dealt with the servants while the other broke in through the window?"

The commissioner (triumphantly): "It did occur to me, my dear brainy monsieur, indeed it did. That is precisely the assumption that the murderer wanted us to make. It's perfectly obvious he was simply trying to confuse the trail! After he poisoned the servants, he left the pantry and went upstairs, where he ran into the master of the house. Very probably the thief simply smashed in the glass of the display case because he thought there was no one else in the house. When his lordship came out of his bedroom to see what all the noise was about, he was murdered. Following this unexpected encounter, the culprit beat a hasty retreat, not through the door, but through the window of the conservatory. Why? In order to pull the wool over our eyes and make it seem as though there were two of them. You fell for his little trick hook, line, and sinker. But old papa Gauche is not so easily taken in."

The commissioner's words were greeted with general approval. Renier-san even said: "Damn it, Commissioner, but you're a dangerous man!" (This is a common turn of speech in various European languages. It should not be taken literally. The lieutenant meant to say that Gauche-san is a very clever and experienced detective.)

Fandorin-san waited for a while and asked: "Then you made a thorough study of the footprints and came to the conclusion that this person jumped down from the window and did not climb up onto the window-sill?"

The commissioner did not answer that, but he gave the Russian a rather angry look.

At this point Stamp-san made a comment that turned the conversation in a new direction.

"One culprit, two culprits—but I still don't understand the most important thing: What was it all done for?" she said. "Clearly not for the Shiva. But what, then? And not for the sake of the scarf, either, no matter how remarkable and legendary it may be!"

Fandorin-san replied to this in a matter-of-fact voice, as if he were saying something perfectly obvious: "But of course, it was precisely for the sake of the scarf, mademoiselle. The Shiva was only taken in order to divert attention. It was then thrown into the Seine from the nearest bridge because it was no longer needed."

The commissioner observed: "For Russian *boyar*s (I have forgotten what this word means; I shall have to look it up in the dictionary), half a million francs may perhaps be a mere trifle, but most people think differently. Two kilograms of pure gold was 'no longer needed'! You really are getting carried away, monsieur diplomat."

Fandorin-san: "Oh, come now, Commissioner, what is half a million francs compared to the treasure of Bagdassar?"

"Gentlemen, enough of this quarreling!" the odious Mme. Kleber exclaimed capriciously. "I was almost killed, and here you are, still harping on the same old tune. Commissioner, while you were so busy tinkering with an old crime, you very nearly had a new one on your hands!"

That woman simply cannot bear it when she is not the center of attention. After what happened yesterday, I try not to look at her—I have a strong urge to jab my finger into the blue vein pulsating on her white neck. One jab would be enough to dispatch the loathsome creature. But, of course, that is one of those evil thoughts that a man must drive out of his head by an effort of will. By confiding my evil thoughts to this diary, I have managed to diminish the violence of my hatred a little.

The commissioner put Mme. Kleber in her place. "Please be quiet, madam," he said sternly. "Let us hear what other fantasies our diplomat has concocted."

Fandorin-san: "The entire story only makes sense if the stolen shawl is especially valuable in some way. That is one. According to what the professor told us, in itself the shawl is of no great value, so it is not a matter of the piece of silk, but of something else connected with it. That is two. As you already know, the shawl is connected with the final will and testament of the rajah Bagdassar, the last owner of the Brahmapur treasure. That is three. Tell me, Professor, was the rajah a zealous servant of the Prophet?"

Sweetchild-sensei (after a moment's thought): "I can't say, exactly . . . He didn't build mosques, and he never mentioned the name of Allah in my company. The rajah liked to dress in European clothes; he smoked Cuban cigars and read French novels . . . Ah, yes, he drank cognac after lunch! So he obviously didn't take religious prohibitions very seriously."

Fandorin-san: "Then that makes four: Although he is not overly devout, Bagdassar makes his son a final gift of a Koran, which for some reason is wrapped in a shawl. I suggest that the shawl was the most important part of this legacy. The Koran was included for the sake of appearances . . . Or possibly the notes made in the margins in Bagdassar's own hand contained instructions on how to find the treasure with the help of the shawl."

Sweetchild-sensei: "But why did it have to be with the help of the shawl? The rajah could have conveyed his secret in the marginalia!"

Fandorin-san: "He could have, but he chose not to. Why? Allow me to refer you to my argument number one: If the shawl were not immensely valuable in some way, it is unlikely that ten people would have been murdered for it. The shawl is the key to five hundred million francs or, if you prefer, fifty million pounds, which is approximately the same. I believe it is the greatest hidden treasure there has ever been in the whole of human history. And by the way, Commissioner, I must warn you that if you are not mistaken and the murderer really is on board the *Leviathan,* more people could be killed. Indeed, the closer you come to your objective, the more likely it becomes. The stakes are too high, and too great a price has already been paid for the key to the mystery."

These words were followed by deadly silence. Fandorin-san's logic seemed irrefutable, and I believe all of us felt shivers run up and down our spines. All of us except one.

The first to recover his composure was the commissioner. He gave a nervous laugh and said: "My, what a lively imagination you have, M. Fandorin. But as far as danger is concerned, you are right. Only you, gentlemen, have no need to quake in your boots. This danger threatens no one but old man Gauche, and he knows it very well. It is part of my profession. But I'm well prepared for it!" And he glanced around at us menacingly, as if he were challenging us to single combat.

The fat old man is laughable. Of everyone there, the only person whom he might be able to get the best of is the pregnant Mme. Kleber. In my mind's eye I glimpsed a tempting picture: The red-faced commissioner had flung the young witch to the floor and was strangling her with his hairy sausage fingers, and Mme. Kleber was expiring with her eyes popping out of her head and her malicious tongue dangling out of her mouth.

"Darling, I'm scared!" I heard the doctor's wife whisper in a thin, squeaky voice as she turned to her husband, who patted her shoulder reassuringly.

The redheaded freak M.S.-san (his name is too long for me to write it in full) raised an interesting question: "Professor, can you describe the shawl in more detail? We know the bird has a hole where its eye should be, and that it's triangle-shaped. Is there anything else remarkable about it?"

I should note that this strange gentleman takes part in the general conversation almost as rarely as I do. But, like the author of these lines, if he does say something, then it is always off the subject, and so the unexpected appropriateness of his question was all the more remarkable.

Sweetchild-sensei: "As far as I recall, apart from the hole and the unique shape there is nothing special about the shawl. It is about the size of a small fan, but it can easily be hidden in a thimble. Such remarkably fine fabric is quite common in Brahmapur."

"Then the key must lie in the eye of the bird and the triangular shape," Fandorin-san concluded with exquisite assurance.

He was truly magnificent.

The more I ponder on his triumph and the whole story in general, the more strongly I feel the unworthy temptation to demonstrate to all of them that Gintaro Aono is also no fool. I too could reveal things that would amaze them. For instance, I could tell Commissioner Gauche certain curious details about yesterday's incident involving the black-skinned savage. Even the wise Fandorin-san has admitted that the matter is not entirely clear to him as yet. What if the "wild Japanese" were suddenly to solve the riddle that is puzzling him? That could be interesting!

Yesterday's insults unsettled me and I lost my composure for a while. Afterward, when I had calmed down, I began comparing facts and weighing the situation up, and I have constructed an entire logical argument that I intend to put to the policeman. Let him work out the rest for himself. This is what I shall tell the commissioner.

First I shall remind him of how Mme. Kleber humiliated me. It was a highly insulting remark, made in public. And it was made at the precise moment when I was about to reveal what I had observed. Did Mme. Kleber perhaps wish to shut me up? This surely appears suspicious, monsieur commissioner.

To continue. Why does she pretend to be weak, when she is as fit as a sumo wrestler? You will say this is an irrelevant detail. But I shall tell you, monsieur detective, that a person who is constantly pretending must be hiding something. Take me, for instance. (Ha-ha. Of course, I shall not say that.)

Then I shall point out to the commissioner that European women have very delicate white skin. Why did the Negro's powerful fingers not leave even the slightest mark on it? Is that not strange?

And, finally, when the commissioner decides I have nothing to offer him but the vindictive speculations of an oriental mind bent on vengeance,

I shall tell him the most important thing, which will immediately make our detective sit up and take notice.

"M. Gauche," I shall say to him with a polite smile, "I do not possess your brilliant mind, and I am not attempting, hopeless ignoramus that I am, to interfere in your investigation, but I regard it as my duty to draw your attention to a certain circumstance. You yourself say that the murderer from the Rue de Grenelle is one of us. M. Fandorin has expounded a convincing account of how Lord Littleby's servants were killed. Vaccinating them against cholera was a brilliant subterfuge. It tells us that the murderer knows how to use a syringe. But what if the person who came to the mansion on the Rue de Grenelle were not a male doctor, but a woman, a nurse? She would have aroused even less suspicion than a man, would she not? Surely you agree? Then let me advise you to take a casual glance at Mme. Kleber's arms when she is sitting with her viper's head propped on her hand and her wide sleeve slips down to the elbow. You will observe some barely visible points on the inner flexure, as I have observed. They are needle marks, monsieur commissioner. Ask Dr. Truffo if he is giving Mme. Kleber any injections, and the venerable physician will tell you what he has already told me today: No, he is not, for he is opposed in principle to the intravenous injection of medication. And then, oh wise Gauche-sensei, you will add two and two, and you will have something for your gray head to puzzle over." That is what I shall tell the commissioner, and then he will take Mme. Kleber more seriously.

A European knight would say that I had behaved villainously, but that would merely demonstrate his own limitations. That is precisely why there are no knights left in Europe, but the samurai are still among us. Our lord and emperor may have set the different estates on one level and forbidden us to wear two swords in our belts, but that does not mean the calling of a samurai has been abolished. Quite the opposite; the entire Japanese nation has been elevated to the estate of the samurai in order to prevent us from boasting to one another about our noble origins. We all stand together against the rest of the world. Oh, you noble European knight (who has never existed except in novels)! In fighting with men, use the weapons of a man, but in fighting with women, use the weapons of a woman. That is the samurai code of honor, and there is nothing villainous in it, since women know how to fight every bit as well as men. What contradicts the honor of the samurai is to employ the weapons of a man against a woman or the weapons of a woman against a man. I would never sink as low as that.

I am still uncertain whether the maneuver I am contemplating is worthwhile, but my state of mind is incomparably better than it was yesterday. So much so that I have even managed to compose a decent haiku without any difficulty:

> *The moonlight glinting,*
> *Bright upon the steely blade,*
> *A cold spark of ice.*

Clarissa Stamp

CLARISSA GLANCED AROUND with a bored look on her face to see if anyone was watching, and only then did she peep cautiously around the corner of the deckhouse.

The Japanese was sitting alone on the quarterdeck with his legs folded up underneath him. His head was thrown back and she could see the whites of his eyes glinting horribly between the half-closed lids. The expression on his face was absolutely impassive—inhumanly dispassionate.

Br-r-r! Clarissa shuddered. What a strange specimen this Mr. Aono was. Here on the boat deck, located just one level above the first-class cabins, no one was taking the air except a gaggle of young girls skipping rope and two nursemaids exhausted by the heat who were sheltering in the shade of a snow-white launch. Who but children and a crazy oriental would be out in such scorching heat? The only structures higher than the boat deck were the control room, the bridge, and, of course, the funnels, masts, and sails. The white canvas sheets were swollen taut by a following wind, and *Leviathan* was making straight for the liquid-silver line of the horizon, puffing smoke into the sky as it went, while all around, the Indian Ocean lay spread out like a slightly crumpled tablecloth patterned in shimmering patches of bright bottle green. From up here she could see that the earth really was round: The rim of the horizon was clearly lower than the *Leviathan*, and the ship seemed to be running downhill toward it.

But Clarissa had not drenched herself in perspiration for the sake of the sea view. She wanted to see what Mr. Aono was up to. Where did he disappear to with such unfailing regularity after breakfast?

And she was right to have been curious. Look at him now, the very image of the inscrutable oriental! A man with such a motionless, pitiless mask for a face was capable of absolutely anything. The members of the yellow race were certainly not like us, and it was not simply a matter of the shape of their eyes. On the outside they looked very much like people, but on the inside they were a different species altogether. After all, wolves looked like dogs, didn't they, but their nature was quite different. Of course, the yellow-skinned races had a moral code of their own, but it was so alien to Christianity that no normal person could possibly understand it. It would be better if they didn't wear European clothes or learn how to use cutlery—that created a dangerous illusion of civilization, when there were things we couldn't possibly imagine going on under that slickly parted black hair and those yellow foreheads.

The Japanese stirred almost imperceptibly and blinked, and Clarissa hastily ducked back out of sight. Of course, she was behaving like an absolute fool, but she couldn't just do nothing! This nightmare couldn't be allowed to go on forever. The commissioner had to be nudged in the right direction; otherwise there was no way of telling how it all might end. Despite the heat, she felt a chill tremor run through her.

There was obviously something mysterious about Mr. Aono's character and behavior. Like the mystery of the crime in the Rue de Grenelle. It was strange that Gauche had still not realized that all the signs pointed to the Japanese as the main suspect.

What kind of officer was he? How could he have graduated from St. Cyr if he knew nothing about horses? One day, acting purely out of humanitarian motives, Clarissa had decided to involve the oriental in the general conversation and started talking about a subject that should have been of interest to a military man—training and racing horses, the merits and shortcomings of the Norfolk trotter. He was no officer! She had asked him: "Have you ever taken part in a steeplechase?" He replied that officers of the Imperial Army were absolutely forbidden to become involved in politics. He simply had no idea what a steeplechase was! Of course, who could tell what kind of officers they had in Japan—perhaps they rode around on sticks of bamboo—but how could an alumnus of St. Cyr possibly be so ignorant? No, it was quite out of the question.

She had to bring this to Gauche's attention. Or perhaps she ought to wait and see if she could discover something else suspicious?

And what about that incident yesterday? Clarissa had taken a stroll along the corridor past Mr. Aono's cabin after she heard some extremely strange noises. There was a dry crunching sound coming from inside the cabin, as if someone were smashing furniture with precise, regular blows. Clarissa had screwed up her courage and knocked.

The door had opened with a jerk and the Japanese appeared in the doorway—entirely naked except for a loincloth! His swarthy body was gleaming with sweat; his eyes were swollen with blood.

When he saw Clarissa standing there, he hissed through his teeth: *"Chikusho!"*

The question she had prepared in advance ("Mr. Aono, do you by any chance happen to have with you some of those marvelous Japanese prints I've heard so much about?") flew right out of her head, and Clarissa froze, stupefied. Now he would drag her into the cabin and throw himself on her! And afterward he would chop her into pieces and throw her into the sea. Nothing could be simpler. And that would be the end of Miss Clarissa Stamp, the well-brought-up English lady, who might not have been very happy, but had still expected so much from her life.

Clarissa mumbled that she had knocked at the wrong door. Aono stared at her without speaking. He gave off a sour smell.

Probably she ought to have a word with the commissioner, after all.

BEFORE AFTERNOON TEA she ambushed the detective outside the doors of the Windsor salon and began sharing her ideas with him, but the way the lout listened was very odd: He kept darting sharp, mocking glances at her, as though he were listening to a confession of some dark misdeed that she had committed.

At one point he muttered into his mustache: "Ah, how eager you all are to tell tales on one another."

When she had finished, he suddenly asked out of the blue: "And how are Mama and Papa keeping?"

"Whose, Mr. Aono's?" Clarissa asked in amazement.

"No, mademoiselle, yours."

"I was orphaned as a child," she replied, glancing at the policeman in alarm. Good God, this was no ship; it was a floating lunatic asylum.

"That's what I needed to establish," said Gauche with a nod of satisfaction, then the boor began humming a song Clarissa didn't know and walked into the salon ahead of her, which was incredibly rude.

That conversation had left a bad taste in her mouth. For all their much-vaunted gallantry, the French were not gentlemen. Of course, they could dazzle you and turn your head, make some dramatic gesture like sending a hundred red roses to your hotel room (Clarissa winced as she thought of that), but they were not to be trusted. Although the English gentleman might appear somewhat insipid by comparison, he knew the meaning of the words "duty" and "decency." But if a Frenchman wormed his way into your trust, he was certain to betray it.

These generalizations, however, had no direct relevance to Commissioner Gauche. And, moreover, the reason for his bizarre behavior was revealed at the dinner table in a most alarming manner.

Over dessert, the detective, who had thus far preserved a most untypical silence that had set everyone's nerves on edge, suddenly stared hard at Clarissa and said: "Yes, by the way, Mlle. Stamp" (although she had not said anything), "you were asking me recently about Marie Sanfon. You know—the little lady who was supposedly seen with Lord Littleby shortly before he died."

Clarissa started in surprise, and everyone else fell silent and began staring curiously at the commissioner, recognizing that special tone of voice in which he began his leisurely "little stories."

"I promised to tell you something about that individual at some time. And now the time has come," Gauche continued, his eyes still fixed on Clarissa, and the longer he looked, the less she liked it. "It will be a rather long story, but you won't be bored, because it concerns a quite extraordinary woman. And, in any case, we are in no hurry. Here we all are, sitting comfortably, eating our cheese and drinking our orangeade. But if anyone has business to attend to, do leave by all means; papa Gauche won't be offended."

No one moved.

"Then shall I tell you about Marie Sanfon?" the commissioner asked with feigned bonhomie.

"Oh, yes! You must!" they all cried.

Only Clarissa said nothing, aware that this topic had been broached for a reason; it was intended exclusively for her ears. Gauche did not even attempt to disguise the fact.

He smacked his lips in anticipation and took out his pipe without bothering to ask permission from the ladies.

"Then let me start at the beginning. Once upon a time in the Belgian town of Bruges there lived a little girl by the name of Marie. The little girl's parents were honest, respectable citizens who went to church, and they doted on their little golden-haired darling. When Marie was five years old, her parents presented her with a little brother, the future heir to the Sanfon and Sanfon brewery, and the happy family began living even more happily, until suddenly disaster struck. The infant boy, who was barely a month old, fell out of a window and was killed. The parents were not at home at the time; they had left the children alone with their nanny. But the nanny had gone out for half an hour to see her sweetheart, a fireman, and during her brief absence a stranger in a black cloak and black hat burst into the house. Little Marie managed to hide under the bed, but the man in black grabbed her little brother out of his cradle and threw him out the window. Then he simply vanished without trace."

"Why are you telling us such terrible things?" Mme. Kleber exclaimed, clutching at her belly.

"Why, I have hardly even begun," said Gauche, gesturing with his pipe. "The best—or the worst—is yet to come. After her miraculous escape, little Marie told Mama and Papa about the 'black man.' They turned the entire district upside down searching for him, and in the heat of the moment they even arrested the local rabbi, since he naturally always wore black. But there was one strange detail that kept nagging at M. Sanfon: Why had the criminal moved a stool over to the window?

"Oh, God!" Clarissa gasped, clutching at her heart. "Surely not!"

"You are quite remarkably perceptive, Mlle. Stamp," the commissioner said with a laugh. "Yes, it was little Marie who had thrown her own baby brother out the window."

"How terrible!" Mrs. Truffo felt it necessary to interject. "But why?"

"The girl did not like the way everyone was paying so much attention to the baby, while they had forgotten all about her. She thought that if she got rid of her brother, then she would be Mama and Papa's favorite again," Gauche explained calmly. "But that was the first and the last time Marie Sanfon ever left a clue and was found out. The sweet child had not yet learned to cover her tracks."

"And what did they do with the infant criminal?" asked Lieutenant Renier, clearly shaken by what he had heard. "They couldn't try her for murder, surely?"

"No, they didn't try her." The commissioner smiled craftily at Clarissa. "The shock, however, was too much for her mother, who lost her mind and was committed to an asylum. M. Sanfon could no longer bear the sight of the little daughter who was the cause of his family's calamitous misfortune, so he placed her with a convent of the Gray Sisters of St. Vincent, and the girl was brought up there. She was best at everything, in her studies and in her charity work. But most of all, they say, she liked to read books. The novice nun was just seventeen years old when a disgraceful scandal occurred at the convent." Gauche glanced into his file and nodded. "I have the date here. The seventeenth of July, 1866. The archbishop of Brussels himself was staying with the Gray Sisters when the venerable prelate's ring with a massive amethyst disappeared from his bedroom. It had supposedly belonged to St. Louis himself. The previous evening, the monseigneur had summoned the two best pupils, our Marie and a girl from Arles, to his chambers for a talk. Suspicion naturally fell on the two girls. The mother superior organized a search and the ring's velvet case was discovered under the mattress of the girl from Arles. The thief lapsed into a stupor and would not answer any questions, and she was escorted to the punishment cell. When the police arrived an hour later, they were unable to question the criminal—she had strangled herself with the belt of her habit."

"I've guessed it—the whole thing was staged by that abominable Marie Sanfon!" Milford-Stokes exclaimed. "A nasty story, very nasty!"

"Nobody knows for certain, but the ring was never found," the commissioner said with a shrug. "Two days later, Marie came to the mother superior in tears and said everyone was giving her strange looks and begged to be released from the convent. The mother superior's feelings for her former favorite had also cooled somewhat, and she made no effort to dissuade her."

"They should have searched the little dove at the gates," said Dr. Truffo with a regretful sigh. "You can be sure they would have found the amethyst somewhere in her skirts."

When he translated what he had said to his wife, she jabbed him with her elbow, evidently regarding his remark as somehow indecent.

"Either they didn't search her or they searched her and found nothing, I don't know which. In any case, after she left the convent, Marie chose to go to Antwerp, which, as you are aware, is regarded as the world capital of precious stones. The former nun suddenly grew rich and ever since has lived in the grand style. Sometimes, just occasionally, she has been left without a sou to her name, but not for long. With her sharp mind and brilliant skill as an actress, combined with a total lack of moral scruples [at this point the commissioner raised his voice and then paused] she has always been able to obtain the means required for a life of luxury. The police of Belgium, France, England, the United States, Brazil, Italy, and a dozen other countries have detained Marie Sanfon on numerous occasions on suspicion of all sorts of offenses, but no charges have ever been brought against her. Always it turns out that either no crime has actually been committed or there is simply not enough evidence. If you like, I could tell you about a couple of episodes from her distinguished record. Are you not feeling bored yet, Mlle. Stamp?"

Clarissa did not reply; she felt it was beneath her dignity. But in her heart she felt alarmed.

"Eighteen seventy," Gauche declared after another glance into his file. "The small but prosperous town of Fettburg in German-speaking Switzerland. The chocolate and ham industries. Eight and a half thousand pigs versus four thousand inhabitants. A land of rich, fat idiots—I beg your pardon, Mme. Kleber, I did not mean to insult your homeland," said the policeman, suddenly realizing what he had said.

"Never mind," said Mme. Kleber with a careless shrug. "I come from

French-speaking Switzerland. And anyway, the area around Fettburg really is full of simpletons. I believe I have heard this story; it is very funny. But never mind—carry on."

"Some might think it funny," Gauche sighed reproachfully, and suddenly he winked at Clarissa, which was going too far altogether. "One day the honest burghers of the town were thrown into a state of indescribable excitement when a certain peasant by the name of Möbius, who was known in Fettburg as an idler and a numskull, boasted he had sold his land, a narrow strip of stony wasteland, to a certain grand lady who styled herself the 'comtesse de Sanfon.' This damn fool of a countess had shelled out three thousand francs for thirty acres of barren land on which not even thistles would grow. But there were people smarter than Möbius on the town council, and they thought his story sounded suspicious. Why would a countess want thirty acres of sand and rock? Something fishy was going on. So they dispatched the very smartest of the town's citizens to Zurich to find out what was what, and he discovered that the comtesse de Sanfon was well known there as woman who knew how to enjoy life on a grand scale. Even more interesting, she often appeared in public in the company of Mr. Goldsilber, the director of the state railway company. The director and the countess were rumored to be romantically involved. Then, of course, the good burghers guessed what was going on. The little town of Fettburg had been dreaming for a long time of having its own railway line, which would make it cheaper to export its chocolate and ham. The wasteland acquired by the countess just happened to run from the nearest railway station to the forest, where the communal land began. Suddenly everything was clear to the city fathers: Having learned from her lover about plans to build a railway line, the countess had bought the key plot of land, intending to turn a handsome profit. An outrageously bold plan began to take shape in the good burghers' heads. They dispatched a deputation to the countess, which attempted to persuade her excellency to sell the land to the noble town of Fettburg. The beautiful lady was obstinate at first, claiming she knew nothing about any branch railway line, but when the burgomaster hinted subtly that the affair smacked of a conspiracy between her excellency and his excellency the director of state railways, which was a matter that fell within the competence of the courts, the woman's nerve finally gave way and she agreed. The wasteland was divided into thirty one-acre lots and auctioned off to the citizens of the town. The Fettburgers almost came to blows over it, and the price for some lots rose as high as fifteen thousand francs. Altogether the countess received . . ." The commissioner ran his finger along a line of print. "A little less than two hundred eighty thousand francs."

Mme. Kleber laughed out loud and gestured to Gauche as if to say: I'm saying nothing—go on, go on.

"Weeks went by, then months, and still the construction work had not started. The citizens of the town sent an inquiry to the government and received a reply that no branch line to Fettburg was planned for the next fifteen years. They went to the police and explained what had happened and said it was highway robbery. The police listened to the victims' story with sympathy, but there was nothing they could do about it: Mlle. Sanfon had said that she knew nothing about any railway line and she had not wanted to sell the land. The sales were properly registered; everything was perfectly legal. As for calling herself a countess, that was not a very nice thing to do, but unfortunately it was not a criminal offense."

"Very clever!" laughed Renier. "Indeed it was all perfectly legal."

"But that's nothing," said the commissioner, leafing through his papers again. "I have another story here—it is absolutely fantastic. The action is set in the Wild West of America in 1873. Miss Cleopatra Frankenstein, the world-famous necromancer and Grand Dragoness of the Maltese Lodge, whose name according to her passport is 'Marie Sanfon,' arrives in the goldfields of California. She informs the prospectors that she has been guided to this wild spot by the voice of Zarathushtra, who has ordered his faithful handmaiden to carry out a great experiment in the town of Golden Nugget. Apparently, at that precise longitude and latitude the cosmic energy was focused in such a way that on a starry night, with the help of a few cabbalistic formulae, it was possible to resurrect someone who had already crossed the Great Divide between the Kingdom of the Living and the Kingdom of the Dead. And Cleopatra intended to perform this miracle that very night, in public and entirely without charge, because she was no circus conjurer but the medium of the Supreme Spheres. And what do you think?" Gauche asked, pausing for effect. "Before the eyes of five hundred bearded onlookers, the Dragoness worked her magic over the burial mound of Red Coyote, the legendary Indian chief who had died a hundred years earlier, and suddenly the earth began to stir—it gaped asunder, you might say—and an Indian brave in a feather headdress emerged from the mound, complete with a tomahawk and painted face. The onlookers trembled, and Cleopatra, in the grip of her mystical trance, screeched: 'I feel the power of the cosmos in me! Where is the town cemetery? I will bring everyone in it back to life.' It says in this article," the policeman explained, "that the cemetery in Golden Nugget was vast, because in the goldfields someone was dispatched to the next world every day of the week. Apparently the headstones outnumbered the town's living inhabitants. When the prospectors imagined what would happen if all those troublemakers, drunks, and gallows-dancers suddenly rose from their graves, panic set in. The situation was saved by the justice of the peace, who stepped forward and asked politely whether the Dragoness would agree to halt her great experiment if the town's inhabitants gave her a saddlebag full of gold dust as a modest donation toward the needs of occult science."

"Well, did she agree?" chuckled the lieutenant.

"Yes. For two saddlebags of gold."

"And what became of the Indian chief?" asked Fandorin with a smile. He had a quite wonderful smile, except that it was too boyish, thought Clarissa. As they said in Suffolk: A grand pie, but not for your mouth.

"Cleopatra Frankenstein took the Indian chief with her," Gauche replied with a serious expression. "For purposes of scientific research. They say someone cut his throat during a drunken brawl in a Denver bordello."

"This Marie Sanfon really is a very interesting character," mused Fandorin. "Tell us more about her. It's a long way from all these clever frauds to cold-blooded mass murder."

"Oh, please, that's more than enough already," protested Mrs. Truffo, turning to her husband. "My darling, it must be awfully tiresome for you to translate all this nonsense."

"You are not obliged to stay, madam," said commissioner Gauche, offended by the English word "nonsense."

Mrs. Truffo batted her eyelids indignantly, but she had no intention of leaving.

"M. le Cosaque is right," Gauche acknowledged. "Let me try to dig out a more vicious example."

Mme. Kleber laughed and cast a glance at Fandorin, and, nervous as she was, even Clarissa was unable to restrain a smile—the diplomat was so very unlike a wild son of the steppe.

"Here we are—listen to this story about the black baby. It's a recent case, from the year before last, and we have a detailed report of the outcome." The detective glanced through several sheets of paper clipped together, evidently to refresh his memory of the story. He chuckled. "This is something of a masterpiece. I have all sorts of things in my little file, ladies and gentlemen." He stroked the black-calico binding lovingly with the stumpy fingers of his plebeian hand. "Papa Gauche made thorough preparations for his journey; he didn't forget a single piece of paper that might come in useful. The embarrassing events I am about to relate to you never reached the newspapers—what I have here is the police report. All right. In a certain German principality (I won't say which, because this is a delicate matter), a certain family of great note was expecting an addition to its number. It was a long and difficult birth. The delivering physician was a certain highly respected Dr. Vogel. Eventually the bedroom was filled with a sound of an infant wailing. The grand duchess lost consciousness for several minutes because she had suffered so much, and then she opened her eyes and said to the doctor: 'Ah, Herr Professor, show me my little child.' With an expression of extreme embarrassment, Dr. Vogel handed her highness the charming baby that was bawling so loudly. Its skin was the color of light coffee. When the grand duchess fainted again, the doctor glanced out the door and beckoned with his finger to the grand duke, which of course was a gross violation of court etiquette."

It was obvious the commissioner was taking great pleasure in telling this story to the prim and proper Windsorites. A police report was unlikely to contain such details—Gauche was clearly allowing himself to fantasize at will. He lisped when he spoke the countess's part and deliberately selected words that had a pompous ring to them: He obviously thought that made the tale sound funnier. Clarissa did not consider herself an aristocrat, but even she winced at the bad taste of his scoffing at royalty. Sir Reginald, a baronet and the scion of an ancient line, also knitted his brows in a scowl, but this reaction only seemed to inspire the commissioner to greater efforts.

"His highness, however, did not take offense at his physician, because this was a moment of tremendous pathos. Positively overwhelmed by a rising tide of paternal and conjugal feelings, he went dashing into the bedroom. You can imagine for yourselves the scene that followed: The crowned monarch swearing like a trooper, the grand duchess sobbing and making excuses and swooning by turns, the little Negro child bawling his lungs out, and the court physician frozen in reverential horror. Eventually his highness controlled himself and decided to postpone the investigation into her highness's behavior until later. In the meantime, the business had to be hushed up. But how? Flush the child down the toilet?" Gauche put his hand over his mouth, acting the fool. "I beg your pardon, ladies, it just slipped out. It was impossible to get rid of the child—the entire principality had been eagerly awaiting his birth. In any case, it would have been a sin. If he called his advisers together, they might let the cat out of the bag. What was he going to do? And then Dr. Vogel coughed deferentially into his hand and suggested a way of saving the situation. He said he knew a lady by the name of Fräulein von Sanfon who could work miracles—even pluck a phoenix from the sky for the prince if he needed it, let alone find him a newborn white baby. The fräulein knew how to keep her mouth shut, and, being a very noble individual, she would of course not take any money for her services, but she did have a great fondness for old jewels . . . Anyway, within a couple of hours a fine bouncing baby boy, whiter than a little suckling piglet, with white hair, was reposing on the satin sheets of the cradle, and the poor little Negro child was taken from the palace. They told her highness that the innocent child would be transported to southern climes and placed with a good family. And so everything was settled as well as could possibly be managed. The grateful duke gave the doctor a monogrammed diamond snuffbox for Fräulein von Sanfon, together with a note of gratitude and an oral request to depart the principality and never return. Which the considerate maiden immediately did." Gauche chuckled, unable to restrain himself. "The next morning, after a row that had lasted all night, the grand duke finally decided to take a closer look at his new son and heir. He squeamishly lifted the boy out of the cradle and turned him this way

and that, and suddenly on his pink little backside—begging your pardon—
he saw a birthmark shaped like a heart. His highness had one exactly like it
on his own hindquarters, and so did his grandfather, and so on to the seventh generation. Totally confused, the duke sent for his physician, but Dr.
Vogel had set out from the castle for parts unknown the previous night,
leaving behind his wife and eight children." Gauche burst into hoarse
laughter, then began coughing and waving his hands in the air. Someone
else chuckled uncertainly, and Mme. Kleber put her hand to her mouth.

"The investigation that followed soon established that the court doctor
had been behaving strangely for some time, and had even been seen in the
gambling houses of neighboring Baden—in the company, moreover, of a
certain young woman whose description closely matched that of Fräulein
von Sanfon." The detective assumed a more serious expression. "The doctor was found two days later in a hospital in Strasbourg. Dead. He'd taken
a fatal dose of laudanum and left a note: 'I alone am to blame for everything.' A clear case of suicide. The identity of the true culprit was obvious,
but how could you prove it? As for the snuffbox, it was a gift from the
grand duke, and there was a note to go with it. It would not have been
worth their highnesses' while to take the case to court. The greatest mystery, of course, was how they managed to swap the newborn prince for the
little Negro baby and where they could have found a chocolate-colored
child in a country of people with blue eyes and blond hair. But then, according to some sources, shortly before the incident described, Marie Sanfon had a Senegalese maid in her service."

"Tell me, Commissioner," Fandorin said when the laughter stopped
(four people were laughing: Lieutenant Renier, Dr. Truffo, Professor
Sweetchild, and Mme. Kleber), "is Marie Sanfon so remarkably good-
looking that she can turn any man's head?"

"No, she is nothing of the kind. It says everywhere that her appearance
is perfectly ordinary, with absolutely no distinctive features." Gauche cast
a lingering challenging glance in Clarissa's direction. "She changes the
color of her hair, her behavior, her accent, and the way she dresses with the
greatest of ease. But evidently there must be something exceptional about
this woman. In my line of work, I've seen all sorts of things. The most dev-
astating heartbreakers are not usually great beauties. If you saw them in a

photograph, you would never pick them out, but when you meet them you can feel your skin creep. It's not a straight nose and long eyelashes that a man goes for; it's a certain special smell."

"Oh, Commissioner," Clarissa objected at this vulgar comment. "There are ladies present."

"There are certainly suspects present," Gauche parried calmly. "And you are one of them. How do I know that Mlle. Sanfon is not sitting at this very table?"

He fixed his eyes on Clarissa's face. This was becoming more and more like a bad dream. She could hardly catch her breath.

"If I have c-calculated correctly, then this person should be twenty-nine now?"

Fandorin's calm, almost indifferent question roused Clarissa to take a grip on herself, and casting female vanity aside, she cried out: "There is no point in staring at me like that, monsieur detective! You are obviously paying me a compliment that I do not deserve. I am almost ten years older than your adventuress! And the other ladies present are hardly suited to the role of Mlle. Sanfon. Mme. Kleber is too young and Mrs. Truffo, as you know, does not speak French!"

"For a woman of Marie Sanfon's skill, it is a very simple trick to add or subtract ten years from her age," Gauche replied slowly, staring at Clarissa as intently as ever. "Especially if the prize is so great and failure smacks of the guillotine. So, have you really never been to Paris, Mlle. Stamp? Somewhere in the region of the Rue de Grenelle, perhaps?"

Clarissa turned deathly pale.

"At this point, I feel obliged to intervene as a representative of the Jasper-Artaud Partnership," Renier interrupted irritably. "Ladies and gentlemen, I can assure you there is absolutely no way that any swindler or crook with an international reputation could have joined our cruise. The company guarantees there are no cardsharps or loose women on board the *Leviathan*, let alone adventuresses known to the police. You can understand why. A maiden voyage is a very great responsibility. A scandal is the very last thing we need. Captain Cliff and I personally checked and rechecked the passenger lists, and whenever necessary we made inquiries— including some to the French police, monsieur commissioner. The captain and I are prepared to vouch for everyone present here. We do not wish to prevent you from carrying out your professional duty, M. Gauche, but you are simply wasting your time. And French taxpayers' money."

"Well, now," growled Gauche, "that only time will tell."

Following which, to everyone's relief, Mrs. Truffo struck up a conversation about the weather.

Reginald Milford-Stokes

10 April 1878
22 hours, 31 minutes
In the Arabian Sea
17° 06' 28" N 59° 48' 14" E

My passionately beloved Emily,

This infernal ark is controlled by the forces of evil; I can sense it in every fiber of my tormented soul. Although I am not sure a criminal such as I can have a soul. Writing that has set me thinking. I remember that I have committed a crime, a terrible crime that can never ever be forgiven, but the strange thing is, I have completely forgotten what it was I did. And I very much do not want to remember.

At night, in my dreams, I remember it very well—otherwise how can I explain why I wake up in such a terrible state every morning? How I long for our separation to be over! I feel that if it lasts for even a little longer, I shall lose my mind. I sit in the cabin and stare at the minute hand of the chronometer, but it doesn't move. Outside on the deck I heard someone say, "It's the tenth of April today," and I couldn't grasp how it could possibly be April and why it had to be the tenth. I unlocked the trunk and saw that the letter I wrote to you yesterday was dated the ninth of April and the one from the day before yesterday was dated the eighth. So they're right. It is April. The tenth.

For several days now I have been keeping a close eye on Professor

Sweetchild (if he really is a professor). He is a very popular man with our group in Windsor, an inveterate old windbag who loves to flaunt his knowledge of history and oriental matters. Every day he comes up with new, fantastic stories of hidden treasure, each more improbable than the last. And he has nasty, shifty, piggy little eyes. Sometimes there is an insane gleam in them. If only you could hear how sensual his voice sounds when he talks about precious stones. He has a positive mania for diamonds and emeralds.

Today at breakfast Dr. Truffo suddenly stood up, clapped his hands loudly, and announced in a solemn voice that it was Mrs. Truffo's birthday. Everybody oohed and aahed and began congratulating her, and the doctor himself publicly presented his plain-faced spouse with a gift for the occasion, a pair of topaz earrings in exceptionally bad taste. What terrible vulgarity, to make a spectacle of giving a present to one's own wife! Mrs. Truffo, however, did not seem to think so. She became unusually lively and appeared perfectly happy, and her dismal features turned the color of a grated carrot. The lieutenant said: "Oh, madam, if we had known about this happy event in advance, we would certainly have prepared some surprise for you. You have only your own modesty to blame." The empty-headed woman turned an even more luminous shade and muttered bashfully: "Would you really like to make me happy?" The response was a general lazy mumble of goodwill. "Well, then," she said, "let's play my favorite game, lotto. In our family we always used to take out the cards and the bag of counters on Sundays and church holidays. It's such wonderful fun! Gentlemen, it will really make me very happy if you play!" It was the first time I had heard the doctor's wife speak at such length. For an instant I thought she was making fun of us, but no, Mrs. Truffo was entirely serious. There was nothing to be done. Only Renier managed to slip out, supposedly because it was time for him to go on watch. The churlish commissioner also attempted to cite some urgent business or other as an excuse, but everyone stared at him so reproachfully that he gave in with a bad grace and stayed.

Mr. Truffo went to fetch the equipment for this idiotic game and the torment began. Everyone dejectedly set out their cards, glancing longingly at the sunlit deck. The windows of the salon were wide open, but we sat there playing out a scene from the nursery. We set up a prize fund to which everyone contributed a guinea—"To make things more interesting" as the elated birthday girl said. Our leading lady should have had the best chance of winning, since she was the only one who was watching eagerly as the numbers were drawn. I had the impression that the commissioner would have liked to win the jackpot, too, but he had difficulty understanding the childish little rhymes that Mrs. Truffo kept spouting—for her sake on this occasion we spoke English.

The pitiful topaz earrings, which are worth ten pounds at the most, prompted Sweetchild to turn to his obsession again. "An excellent present, sir!" he declared to the doctor, who beamed in delight, but then Sweetchild spoiled everything with what he said next. "Of course, topazes are cheap nowadays, but who knows, perhaps their price will shoot up in a hundred years or so. Precious stones are so unpredictable! They are a genuine miracle of nature, unlike those boring metals, gold and silver. Metal has no soul or form, it can be melted down, while each stone has a unique personality. But it is not just anyone who can find them, only those who stop at nothing and are willing to follow their magical radiance to the ends of the earth, or even beyond, if necessary." These bombastic sentiments were accompanied by Mrs. Truffo calling out the numbers on the counters in her squeaky voice. While Sweetchild was declaiming, "I shall tell you the legend of the great and mighty conqueror Mahmud Gaznevi, who was bewitched by the brilliant luster of diamonds and put half of India to fire and the sword in his search for these magical crystals," Mrs. Truffo said: "Eleven, gentlemen. Drumsticks!" And so it went on.

But I shall tell you Sweetchild's legend of Mahmud Gaznevi anyway. It will give you a better understanding of this storyteller. I can even attempt to convey his distinctive manner of speech.

"In the year (I don't remember which) of our Lord Jesus Christ, which according to the Moslem chronology was (and of course I don't remember that), the mighty Gaznevi learned that in Sumnat on the peninsula of Guzzarat (I think that was it) there was a holy shrine that housed an immense idol worshiped by hundreds of thousands of people. The idol jealously guarded the borders of that land against foreign invasions, and anyone who stepped across them with a sword in his hand was doomed. This shrine belonged to a powerful Brahman community, the richest in all India. And these Brahmans of Sumnat also possessed an immense number of precious stones. But, unafraid of the power of the idol, the intrepid conqueror gathered his forces together and launched his campaign. Mahmud hewed off fifty thousand heads, reduced fifty fortresses to ruins, and finally burst into the Sumnat shrine. His soldiers defiled the holy site and ransacked it from top to bottom, but they could not find the treasure. Then Gaznevi himself approached the idol, swung his great mace, and smote its copper head. The Brahmans fell to the floor before their conqueror and offered him a million pieces of silver if only he would not touch their god. Mahmud laughed and smote the idol again. It cracked. The Brahmans began wailing more loudly than ever and promised this terrible ruler ten million pieces of gold. But the heavy mace was raised once again and it struck for a third time. The idol split in half and the diamonds and precious stones that had been concealed within it spilled out on to the floor in a gleaming torrent. The value of that treasure was beyond all calculation."

At this point Mr. Fandorin announced with a slightly embarrassed expression that he had a full card. Everyone except Mrs. Truffo was absolutely delighted and was on the point of leaving when she begged us so insistently to play another round that we had to stay. It started up again: "Thirty-nine—pig and swine! Twenty-seven—I'm in heaven!" and more drivel of the same kind.

But now Mr. Fandorin began speaking, and he told us another story in his gentle, rather ironic manner, an Arab fairy tale that he had read in an old book. Here is the fable as I remember it.

"Once upon a time three Maghreb merchants set out into the depths of the Great Desert, for they had learned that far, far away among the shifting sands, where the caravans do not go, there was a Great Treasure, the equal of which mortal eyes had never seen. The merchants walked for forty days, tormented by great heat and weariness, until they had only one camel each left—the others had all collapsed and died. Suddenly they saw a tall mountain ahead of them, and when they grew close to it they could not believe their eyes: The entire mountain consisted of silver ingots. The merchants gave thanks to Allah, and one of them stuffed a sack full of silver and set off back the way they had come. But the others said: 'We shall go farther.' They walked for another forty days, until their faces were blackened by the sun and their eyes were red and inflamed. Then another mountain appeared ahead of them, this time of gold. The second merchant exclaimed: 'Not in vain have we endured so many sufferings! Glory be to the Most High!' He stuffed a sack full of gold and asked his comrade: 'Why are you just standing there?' The third merchant replied: 'How much gold can you carry away on one camel?' The second said: 'Enough to make me the richest man in our city.' 'That is not enough for me,' said the third. 'I shall go farther and find a mountain of diamonds. And when I return home, I shall be the richest man in the entire world.' He walked on, and his journey lasted another forty days. His camel lay down and rose no more, but the merchant did not stop, since he was stubborn and believed in the mountain of diamonds, and everyone knows that a single handful of diamonds is more valuable than a mountain of silver or a hill of gold. Then the third merchant beheld a wondrous sight ahead of him: A man standing there doubled over in the middle of the desert, bearing a throne made of diamonds on his shoulders, and squatting on the throne was a monster with a black face and burning eyes. 'Joyous greetings to you, O worthy traveler,' croaked the doubled-over man. 'Allow me to introduce Marduf, the demon of avarice. Now you will bear him on your shoulders until another as avaricious as you and I comes to take your place.' "

The story was broken off at that point, because once again Mr. Fandorin had a full card, so our hostess failed to win the second jackpot, too. Five seconds later Mrs. Truffo was the only person left at the table—everyone else had disappeared in a flash.

I keep thinking about Mr. Fandorin's story. It is not as simple as it seems.

That third merchant is Sweetchild. Yes, when I heard the end of the story, I suddenly realized how dangerous a madman he is! An uncontrollable passion rages in his soul, and if anyone should know what that means, it is me. I have been gliding around after him like an invisible shadow ever since we left Aden.

I have already told you, my precious Emily, that I spent the time we were moored there very profitably. I'm sure you must have thought I meant I had bought a new navigational instrument to replace the one that was stolen. Yes, I now have a new sextant and I am checking the ship's course regularly once again, but what I meant was something quite different. I was simply afraid to commit my secret to paper. What if someone were to read it? For, after all, I am surrounded by enemies on all sides. But I have a resourceful mind, and I have invented a fine stratagem: Starting today I am writing in milk. To the eye of a stranger it will seem like a clean sheet of paper, quite uninteresting, but my quick-witted Emily will warm the sheets on the lamp shade to make the writing appear! What a fine dodge, eh?

Well then, about Aden. While I was still on the steamer, before they let us go ashore, I noticed that Sweetchild was nervous; more than simply nervous, he was positively jumping up and down with excitement. It began soon after Fandorin announced that the shawl stolen from Lord Littleby was the key to the mythical treasure of the Emerald Rajah. The professor became terribly agitated, started muttering to himself, and kept repeating: "Ah, I must get ashore soon." But what for, that was the question!

I decided to find out.

Pulling my black hat with the wide brim well down over my eyes, I set off to follow Sweetchild. It could not have gone better at first: He didn't glance round once and I had no trouble trailing him to the square behind the little customs house. But there I was in for an unpleasant surprise. Sweetchild called one of the local cabbies and drove off with him. His barouche was moving rather slowly, but I could not go running after it; that would have been unseemly. Of course, there were other barouches on the square, and I could easily have got into any of them, but you know, my dearest, how heartily I detest open carriages. They are the devil's own invention and only reckless fools ride in them. Some people (I have seen it with my own eyes more than once) even take their wives and innocent children with them. How long can it be before disaster strikes? The two-wheelers so popular at home in Britain are especially dangerous. Someone once told me (I can't recall who it was at the moment) that a certain young man from a very decent family, with a good position in society, was rash enough to take his young wife for a ride in one of those two-wheelers when she was eight months pregnant. It ended badly, of course: The mad fool lost control of the horses, which bolted, and the carriage overturned. The young man was all right, but his wife went into premature labor. They were unable to save her or the child. And all because of his recklessness. They could have gone for a walk or taken a ride in a boat. If it comes to that, one can take a ride on a train. In Venice they take rides in gondolas. We were there, remember? Remember how the water lapped at the steps of the hotel?

I am finding it hard to concentrate; I am constantly digressing. And so Sweetchild rode off in a carriage, and I was left standing beside the customs house. But do you think I lost my head? Not at all. I thought of something that calmed my nerves almost instantly. While I was waiting for Sweetchild, I went into a sailors' shop and bought a new sextant, even better than the old one, and a splendid navigational almanac with astronomical formulae. Now I can calculate the ship's position much faster and more precisely. See what a sly fellow I am!

I waited for six hours and thirty-eight minutes. I sat on a rock and looked at the sea, thinking about you.

When Sweetchild returned, I pretended to be dozing. He slipped past me, certain that I had not seen him.

The moment he disappeared round the corner of the customs house, I dashed across to his cabby. For six pence the Bengali told me where our dear professor had been. You must admit, my sweet Emily, that I handled this business most adroitly.

The information I received only served to corroborate my initial suspicions. Sweetchild had asked to be taken from the port directly to the telegraph office. He spent half an hour there, and then went back to the post office building another four times. The cabby said: "Sahib very-very worried. Run backward and forward. Sometimes say: Take me to bazaar, then tap me on back—take me back, post office, quick-quick." It seems quite clear that Sweetchild first sent off an urgent message to someone and then waited impatiently for an answer. The Bengali said that the last time he came out of the post office he was "not like himself, he wave paper" and told the cabby to drive him back to the ship. His reply must have arrived.

I do not know what was in it, but it is perfectly clear that the professor, or whoever he really is, has accomplices.

That was two days ago. Since then Sweetchild has been a changed man. As I have already told you, he speaks of nothing but precious stones all the time, and sometimes he suddenly sits down on the deck and starts drawing something, either on his cuff or his handkerchief.

This evening there was a ball in the grand salon. I have already described this majestic hall, which appears to have been transported here from Versailles or Buckingham Palace. There is gilt everywhere and the walls are covered from top to bottom with mirrors. The crystal electric chandeliers tinkle melodically in time to the gentle rolling of the ship. The orchestra (a perfectly decent one, by the way) mostly played Viennese waltzes, and as you know, I regard that dance as indecent, so I stood in the corner, keeping an eye on Sweetchild. He was enjoying himself greatly, inviting one lady after another to dance, skipping about like a goat and trampling on their feet outrageously, but he did not notice at all. I myself was even distracted, recalling how you and I once used to dance, and how elegant your arm looked in its white glove as it lay on my shoulder. Suddenly I saw Sweetchild stumble and drop his partner; then, without even bothering to apologize, he fairly raced across almost to the tables with the hors d'oeuvres, leaving his partner standing bewildered in the middle of the hall. I must admit that this sudden attack of uncontrollable hunger struck me as rather strange, too.

Sweetchild, however, did not even glance at the dishes of pies, cheese, and fruit. He grabbed a paper napkin out of a silver napkin holder, hunched over the table, and began furiously scribbling something on it. He has become completely obsessed, and obviously no longer feels it necessary to guard his secret, even in a crowded room! Consumed by curiosity, I began strolling casually in his direction. But Sweetchild had already straightened up and folded the napkin twice, evidently intending to put it in his pocket. Unfortunately, I was too late to glance at it over his shoulder. I stamped my foot furiously and was about to turn back when I noticed Mr. Fandorin coming over to the table with two glasses of champagne. He handed one to Sweetchild and kept the other for himself. I heard the Russian say: "Ah, my dear professor, how terribly absentminded you are! You have just put a dirty napkin in your pocket." Sweetchild was embarrassed; he took the napkin out, crumpled it into a ball, and threw it under the table. I immediately joined them and deliberately struck up a conversation about fashion, knowing the Indologist would soon grow bored and leave. Which is exactly what happened.

No sooner had he made his apologies and left us alone than Fandorin whispered to me conspiratorially: "Well, Sir Reginald, which of us is going to crawl under the table?" I realized that the diplomat was as suspicious of the professor's behavior as I was. We understood each other completely in an instant. "Yes, it is not exactly convenient," I agreed. Mr. Fandorin glanced around and then suggested: "Let us do this thing fairly and honestly. If one of us can come up with a reasonable pretext, the other will crawl after the napkin." I nodded and started thinking, but nothing appropriate came to mind. "Eureka!" whispered Fandorin, and with a movement so swift that I could barely see it, he unfastened one of my cuff links. It fell on the floor and the diplomat pushed it under the table with the toe of his shoe. "Sir Reginald," he said loudly enough for people standing nearby to hear, "I believe you have dropped a cuff link."

An agreement is an agreement. I squatted down and glanced under the table. The napkin was lying quite close, but the damned cufflink had skidded right across to the wall, and the table was rather wide. Imagine the scene: your husband crawling under the table on all fours, presenting the crowded hall with a view that was far from edifying. On my way back I got into a rather embarrassing fix. When I stuck my head out from under the table, I saw two young ladies directly in front of me, engaged in lively conversation with Mr. Fandorin. When they spotted my red head at the level of their knees, the ladies squealed in fright, but my perfidious companion merely said calmly: "Allow me to introduce Baronet Milford-Stokes." The ladies gave me a distinctly chilly look and left without saying a word. I leapt to my feet, absolutely bursting with fury, and exclaimed: "Sir, you deliberately stopped them so that you could make fun of me!" Fandorin replied with an innocent expression: "I did stop them deliberately, but not at all in order to make fun of you. It simply occurred to me that their skirts would conceal your daring raid from the eyes of the hall. But where is your booty?"

My hands trembled impatiently as I unfolded the napkin, revealing a strange sight. I am drawing it from memory.

What are these geometrical figures? What does the zigzagging line mean? And why are there three exclamation marks?

I cast a stealthy glance at Fandorin. He tugged at his earlobe and muttered something I didn't catch. I expect it was in Russian.

"What do you make of it?" I asked. "Let's wait for a while," the diplomat replied, a mysterious expression on his face. "He's getting close."

Who is getting close? Sweetchild? Close to what? And is it a good thing that he is getting close?

I had no chance to ask these questions, because at that moment there was a commotion in the hall and everyone started applauding. Then M. Driet, the captain's social director, began shouting deafeningly through a megaphone: "Ladies and gentlemen, the grand prize in our lottery goes to cabin number eighteen!" I had been so absorbed in the operation with the mysterious napkin that I had paid absolutely no attention to what was going on in the hall. It turned out that they had stopped dancing and set up the draw for the charity raffle in aid of fallen women (I wrote to you about this idiotic undertaking in my letter of the third of April). You are well aware how I feel about charity and fallen women, so I shall refrain from further comment.

The announcement had a strange effect on my companion—he frowned and ducked, lowering his head. I was surprised for a moment, and then I remembered that number eighteen is Mr. Fandorin's cabin. Just imagine that, he was the lucky winner again!

"This is becoming quite intolerable," our favorite of fortune mumbled, stammering more than usual. "I think I shall take a walk." He started backing away toward the door, but Mme. Kleber called out in her clear voice: "That's Mr. Fandorin from our salon! There he is, gentlemen! In the white dinner jacket with the red carnation! Mr. Fandorin, where are you going? You've won the grand prize!"

Everyone turned to look at the diplomat and began applauding more loudly than ever as four stewards carried the grand prize into the hall: an exceptionally ugly grandfather clock modeled after Big Ben. It was an absolutely repulsive construction of carved oak one and a half times the height of a man, and it must have weighed at least forty stone. I thought I caught a glimpse of something like horror in Mr. Fandorin's eyes. I must say I cannot blame him.

After that it was impossible to carry on talking, so I came back here to write this letter.

I have the feeling something terrible is about to happen; the noose is tightening around me. But you pursue me in vain, gentlemen, I am ready for you!

However, the hour is already late and it is time to take a reading of our position.

Good-bye, my dear, sweet, infinitely adored Emily.

Your loving

Reginald Milford-Stokes

Renate Kleber

RENATE LAY IN wait for the Watchdog (that was what she had christened Gauche once she discovered what the old bore was really like) outside his cabin. It was clear from the commissioner's wrinkled features and tousled gray hair that he had only just risen from his slumbers—he must have collapsed into bed immediately after lunch and snoozed into the evening.

Renate deftly grabbed hold of the detective's sleeve, lifted herself up on tiptoe, and blurted out: "Wait till you hear what I have to tell you!"

The Watchdog gave her a searching look, crossed his arms, and said in an unpleasant voice: "I shall be very interested to hear it. I've been meaning to have a word with you for some time, madam."

Renate found his tone of voice slightly alarming, but she decided it didn't really mean anything—the Watchdog must be suffering from indigestion, or perhaps he'd been having a bad dream.

"I've done your job for you," Renate boasted, glancing around to make sure no one was listening. "Let's go into your cabin; we won't be interrupted there."

The Watchdog's abode was maintained in perfect order. The familiar black file reposed impressively in the center of the desk, a neat pile of paper and several precisely sharpened pencils lying beside it. Renate surveyed the room curiously, turning her head this way and that, noting the shoe brush and tin of polish and the shirt collars hung up to dry on a piece of string. The man with the big mustache was obviously a penny-pincher—he polished his own shoes and did a bit of laundry to avoid having to give tips to the attendants.

"Right, then, out with it—what have you got for me?" the Watchdog growled irritably, clearly displeased by Renate's inquisitiveness.

"I know who the criminal is," she announced proudly.

This news failed to produce the anticipated effect on the detective. He sighed and asked: "Who is it?"

"Need you ask? It's so obvious a blind man could see it," Renate said, fluttering her hands as she sat down in an armchair. "All the newspapers said that the murder was committed by a lunatic. No normal person could possibly do anything so insane, could they? And now just think about the people we have sitting round our table. It's a choice collection of course, perfectly matching blooms, bores and freaks every last one of them, but there's only one lunatic."

"Are you hinting at the baronet?" asked the Watchdog.

"Finally you've got it!" said Renate with a pitying nod. "Why, it's as clear as day. Have you seen his eyes when he looks at me? He's a wild beast, a monster! I'm afraid to walk down the corridors. Yesterday I ran into him on the stairs when there wasn't a soul around. It gave me such a twinge in here!" She put one hand over her belly. "I've been watching him for a long time. At night he keeps the light on in his cabin and his curtains tightly closed. But yesterday they were open just a tiny little crack, so I peeped in. He was standing there in the middle of the cabin, waving his arms about and making ghastly faces and wagging his finger at somebody. It was so frightening! Later on, in the middle of the night, my migraine started up again, so I went out for a breath of fresh air, and there I saw the lunatic standing on the forecastle, looking up at the moon through some kind of metal contraption. That was when it dawned on me. He's one of those maniacs whose bloodlust rises with the full moon. I've read about them! Why are you looking at me as if I was some kind of idiot? Have you taken a look at the calendar recently?" Renate triumphantly produced a pocket calendar from her purse. "Look at this, I've checked it. On the fifteenth of March, when ten people were killed in the Rue de Grenelle, it was a full moon. See, it's written here in black and white: *pleine lune*."

The Watchdog looked, all right, but he didn't seem very interested.

"Why are you eyeing it like a dozy owl?" Renate asked angrily. "Don't you understand that today there's a full moon, too? While you're sitting around doing nothing, he'll go crazy again and brain somebody else. And I know who it will be—me. He hates me." Her voice trembled hysterically. "Everyone on this loathsome steamer wants to kill me! That African attacked me, that oriental of ours keeps glaring and grinding his teeth at me, and now it's this crazy baronet!"

The Watchdog merely gazed at her with his dull, unblinking eyes, and Renate waved her hand in front of his nose.

"Hallo! M. Gauche! You haven't fallen asleep, have you?"

The old man grabbed her wrist in a firm grip. He moved her hand aside and said sternly: "I'll tell you what, my dear. Stop playing the fool. I'll deal with our redheaded baronet, but I want you to tell me about your syringe. And no fairy tales—I want the truth!" He growled out the words so fiercely that she shrank back from him in alarm.

AT SUPPER SHE sat staring down into her plate. She always had an excellent appetite, but today she had hardly even touched her sautéed eels. Her eyes were red and swollen and every now and then her lips trembled slightly.

But the Watchdog was in a genial, even magnanimous mood. He looked at Renate frequently and with some severity, but his glance was fatherly rather than hostile. Commissioner Gauche was not as fierce as he liked to appear.

"A very impressive piece," he said with an envious glance at the Big Ben clock standing in the corner of the salon. "Some people have all the luck."

The monumental prize was too big to fit in Fandorin's cabin, and so it had been installed temporarily in Windsor. The oak tower continually ticked, jangled, and wheezed deafeningly, and on the hour it boomed out a noise that caught everyone by surprise, making them gasp. At breakfast, when Big Ben informed everyone (ten minutes late) that it was nine o'clock, the doctor's wife almost swallowed a teaspoon. In addition to all of this, the base of the tower was obviously a bit too narrow, and every strong wave set it swaying menacingly. Now, for instance, when the wind had freshened and the white curtains at the windows had begun waving in surrender, Big Ben's squeaky motions had become positively alarming.

The Russian seemed to take the commissioner's genuine admiration for irony and began making apologetic excuses.

"I t-told them to give the clock to fallen women, too, but M. Driet was adamant. I swear by Christ, Allah, and Buddha that when we g-get to Calcutta I shall leave this monster on the steamer. I won't permit that nightmare to be foisted on me!"

He squinted anxiously at Lieutenant Renier, who remained diplomatically silent. Then the diplomat turned to Renate for sympathy, but all she gave him in reply was a severe, sullen glance. In the first place, she was in a very bad mood; in the second, Fandorin had been out of favor with her for some time.

There was a story behind that.

It all started when Renate noticed that the sickly Mrs. Truffo positively blossomed whenever she was near the sweet little diplomat. And Mr. Fandorin himself seem to belong to that common variety of handsome males who manage to discover something fascinating in every dull woman they meet, and never neglect a single one. In principle Renate regarded this sub-species of men with respect, and actually found its members quite attractive. It would be very interesting to know what precious ore the blue-eyed, brown-haired Russian had managed to unearth in the dismal doctor's wife. There certainly could be no doubt he felt distinctly interested in her.

A few days earlier, Renate had witnessed an amusing scene played out by two actors: Mrs. Truffo (in the role of female vamp) and Mr. Fandorin (in the role of perfidious seducer). The audience had consisted of one young lady (quite exceptionally attractive, despite being in a certain delicate condition) who was concealed behind the tall back of a deck chair and following the action in her makeup mirror. The action was set at the stern of the ship. The time was a romantic sunset. The play was performed in English.

The doctor's wife had executed her lumbering approach to the diplomat with all the elephantine grace of a typical British seduction (both dramatis personae were standing at the rail, in profile to the aforementioned deck chair). Mrs. Truffo began, as was proper, with the weather.

"The sun is so very bright in these southern latitudes!" she bleated with passionate feeling.

"Oh, yes," replied Fandorin. "In Russia at this time of the year the snow has still not melted, and here the temperature is already thirty-five degrees Celsius, and that is in the shade. In the sunlight it is even hotter."

The preliminaries having been successfully concluded, Mrs. Goatface felt she could legitimately broach a more intimate subject.

"I simply don't know what to do!" she began in a modest tone appropriate to her theme. "I have such white skin! This insufferable sun will ruin my complexion or even, God forbid, give me freckles."

"The problem of f-freckles is one that worries me as well," the Russian replied in all seriousness. "But I was prudent and brought along a lotion made of extract of Turkish camomile. Look, my suntan is even and there are no freckles at all."

The cunning serpent presented his pretty little face temptingly to the respectable married woman.

Mrs. Truffo's voice trembled treacherously.

"Indeed, not a single freckle . . . And your eyebrows and eyelashes are barely bleached. You have a wonderful epithelium, Mr. Fandorin, quite wonderful!"

Now he'll kiss her, Renate predicted, seeing that the distance separating the diplomat's epithelium from the flushed features of the doctor's wife was a mere five centimeters.

But her prediction was mistaken.

Fandorin stepped back and said: "Epithelium? Are you familiar with the science of physiology?"

"A little," Mrs. Truffo replied modestly. "Before I was married, I had some involvement with medicine."

"Indeed? How interesting! You really must t-tell me about it!"

Unfortunately Renate had not been able to follow the performance all the way to its conclusion—a woman she knew had sat down beside her and she had been obliged to break off her surveillance.

However, the clumsy assault by the doctor's foolish wife had piqued Renate's own vanity. Why should she not ply her own charms on this nice-looking Russian bear cub? Purely out of sporting interest, naturally, and in order to maintain the skills without which no self-respecting woman could get by. Renate had no interest in the thrill of romance. In fact, in her present condition the only feeling that men aroused in her was nausea.

In order to while away the time (Renate's phrase was "to speed up the voyage"), she worked out a simple plan. Small-scale naval maneuvers, code name "Bear Hunt." In fact, of course, men were actually more like members of the canine family. Everybody knew they were primitive creatures who could be divided into three main types: jackals, sheepdogs, and gay dogs. There was a different approach for each type.

The jackal fed on carrion—that is, he preferred easy prey. Men of that kind went for the readily available.

And so the very next time they were alone together, Renate complained to Fandorin about M. Kleber, the tedious banker whose head was full of nothing but figures, the bore who had no time for his young wife. Any halfwit would have realized that here was a woman literally pining under the tedium of her empty life, ready to swallow any hook, even an unbaited one.

That didn't work, and she had to waste a lot of time parrying inquisitive questions about her husband's bank.

Very well, so next Renate set her trap for a sheepdog. This category of men loved weak, helpless women. All they really wanted was to be allowed to rescue and protect you. A fine subspecies, very useful to have around. The main thing here was not to overdo the physical weakness—men were afraid of sick women.

Renate had swooned a couple of times from the heat, slumping gracefully against the ironclad shoulder of her knight and protector. Once she had been unable to open the door to her cabin because the key had got stuck. On the evening of the ball, she had asked Fandorin to protect her from a tipsy (and entirely harmless) major of dragoons.

The Russian had lent her his shoulder, opened the door, and sent the dragoon packing, but he himself had not betrayed the slightest sign of amorous interest, the louse.

Could he in fact be a gay dog? Renate wondered. You certainly wouldn't think so to look at him. This third type of man was the least complicated, and entirely devoid of imagination. Only a coarsely sensual stimulus, such as a chance glimpse of an ankle, had any effect on them. On the other hand, many great men and even cultural luminaries belonged to precisely this category, so it was certainly worth a try.

With gay dogs the approach was elementary. Renate asked the diplomat to come and see her at precisely midday, so that she could show him her watercolors (which were nonexistent). At one minute to twelve the huntress was already standing in front of her mirror, dressed only in her bodice and pantaloons.

When there was a knock at the door she called out: "Come in, come in, I've been waiting!"

Fandorin stepped inside and froze in the doorway. Without turning round, Renate wiggled her rear at him and displayed her naked back to its best advantage. The wise beauties of the eighteenth century had discovered that it was not a dress open down to the navel that produced the strongest effect on men, but an open neck and a bare back. Obviously the sight of a defenseless spine roused the predatory instinct in the human male.

The diplomat seemed to have been affected. He stood there looking, not turning away. Pleased with the effect, Renate said capriciously: "What are you doing over there, Jenny? Come here and help me on with my dress. I'm expecting a very important guest any minute."

How would any normal man have behaved in this situation?

The more forward kind would have come up behind her without saying a word and kissed the soft curls on the back of her neck.

The average, fair-to-middling kind would have handed her the dress and giggled bashfully.

At that point Renate would have decided the hunt had been successfully concluded. She would have pretended to be embarrassed, thrown the insolent creature out, and lost all further interest in him. But Fandorin's response was unusual.

"It's not Jenny," he said in a disgustingly calm voice. "It is I, Erast Fandorin. I shall wait outside while you g-get dressed."

He was either one of the rare seduction-proof variety or a secret pervert. In the latter case, the Englishwomen were simply wasting their time and effort. But Renate's keen eye had not detected any of the characteristic signs of perversion. Apart, that was, from his strange predilection for secluded conversations with the Watchdog.

But this was all trivial nonsense. She had more serious reasons for being upset.

AT THE VERY moment Renate finally decided to plunge her fork into the cold sautée, the doors crashed open and the bespectacled professor burst into the dining room. He always looked a little wild—either his jacket was buttoned crookedly or his shoelaces were undone—but today he looked a real mess: His beard was disheveled, his tie had slipped over to one side, his eyes were bulging out of his head, and a suspender was dangling from under the flap of his jacket. Obviously something quite extraordinary must have happened. Renate instantly forgot her own troubles and stared curiously at the learned scarecrow.

Sweetchild spread his arms like a ballet dancer and shouted: "Eureka, gentlemen! The mystery of the Emerald Rajah is solved!"

"Oh, no," groaned Mrs. Truffo. "Not again!"

"Now I can see how it all fits together," said the professor, launching abruptly into an incoherent explanation. "After all, I was there—why didn't I realize it before? I kept thinking about it, going round and round in circles, but it just didn't add up. In Aden I received a telegram from an acquaintance of mine in the French Ministry of the Interior. He confirmed my suspicions, but I still couldn't make any sense of the eye, and most important, I couldn't work out who it could be. That is, I more or less know who, but how? How was it done? But now it has suddenly dawned on me!" He ran over to the window. A curtain fluttering in the wind enveloped him like a white shroud, and the professor impatiently pushed it aside. "I was standing at the window of my cabin, knotting my tie, and I saw the waves, crest after crest all the way to the horizon. And then suddenly it hit me! Everything fell into place—about the shawl, and about the son! It's a matter of clerical work pure and simple. Dig around in the registers at the École Maritime and you'll find him!"

"I don't understand a word," growled the Watchdog. "You're raving. What's this about some school or other?"

"Oh, no, this is very, very interesting," exclaimed Renate. "I just love trying to solve mysteries. But, my dear professor, this will never do. Sit down at the table, have some wine, catch your breath, and tell us everything from the beginning, calmly and clearly. After all, you have such a wonderful way with a story. But first someone must bring me my shawl so I don't catch a chill in this draft."

"Let me close the windows on the windward side, and the draft will stop immediately," Sweetchild suggested. "You are right, madam, I should tell you the whole thing starting from the beginning."

"No, don't close the windows—it will be too stuffy. Well, gentlemen?" Renate inquired capriciously. "Who will fetch my shawl from my cabin? Here is the key! Monsieur baronet?"

Of course the Ginger Lunatic did not stir, and Renier leapt to his feet.

"Professor, I implore you, do not start without me!" he said. "I shall be back in a moment."

"And I'll go get my knitting," said the doctor's wife with a sigh.

She got back first and began deftly clacking away with her needles. She waved her hand at her husband to tell him there was no need to translate.

Meanwhile Sweetchild was readying himself for his moment of triumph. Having taken Renate's advice to heart, he seemed determined to expound his discoveries as spectacularly as possible.

There was complete silence at the table, with everyone watching the speaker and following each movement he made.

Sweetchild took a sip of red wine and began walking backward and forward across the room. Then he halted, picturesquely posed in profile to his audience, and began.

"I have already told you about that unforgettable day when Rajah Bagdassar invited me into his palace in Brahmapur. It was a quarter of a century ago, but I remember everything quite clearly, down to the smallest detail. The first thing that struck me was the appearance of the palace. Knowing that Bagdassar was one of the richest men in the world, I had been expecting to see oriental luxury on a grand scale. But there was nothing of the kind. The palace buildings were rather modest, without any ornamental refinements. And the thought came to me that the passion for precious stones that was hereditary in this family, handed down from father to son, must have displaced every other vainglorious ambition. Why spend money on walls of marble when you could buy another sapphire or diamond instead? The Brahmapur palace was squat and plain, essentially the same kind of clay casket in which that indescribable distillation of magical luminescence was kept. No marble and alabaster could ever have rivaled the blinding radiance of those stones." The professor took another sip of wine and adopted a thoughtful pose.

Renier arrived, puffing and panting, respectfully laid Renate's shawl across her shoulders, and remained standing beside her.

"What was that about marble and alabaster?" he asked in a whisper.

"It's about the Brahmapur palace—let me listen," said Renate with an impatient jerk of her chin.

"The décor of the palace was also very simple," Sweetchild continued. "Over the centuries the halls and rooms had changed in appearance many times, and the only part of the palace that seemed interesting to me from a historical point of view was the upper level, consisting of four halls, each of which faced one of the points of the compass. At one time the halls had been open galleries, but during the last century they had been glassed in. At the same time the walls were decorated with quite fascinating frescoes depicting the mountains that surround the valley on all sides. The landscape is reproduced with astonishing realism, so that the mountains seem to be reflected in a mirror. From the philosophical point of view, this mirror imaging must surely represent the duality of existence and—"

Somewhere nearby a ship's bell began clanging loudly. They heard people shouting, and a woman screamed.

"My God, it's the fire alarm!" shouted the lieutenant, dashing for the door. "That's all we need now!"

They dashed after him in a tight bunch.

"What's happening?" the startled Mrs. Truffo inquired. "Have we been boarded by pirates?"

Renate sat there for a moment with her mouth open, then let out a bloodcurdling squeal. She grabbed the tail of the commissioner's coat and stopped him running out after the others.

"M. Gauche, don't leave me!" she begged him. "I know what a fire on board ship means, I've read about it! Now everyone will dash to the lifeboats and people will be crushed to death, and I'm a weak pregnant woman, I'll just be swept aside! Promise you'll look after me!"

"What's that about lifeboats?" the old man mumbled anxiously. "What kind of nonsense is that? I've been told the firefighting arrangements on the *Leviathan* are exemplary. Why, the ship even has a special fire officer. Stop shaking, will you? Everything will be all right." He tried to free himself, but Renate was clutching his coattail in a grip of iron. Her teeth were chattering loudly.

"Let go of me, little girl," the Watchdog said in a soothing voice. "I won't go anywhere. I'll just take a look at the deck through the window."

But no, Renate's fingers didn't release their grip.

The commissioner was proved right. After two or three minutes there was the sound of leisurely footsteps and loud voices in the corridor, and one by one the Windsorites began to return.

They had still not recovered from their shock, so they were laughing a lot and talking more loudly than usual.

The first to come in were Clarissa Stamp, the Truffos, and Renier, whose face was flushed.

"It was nothing at all," the lieutenant announced. "Someone threw a burning cigar into a litter bin that had an old newspaper in it. The fire spread to a door curtain, but the crew was alert and they put the flames out in a moment . . . But I see that you were all prepared for a shipwreck," he said with a laugh, glancing significantly at Clarissa.

She was clutching her purse and a bottle of orangeade.

"Well, orangeade in order not to die of thirst in the middle of the ocean," Renier guessed. "But what is the purse for? You wouldn't have much use for it in a lifeboat."

Renate giggled hysterically, and Miss Old Maid, embarrassed, put the bottle back on the table. The Truffos were also well equipped: The doctor had managed to grab his bag of medical instruments and his wife was clutching a blanket to her breast.

"This is the Indian Ocean, madam; you would hardly have frozen to death," Renier said with a serious expression, and the stupid goat idiotically nodded her head.

The Japanese appeared holding a pathetic, bright-colored bundle . . . What could he have in there, a traveling hara-kiri kit?

The lunatic came in looking disheveled, clutching a small box—the kind normally used for holding writing instruments.

"Who were you planning to write to, Mr. Milford-Stokes? Ah, I understand! When Miss Stamp had drunk her orangeade, we could have stuck a letter in the bottle and sent it floating off across the ocean waves," suggested the lieutenant, who was obviously acting so jovially out of a sense of relief.

Now everyone was there except the professor and the diplomat.

"M. Sweetchild is no doubt packing his scholarly works, and monsieur le Russe is lighting the samovar for a final cup of tea," said Renate, infected by the lieutenant's lighthearted mood.

And there was the Russian, speak of the devil. He stood by the door, his handsome face as dark as a storm cloud.

"Well, M. Fandorin, have you decided to take your prize with you in the boat?" Renate inquired provocatively.

Everyone roared with laughter except the Russian, who failed to appreciate the joke, even though it was rather witty.

"Commissioner Gauche," he said quietly. "Would you be so kind as to step out into the corridor? As quickly as you can."

It was strange, but when he spoke these words the diplomat did not stammer once. Perhaps the nervous shock had cured him? Such things did happen.

Renate was on the point of joking about that, too, but she bit her tongue. It would probably have been going too far.

"What's all the hurry?" the Watchdog asked gruffly. "Another teller of tales. Later, young man, later. First I want to hear the rest of what the professor has to say. Where has he got to?"

Fandorin looked at the commissioner expectantly, but when he realized the old man was feeling obstinate and had no intention of going out into the corridor, he shrugged and said: "The professor will not be joining us."

Gauche scowled.

"And why would that be?"

"What do you mean, he won't be joining us?" Renate put in. "He stopped just when it was getting interesting! It's not fair!"

"Professor Sweetchild has just been murdered," the diplomat announced coolly.

"What's that?" the Watchdog roared. "Murdered? What do you mean, murdered?"

"I believe it was done with a surgical scalpel," the Russian replied with remarkable composure. "His throat was cut very neatly."

Commissioner Gauche

⌇⌇⌇

"ARE THEY EVER going to let us go ashore?" Mme. Kleber asked plaintively. "Everyone else is out strolling round Bombay, and we're just sitting here doing nothing."

The curtains were pulled across the windows to keep out the searing rays of the sun that scorched the deck and made the air sticky and suffocating. But although it was hot and stuffy in the Windsor salon, everyone sat there patiently, waiting for the truth to be revealed.

Gauche took out his watch—a presentation piece with a profile portrait of Napoleon III on it—and replied vaguely.

"Soon, ladies and gentlemen. I'll let you out soon. But not all of you."

At least he knew what he was waiting for: Inspector Jackson and his men were conducting a search. The murder weapon itself was probably lying at the bottom of the ocean, but some clues might have been left. They must have been. Of course, there was plenty of circumstantial evidence, anyway, but hard evidence always made a case look better. It was about time Jackson put in an appearance . . .

The *Leviathan* had reached Bombay at dawn. Since the evening of the previous day, all the Windsorites had been confined to their cabins under house arrest, and immediately the ship arrived in port, Gauche had contacted the authorities, informed them of his own conclusions, and requested their assistance. They had sent Jackson and a team of constables. *Come on, Jackson, get a move on,* thought Gauche, wishing the inspector would stop dragging his feet. After a sleepless night, the commissioner's head felt as heavy as lead and his liver had started playing up, but despite everything he was feeling pleased with himself. He had finally unraveled the knots in this tangled thread, and now he could see where it led to.

At half past eight, after finalizing his arrangements with the local police and spending some time at the telegraph office, Gauche had ordered the detainees assembled in the Windsor salon—it would be more convenient for the search. He hadn't even made an exception for Renate, who had been sitting beside him at the time of the murder and could not possibly have cut the professor's throat. The commissioner had been watching over his prisoners for more than three hours now, occupying a strategic position in the deep armchair opposite his *client,* and there were two armed policemen standing outside the door of the salon, where they could not be seen from inside.

The detainees were all too sweaty and nervous to make conversation. Renier dropped in from time to time, nodded sympathetically to Renate, and went off again about his business. The captain looked in twice, but he didn't say anything—he just gave the commissioner a savage glance, as if this whole mess was papa Gauche's fault.

The professor's deserted chair was like the gap left by a missing tooth. The Indologist himself was ashore, in the chilly vault of the Bombay municipal morgue. The thought of the dark shadows and the blocks of ice almost made Gauche envy the dead man. Lying there, with all his troubles behind him, no sweat-drenched collar chafing into his neck . . .

The commissioner looked at Dr. Truffo, who did not seem very comfortable, either: The sweat was streaming down his olive-skinned face, and his English Fury kept whispering in his ear.

"Why are you looking at me like that, monsieur?" Truffo exploded when he caught the policeman's glance. "Why do you keep staring at me? It's absolutely outrageous! What right do you have? I've been a respectable medical practitioner for fifteen years," he almost sobbed. "What difference does it make if a scalpel was used? Anyone could have done it!"

"Was it really done with a scalpel?" Mlle. Stamp asked timidly.

It was the first time anyone in the salon had mentioned what had happened.

"Yes, only a very-good-quality scalpel produces such a clean incision," Truffo replied angrily. "I inspected the body. Someone obviously grabbed Sweetchild from behind, put one hand over his mouth, and slit his throat with the other. The wall of the corridor is splattered with blood just above the height of a man. That's because his head was pulled back—"

"No great strength would have been required, then?" asked the Russian (our homegrown criminologist!). "The element of surprise would have b-been enough?"

The doctor gave a despondent shrug.

"I don't know, monsieur. I've never tried it."

Aha—at last! The door half opened and the inspector's bony features appeared in the gap. The inspector beckoned to the commissioner, who grunted with the effort of hoisting himself out of his armchair.

There was a pleasant surprise waiting for the commissioner in the corridor. Everything had worked out quite splendidly: a thorough job, efficient and elegant. Solid enough to bring the jury in straightaway, no lawyer could demolish evidence like that. Good old papa Gauche, he could still give any young buck a hundred yards' head start. And well done Jackson for his hard work!

The four of them went back into the salon together: the captain, Renier, Jackson, with Gauche bringing up the rear. At this stage he was feeling so pleased with himself that he even started humming a little tune. And his liver had stopped bothering him.

"Well, ladies and gentlemen, this is it," Gauche announced cheerfully, stepping out into the very center of the salon. He put his hands behind his back and swayed on his heels. It was a pleasant feeling to know you were a figure of some importance—even, in your own way, a ruler of destinies. The road had been long and hard, but he had reached the end at last. Now for the most enjoyable part.

"Papa Gauche has certainly had to rack his old brains, but an old hunting dog will always sniff out the fox's den, no matter how confused the trail might be. By murdering Professor Sweetchild, our criminal has finally given himself away—it was an act of despair. I believe that under questioning the murderer will tell me all about the Indian shawl and many other things as well. Incidentally, I should like to thank our Russian diplomat, who without even knowing it helped to set me on the right track with several of his comments and questions."

In his moment of triumph, Gauche could afford to be magnanimous. He nodded condescendingly to Fandorin, who bowed his head without speaking. What a pain these aristocrats were, with all their airs and graces, always so arrogant; you could never get a civil word out of them.

"I shall not be traveling with you any farther. Thanks for the company, as they say, but all things in moderation. The murderer will also be going ashore: I shall hand him over to Inspector Jackson in a moment, here on board the ship."

Everyone in the salon looked warily at the morose, skinny Englishman standing there with his hands in his pockets.

"I am very glad this nightmare is over," said Captain Cliff. "I realize you have had to put up with much unpleasantness, but everything has been sorted out now. The head steward will find you places in different salons if you wish. I hope the remainder of your cruise on board the *Leviathan* will help you to forget this whole sad business."

"Hardly," said Mme. Kleber, answering for all of them. "This whole experience has been far too upsetting for all of us! But please don't keep us in suspense, monsieur commissioner. Tell us who the murderer is, quickly."

The captain was about to add something to what he had said, but Gauche raised his hand to stop him. This time he had earned the right to a solo performance.

"I must confess that at first my list of suspects included every single one of you. The process of elimination was long and difficult, but now I can reveal the most crucial point: Beside Lord Littleby's body we discovered one of the *Leviathan*'s gold emblems—this one here." He tapped the badge on his own lapel. "This little trinket belongs to the murderer. As you know, a gold badge could only have been worn by a senior officer of the ship or a first-class passenger. The officers were immediately eliminated from the list of suspects because they all had their badges and no one had requested the shipping line issue a new emblem to replace one that had been lost. But among the passengers there were four individuals who were not wearing a badge. Mlle. Stamp, Mme. Kleber, M. Milford-Stokes, and M. Aono. I have kept this quartet under particularly close observation. Dr. Truffo found himself here because he is a doctor, Mme. Truffo because husband and wife must not be set asunder, and our Russian diplomat because of his snobbish disinclination to appear like a janitor."

The commissioner lit his pipe and started pacing around the salon.

"I have erred, I confess. At the very beginning, I suspected monsieur le baronet, but I received timely information concerning his . . . circumstances and selected a different target. You, madam!" Gauche swung round to face Mlle. Stamp.

"As I observed," she replied coldly. "But I really cannot see what made me appear so suspicious."

"Oh, come now!" said Gauche, surprised. "In the first place, everything about you indicates that you suddenly became rich only very recently. That in itself is already highly suspicious. In the second place, you lied about never having been in Paris, even though the words 'Hotel Ambassadeur' are written on your fan in letters of gold. Of course you stopped carrying the fan, but old Gauche has sharp eyes. I spotted that trinket of yours straightaway. It is the sort of thing that expensive hotels give to their guests as mementos of their stay. The Ambassador happens to stand on the Rue de Grenelle, only a five-minute walk from the scene of the crime. It is a luxurious hotel, very large, and all sorts of people stay in it—so why is the mademoiselle being so secretive, I asked myself. There is something not right here. And I found I couldn't get the idea of Marie Sanfon out of my head . . ." The commissioner smiled disarmingly at Clarissa Stamp. "Well, I was casting around in the dark for a while, but eventually I hit upon the right trail, so I offer my apologies, mademoiselle."

Gauche suddenly noticed that the redheaded baronet had turned as white as a sheet: His jaw was trembling and his green eyes were glaring at the commissioner balefully.

"What precisely do you mean by . . . my 'circumstances'?" he said slowly, choking on the words in his fury. "What are you implying, mister detective?"

"Come, come," said Gauche, raising a conciliatory hand. "Above all else, you must remain calm. You must not become agitated. Your circumstances are your circumstances and they are no one else's business. I only mentioned them to indicate that you no longer figure among my potential suspects. Where is your emblem, by the way?"

"I threw it away," the baronet replied gruffly, his eyes still shooting daggers at Gauche. "It's repulsive! It looks like a golden leech! And—"

"And it was not fitting for the baronet Milford-Stokes to wear the same kind of name tag as a raggle-taggle bunch of nouveaux riches, was it?" the commissioner remarked shrewdly. "Yet another snob."

Mademoiselle Stamp also seemed to have taken offense.

"Commissioner, your description of exactly what it is that makes me such a suspicious character was most illuminating. Thank you," she said acidly, with a jerk of her pointed chin. "You have indeed tempered justice with mercy."

"When we were still in Aden, I sent a number of questions back to the prefecture by telegram. I could not wait for the replies, because the inquiries that had to be made took some time, but there were several messages waiting for me in Bombay. One of them concerned you, mademoiselle. Now I know that, from the age of fourteen, when your parents died, you lived in the country with a female cousin of your mother. She was rich but miserly. She treated you, her companion, like a slave and kept you on little more than bread and water."

The Englishwoman blushed and seemed to regret ever having made her comment. *Now, my sweet little bird,* thought Gauche, *let us see how deeply you blush at what comes next!*

"A couple of months ago, the old woman died and you discovered she had left her entire estate to you. It is hardly surprising that after so many years under lock and key, you should want to get out and travel a bit, to see the world. I expect you had never seen anything of life except in books?"

"But why did she conceal the fact that she had visited Paris?" Mme. Kleber interrupted rudely. "Because her hotel was on the street where all those people were killed? She was afraid you would suspect her, was that it?"

"No," laughed Gauche. "That was not it. Having suddenly become rich, Mlle. Stamp acted as any other woman would have done in her place—the first thing she did was visit Paris, the capital of the world. To admire the beautiful sights of Paris, to dress in the latest Paris fashion and also, well . . . for romantic adventures."

The Englishwoman had clenched her fingers together nervously. She was gazing at Gauche imploringly, but nothing was going to stop him now—this fine lady should have known better than to look down her nose at a commissioner of the Paris police.

"Mlle. Stamp found romance aplenty. In the Ambassador Hotel she made the acquaintance of an exceptionally suave and handsome gentleman, who is listed in the police files under the name of 'the Vampire.' A shady character who specializes in rich, aging foreign women. The flames of passion were ignited instantly and—as always happens with the Vampire—they were extinguished without warning. One morning, on the thirteenth of March to be exact, mademoiselle, you woke alone and forlorn in a hotel room that you could barely recognize, it was so empty. Your friend had made off with everything except the furniture. They sent me a list of the items that were stolen from you." Gauche glanced into his file. "Number thirty-eight on the list is 'a golden brooch in the form of a whale.' When I read that, I began to understand why Mlle. Stamp does not like to remember Paris."

The foolish woman was a pitiful sight now—she had covered her face with her hands and her shoulders were heaving.

"I never really suspected Mme. Kleber," said Gauche, moving on to the next point on his agenda, "even though she was unable to give a clear explanation of why she had no emblem."

"But why did you ignore what I told you?" the Japanese butted in. "I told you something very important."

"I didn't ignore it!" The commissioner swung round to face the speaker. "Far from it. I had a word with Mme. Kleber, and she gave me an explanation that accounted for everything. She suffered so badly during the first stages of her pregnancy that her doctor prescribed . . . certain sedative substances. Afterward the painful symptoms passed, but the poor woman had already become habituated to the medication, which she took for her nerves and insomnia. She was taking larger and larger doses, and the habit was threatening to get out of hand. I had a fatherly word with

Mme. Kleber, and afterward, under my watchful eye, she threw the vile narcotic into the sea." Gauche cast a glance of feigned severity at Renate, who had stuck out her lower lip like a sulking child. "Remember, my dear, you promised papa Gauche on your word of honor."

Renate lowered her eyes and nodded.

Clarissa erupted. "Ah, what touching concern for Mme. Kleber! Why could you not spare my blushes, monsieur detective? You have humiliated me in front of the entire company."

But the commissioner had no time for her now—he was still gazing at the Japanese, and his gaze was grave and unrelenting. The quick-witted Jackson understood without having to be told that it was time. There was a funereal gleam of burnished steel as he took his hand out of his pocket. He held the revolver with the barrel pointing straight at the oriental's forehead.

"I believe you Japanese think of us as ginger-haired monkeys?" Gauche said in a hostile voice. "I've heard that's what you call Europeans. We are hairy barbarians and you are cunning, subtle, and so highly cultured. White people are not even fit to lick your boots." The commissioner puffed out his cheeks sarcastically and blew out a thick cloud of smoke to one side. "Killing ten monkeys means nothing to you—you don't even think of it as wrong."

Aono sat there tense and still. His face was like stone.

"You accuse me of killing Rord Ritterby and his vassals . . . that is, servants?" the oriental asked in a flat, lifeless voice. "Why do you accuse me?"

"For every possible reason criminal science has to offer, my dear chap," the commissioner declared. Then he turned away from the Japanese, because the speech he was about to make was not intended for this yellow dog; it was intended for History. The time would come when they would print it in the textbooks on criminology.

"First, gentlemen, allow me to present the circumstantial evidence indicating that this person *could* have committed the crimes of which I accuse him." (Ah, but he shouldn't be giving this speech to an audience of ten people; he should be addressing a packed hall in the Palais de Justice!) "And then I shall present to you the evidence which demonstrates beyond all possible doubt that M. Aono not only could have, but actually did murder eleven people—ten on the fifteenth of March in the Rue de Grenelle and one yesterday, the fourteenth of April, on board the steamer *Leviathan*."

As he spoke, an empty space formed around Aono. The Russian was the only one left sitting beside the prisoner, and the inspector was standing just behind him, with his revolver at the ready.

"I hope nobody here has any doubt that the death of Professor Sweetchild is directly connected with the crime in the Rue de Grenelle. As our investigation has demonstrated, the goal of that murder most foul was to steal, not the golden Shiva, but the silk shawl." Gauche scowled sternly, as if to say: *Yes, indeed, the investigation has established the facts, so you can stop making that wry face, monsieur diplomat.* "And that is the key to the hidden treasure of Bagdassar, rajah of Brahmapur. We do not yet know how the accused came to learn the secret of the shawl, and we are all aware that the Orient holds many mysteries impenetrable to our European minds. However, the deceased professor, a genuine connoisseur of oriental culture, succeeded in solving this mystery. He was on the point of sharing his discovery with us when the fire alarm was sounded. Fate itself had sent the criminal a golden opportunity to stop Sweetchild's mouth forever. Afterward all would be silence again, just like at the Rue de Grenelle. But the killer failed to take into account one very important circumstance: This time Commissioner Gauche was on hand, and he is not one to be trifled with. It was a risky move, but it might have worked. The criminal knew that the scholar would dash straight to his cabin to save his papers—that is, his manuscripts. It was there, concealed by the bend in the corridor, that the murderer committed his foul deed. And there we have the first piece of circumstantial evidence." The commissioner raised a finger to emphasize his point. "M. Aono ran out of the salon and therefore he could have committed this murder."

"Not only I," said the Japanese. "Six other people ran out of the saron: M. Renier, M. and Mme. Truffo, M. Fandorin, M. Mirfor-Stokes, and Mlle. Stamp."

"Correct," Gauche agreed. "But I merely wished to demonstrate to the jury, by which I mean the present company, the connection between these two crimes, and also that you *could* have committed yesterday's murder. Now, let us return to the Crime of the Century. M. Aono was in Paris at the time, a fact of which there can be no doubt, and which is confirmed by a telegram I received."

"One and a half mirrion other people were also in Paris," the Japanese interjected.

"Perhaps, but nonetheless we now have our second piece of circumstantial evidence," said Gauche.

"Too circumstantial by far," put in the Russian.

"I won't dispute that." Gauche tipped some tobacco into his pipe before he made his next move. "However, the fatal injections were administered to Lord Littleby's servants by a medico of some sort, and there are certainly not one and a half million medics in Paris, are there?"

No one contested that, but Captain Cliff asked: "True, but what of it?"

"Ah, monsieur le capitaine," said Gauche, his eyes flashing brightly, "the point is that our friend Aono here is not a military man, as he introduced himself to all of us, but a qualified surgeon, a recent graduate from the medical faculty at the Sorbonne! I learned that from the same telegram."

A pause for effect. A muffled hum of voices in the hall of the Palais de Justice, the rustling of the newspaper artists' pencils on their sketch pads: "Commissioner Gauche Plays His Trump Card." Ah, but you must wait for the ace, my friends—the ace is yet to come.

"And now, ladies and gentlemen, we move from circumstantial evidence to hard facts. Let M. Aono explain why he, a doctor, a member of a respected and prestigious profession, found it necessary to pose as an army officer. Why such deception?"

A drop of sweat slithered down the waxen face of the Japanese. Aono said nothing—he certainly hadn't put up much of a fight.

"There is only one answer: He did it to divert suspicion from himself. The murderer was a doctor," the commissioner summed up complacently. "And that brings us to our second piece of hard evidence. Gentlemen, have you ever heard of Japanese boxing?"

"I've not only heard of it, I've seen it," said the captain. "One time in Macao, I saw a Japanese navigator beat three American sailors senseless. He was a puny little tyke, you'd have thought you could knock him over with a feather, but you should have seen the way he skipped around and flung his arms and legs around. He laid three hulking whalers out flat. He hit one of them on the arm with the edge of his hand and twisted the elbow the other way. Broke the bone, can you imagine it? That was some blow!"

Gauche nodded smugly.

"I have also heard that the Japanese possess the secret of killing with their bare hands in combat. They can easily kill a man with a simple jab of the finger. We have all seen M. Aono practicing his gymnastics. Fragments of a shattered gourd—a remarkably hard gourd—were discovered under the bed in his cabin. And there were several whole ones in a sack. The accused obviously used them for perfecting the precision and strength of his blow. I cannot even imagine how strong a man must be to smash a hard gourd with his bare hand, and into several pieces."

The commissioner surveyed his assembled audience before introducing his second piece of evidence.

"Let me remind you, ladies and gentlemen, that the skull of the unfortunate Lord Littleby was shattered into several fragments by an exceptionally strong blow with a blunt object. Now would you please observe the calluses on the hands of the accused."

The Japanese snatched his small, sinewy hands off the table.

"Don't take your eyes off him, Jackson. He is very dangerous," warned Gauche. "If he tries anything, shoot him in the leg or the shoulder. Now let me ask M. Aono what he did with his gold emblem. Well, have you nothing to say? Then let me answer the question myself: The emblem was torn from your chest by Lord Littleby the very moment you struck him a fatal blow to the head with the edge of your hand!"

Aono half opened his mouth, as though he was about to say something, but he only bit his lip with his strong, slightly crooked teeth and closed his eyes. His face took on a strange detached expression.

"And so the picture that emerges of the crime in the Rue de Grenelle is as follows," said Gauche, starting his summation. "On the evening of the fifteenth of March, Gintaro Aono went to Lord Littleby's mansion with the premeditated intention of killing everyone in the house and taking possession of the triangular shawl from the owner's collection. At that time he already had a ticket for the *Leviathan,* which was due to sail for India from Southampton four days later. The defendant was obviously intending to search for the Brahmapur treasure in India. We do not know how he managed to persuade the unfortunate servants to submit to an 'inoculation against cholera.' It is very probable that the accused showed them some kind of forged document from the mayor's office. That would have been entirely convincing because, as I have been informed by telegram, medical students in their final year at the Sorbonne are quite often employed in prophylactic public-health programs. There are quite a lot of orientals among the students and interns at the university, so the evening caller's yellow skin was unlikely to alarm the servants. The most monstrous aspect of the crime is the infernal callousness with which two innocent children were murdered. I have considerable personal experience dealing with the scum of society, ladies and gentlemen. In a fit of rage a criminal thug may toss a baby into a fire, but to kill with such cold calculation, with hands that do not even tremble . . . You must agree, gentlemen, that is not the French way, indeed it is not the European way."

"That's right!" exclaimed Renier, incensed, and Dr. Truffo supported him wholeheartedly.

"After that, everything was very simple," Gauche continued. "Once he was sure the poisonous injections had plunged the servants into a sleep from which they would never wake, the murderer walked calmly up the stairs to the second floor and into the hall where the collection was kept, and there he began helping himself to what he wanted. After all, he was certain the master of the house was away. But an attack of gout had prevented Lord Littleby from traveling to Spa, and he was still at home. The sound of breaking glass brought him out into the hall, where he was murdered in a most barbarous manner. It was this unplanned murder that shattered the killer's diabolical composure. He had almost certainly planned to take several items from the collection in order not to draw attention to the celebrated shawl, but now he had to hurry. We do not know; perhaps his lordship called out before he died and the killer was afraid his cries had been heard in the street. For whatever reason, he took only a golden Shiva that he did not need, then fled in haste without even noticing his *Leviathan* badge had been left behind in the hand of his victim. In order to throw the police off the scent, Aono left the house through the window of the conservatory . . . No, that was not the reason!" Gauche slapped himself on the forehead. "Why did I not think of it before? He could not go back the way he had come if his victim had cried out! For all he knew, passersby were already gathering at the door of the mansion! That was why Aono smashed the window in the conservatory, jumped down into the garden, and then made his escape over the fence. But he need not have been so careful—at that late hour the Rue de Grenelle was empty. If there were any cries, no one heard them."

The impressionable Mme. Kleber sobbed. Mrs. Truffo listened to her husband's translation and blew her nose with some emotion.

Clear, convincing, and unassailable, thought Gauche. *The evidence and the investigative hypotheses reinforce each other perfectly. And old papa Gauche still hasn't finished with you yet.*

"This is the appropriate moment to consider the death of Professor Sweetchild. As the accused has quite rightly observed, in theory the murder could have been committed by six other people apart from himself. Please do not be alarmed, ladies and gentlemen!" The commissioner raised a reassuring hand. "I shall now prove that you did not kill the professor and that he was in fact killed by our slant-eyed friend here."

The blasted Japanese had completely turned to stone. Was he asleep, or what? Or was he praying to his Japanese god? Pray as much as you like, my lad, that old slut Mme. Guillotine will still have your head!

Suddenly the commissioner was struck by an extremely unpleasant thought. What if the English nabbed the Japanese for the murder of Sweetchild? The professor was a British subject, after all. Then the criminal would be tried in an English court and end up on a British gallows instead of under a French guillotine! Anything but that! The Crime of the Century could not be tried abroad! The trial must be held in the Palais de Justice and nowhere else! Sweetchild may have been killed on board an English ship, but there were ten bodies in Paris and only one here. And, in any case, the ship wasn't entirely British property—there were two partners in the consortium!

Gauche was so upset that he lost track of his argument. *Not on your life,* he thought to himself. *You will not have my client. I'll put an end to this farce and then go straight to the French consul. I'll take the murderer to France myself.* And immediately he could see it: the crowded quayside, the police lines, the journalists . . .

But first the case had to be brought to a conclusion.

"Now Inspector Jackson will tell us what was found when the defendant's cabin was searched."

Gauche gestured for Jackson to say his piece.

Jackson launched into a monotonous rigmarole in English, but the commissioner quickly put a stop to that.

"This investigation is being conducted by the French police," he said sternly, "and the official language of this inquiry is also French. Apart from which, monsieur, not everyone here understands your language. And most important of all, I am not sure the accused knows English. You must admit he has a right to know the results of your search."

The protest was made as a matter of principle, in order to put the English in their place right from the start. They had to realize they were the junior partners in this business.

Renier volunteered to act as interpreter. He stood beside the inspector and translated phrase by phrase, enlivening the Englishman's flat, truncated sentences with his own dramatic intonations and expressive gestures.

"Acting on instructions received, a search was carried out. In cabin number twenty-four. The passenger's name is Gintaro Aono. We acted in accordance with the Regulations for the Conduct of a Search in a Confined Space. A rectangular room with a floor area of two hundred square feet. Was divided into twenty squares horizontally and forty-four squares vertically." The lieutenant asked what that meant and then explained it to the others. "Apparently the walls also have to be divided into squares—they tap on them in order to identify secret hiding places, although I can't see how there could be any secret hiding places in a steamship cabin . . . The search was conducted in strict sequence: first vertically, then horizontally. No hiding places were discovered in the walls." At this point Renier gave an exaggerated shrug, as if to say: Who would ever have thought it? "During the examination of the horizontal plane, the following items relevant to the case were discovered. Item one: notes in a hieroglyphic script. They will be translated and studied. Item two: a long dagger of oriental appearance with an extremely sharp blade. Item three: a sack containing eleven Egyptian gourds. And finally, item five: a bag for carrying surgical instruments. The compartment for holding a large scalpel is empty."

The audience gasped. The Japanese opened his eyes and glanced briefly at the commissioner, but still did not speak.

He's going to crack any moment, thought Gauche, but he was wrong. Without getting up off his chair, the oriental swung round to face the inspector standing behind him and struck the hand holding the revolver a sharp blow from below. While the gun was still describing a picturesque arc through the air, the athletic Japanese had already reached the door, but when he jerked it open the two policemen standing outside jammed the barrels of their Colts into his chest. A split second later the inspector's weapon completed its trajectory, crashed down onto the center of the table, and went off with a deafening roar. A jangling sound, smoke, a scream.

Gauche quickly summed up the situation: The prisoner was backing toward the table; Mrs. Truffo was in a dead faint; there seemed to be no other casualties; there was a hole in Big Ben just below the dial and its hands weren't moving. The clock was jangling. The ladies were screaming. But all in all the situation was in hand.

The Japanese was returned to his seat and shackled with handcuffs; the doctor's wife was revived, and everyone returned to their seats. The commissioner smiled and began talking again, demonstrating his superior presence of mind.

"Gentlemen of the jury, you have just witnessed a scene that amounts to a confession of guilt, even though it was played out in a somewhat unusual manner."

He'd made that slip about the jury again, but he didn't bother to correct himself. After all, this was his dress rehearsal.

"As the final piece of evidence, it could not possibly have been more conclusive," Gauche summed up smugly. "And you, Jackson, may consider yourself reprimanded. I told you he was dangerous."

The inspector was as scarlet as a boiled lobster. That would teach him.

Yes, everything had turned out excellently.

The Japanese sat there with three guns pointing at him, pressing his shackled hands to his chest. He had closed his eyes again.

"That is all, Inspector. You can take him away. He can be kept in your lockup for the time being. When all the formalities have been completed, I shall take him to France. Good-bye, ladies and gentlemen—old papa Gauche is disembarking, I wish you all a pleasant journey."

"I am afraid, Commissioner, you will have to travel with us a little farther," the Russian said in his monotone voice.

For a moment Gauche thought he had misheard.

"Eh?"

"M. Aono is not guilty of anything, so the investigation will have to be continued."

The expression on Gauche's face must have looked quite ridiculous—eyes staring wildly, cheeks bright scarlet.

Before the outburst of fury came, the Russian continued with quite astonishing self-assurance.

"Captain, on b-board ship you are the supreme authority. The commissioner has just acted out a mock trial in which he took the part of prosecutor and played it with great conviction. However, in a civilized court, after the prosecution has made its case the defense is offered the floor. With your permission, I should like to take on that assignment."

"Why waste any more time?" the captain asked, surprised. "It all seems cut and dry to me. The commissioner of police explained everything very clearly."

"Putting a passenger ashore is a serious m-matter, and the responsibility is ultimately the captain's. Think what damage will be done to the reputation of your shipping line if it turns out you have made a mistake. And I assure you," said Fandorin, raising his voice slightly, "that the commissioner is mistaken."

"Nonsense!" exclaimed Gauche. "But I have no objections. It might even be interesting. Carry on, monsieur, I'm sure I shall enjoy it."

After all, a dress rehearsal had to be taken seriously. This boy was no fool; he might possibly expose some gaps in the prosecution's logic that needed patching up. Then, if the prosecutor made a mess of things during the trial, Commissioner Gauche would be able to help him out.

Fandorin crossed one leg over the other and clasped his hands around his knee.

"You gave a brilliant and convincing speech. At first sight your arguments appear conclusive. Your logic seems almost beyond reproach, although, of course, the so-called circumstantial evidence is worthless. Yes, M. Aono was in Paris on the fifteenth of March. Yes, M. Aono was not in the salon when the p-professor was killed. In themselves these two facts mean nothing, so let us not even take them into consideration."

"Very well," Gauche agreed sarcastically. "Let us move straight on to the hard facts."

"Gladly. I counted five more or less significant elements. M. Aono is a doctor, but for some reason he concealed that from us. That is one. M. Aono is capable of shattering a hard object, such as a gourd—and perhaps also a head—with a single blow. That is two. M. Aono does not have a *Leviathan* emblem. That is three. A scalpel, which might be the one that killed Professor Sweetchild, is missing from the defendant's medical bag. That is four. And, finally, five: We have just witnessed an attempted escape by the accused, which sets his guilt beyond all reasonable doubt. I don't think I have forgotten anything, have I?"

"There is a number six," put in the commissioner. "He is unable to offer an explanation for any of these points."

"Very well, let us make it six," the Russian readily agreed.

Gauche chuckled: "I'd say that's more than enough for any jury to send this little bird to the guillotine."

Inspector Jackson jerked his head up and growled in English: "To the gallows."

"No, to the gallows," Renier translated.

Ah, the perfidious English! He had nursed a viper at his bosom!

"I beg your pardon," fumed Gauche. "The investigation has been conducted by the French side. So our villain will go to the guillotine!"

"And the decisive piece of evidence, the missing scalpel, was discovered by the British side. He'll be sent to the gallows," the lieutenant translated.

"The main crime was committed in Paris. To the guillotine!"

"But Lord Littleby was a British subject. And so was Professor Sweetchild. It's the gallows for him."

The Japanese appeared not to hear this discussion, which threatened to escalate into an international conflict. His eyes were still closed and his face was completely devoid of all expression. *These yellow devils really are dif-*

ferent from us, thought Gauche. And just think of all the trouble they would have to take with him: a prosecutor, a defense attorney, a jury, judges in robes. Of course, that was the way it ought to be, democracy is democracy after all, but surely this was casting pearls before swine.

When there was a pause, Fandorin asked: "Have you concluded your debate? May I p-proceed?"

"Carry on," Gauche said gloomily, thinking about the battles with the British that lay ahead.

"And let us not d-discuss the shattered gourds, either. They also prove nothing."

This whole comedy was beginning to get on the commissioner's nerves.

"All right. We needn't waste any time on trifles."

"Excellent. Then that leaves five points: He concealed the fact that he is a doctor; he has no emblem; the scalpel is missing; he tried to escape; he offers no explanations."

"And every point enough to have the villain sent . . . for execution."

"The problem is, commissioner, that you think like a European, but M-mister Aono has a different, Japanese, logic, that you have not made any effort to fathom. I, however, have had the honor of conversing with this gentleman, and I have a better idea of how his mind works than you do. M. Aono is not simply Japanese, he is a samurai, and he comes from an old and influential family. This is an important point for this particular case. For five hundred years every man in the clan of Aono was a warrior. All other professions were regarded as unworthy of such a distinguished family. The accused is the third son in the family. When Japan decided to move a little closer to Europe, many noble families began sending their sons abroad to study, and M. Aono's father did the same. He sent his eldest son to England to study for a career as a naval officer, because the principality of Satsuma, where the Aono clan resides, provides officers for the Japanese navy. In Satsuma the navy is regarded as the senior service. Aono senior sent his second son to a military academy in Germany. Following the Franco-German War of 1870, the Japanese decided to restructure their army on the German model, and all their military advisers are Germans. This information about the clan of Aono was volunteered to me by the accused himself."

"And what the devil do we need all these aristocratic details for?" Gauche asked irritably.

"I observed that the accused spoke with pride about his older brothers, but preferred not to talk about himself. I also noticed a long time ago that, for an alumnus of St. Cyr, M. Aono is remarkably ignorant of military matters. And why would he have been sent to a French military academy when he himself had told me that the Japanese army was being organized along German lines? I have formed the following impression. In keeping with the spirit of the times, Aono senior decided to set his third son up in a peaceful, nonmilitary profession and make him into a doctor. From what I have read in books, in Japan the decision of the head of the family is not subject to discussion. The defendant traveled to France to take up his studies in the faculty of medicine, even though he felt unhappy about it. In fact, as a son of the martial clan of Aono, he felt disgraced by having to fiddle with bandages and tinker with clysters! That is why he said he was a soldier. He was simply ashamed to admit his true profession, which he regards as shameful. From a European point of view this might seem absurd, but try to see things through his eyes. How would your countryman D'Artagnan have felt if he had ended up as a physician after dreaming for so long of winning a musketeer's cloak?"

Gauche noticed a sudden change in the Japanese. He had opened his eyes and was staring at Fandorin in a state of obvious agitation, and crimson spots had appeared on his cheeks. Could he possibly be blushing? No, nonsense.

"Ah, how very touching," Gauche snorted. "But I'll let it go. Tell me instead, monsieur counsel for the defense, about the emblem. What did your bashful client do with it? Was he ashamed to wear it?"

"That is absolutely right," the self-appointed lawyer said with a nod. "That is the reason. He was ashamed. Look at what it says on the badge."

Gauche glanced down at his lapel.

"It doesn't say anything. There are just the initials of the Jasper-Artaud Partnership."

"Precisely." Fandorin traced out the three letters in the air with his finger. "J—A—P. The letters spell 'Jap,' the term of abuse that foreigners use for the Japanese. Tell me, Commissioner, how would you like to wear a badge that said 'Frog'?"

Captain Cliff threw his head back and burst into loud laughter. Even the sour-faced Jackson and standoffish Mlle. Stamp smiled. The crimson spots spread even farther across the face of the Japanese.

A terrible premonition gnawed at Gauche's heart. His voice was suddenly hoarse.

"And why can he not explain all this for himself?"

"That is quite impossible. You see—again, as far as I can understand from the books I have read—the main difference between the Europeans and the Japanese lies in the moral basis of their social behavior."

"That's a bit high-flown," said the captain.

The diplomat turned to face him.

"Not at all. Christian culture is based on a sense of guilt. It is bad to sin, because afterward you will be tormented by remorse. The normal European tries to behave morally in order to avoid a sense of guilt. The Japanese also strive to observe certain moral norms, but their motivation is different. In their society, moral restraints derive from a sense of shame. The worst thing that can happen to a Japanese is to find himself in a situation in which he feels ashamed and is condemned or, even worse, ridiculed by society. That is why the Japanese are so afraid of committing any faux pas that offends the social sense of decency. I can assure you that shame is a far more effective civilizing influence than guilt. From M. Aono's point of view, it would be quite unthinkable to speak openly of 'shameful' matters, especially with foreigners. To be a doctor and not a soldier is shameful. To confess that he has lied is even more shameful. And to admit that he, a samurai, could attach any importance to offensive nicknames—why, that is entirely out of the question."

"Thank you for the lecture," said Gauche, with an ironic bow. "And was it shame that made your client attempt to escape from custody, too?"

"That's the point," agreed Jackson, suddenly transformed from enemy to ally. "The yellow bastard almost broke my wrist."

"Once again you have guessed correctly, Commissioner. It is impossible to escape from a steamship; there is nowhere to go. Believing his position to be hopeless and anticipating nothing but further humiliation, my client—as you insist on calling him—undoubtedly intended to lock himself in his cabin and commit suicide according to samurai ritual. Is that not right, M. Aono?" Fandorin asked, addressing the Japanese directly for the first time.

"You would have been disappointed," the diplomat continued gently. "You must have heard that your ritual dagger was taken by the police during their search."

"Ah, you're talking about that—what's it called—hira-kira, hari-kari." Gauche smirked into his mustache. "Rubbish, I don't believe a man could rip his own belly open. If you've really had enough of this world, it's far better to brain yourself against the wall. But I'll let that pass too. There is one piece of evidence you can't shrug off—the scalpel missing from his set of medical instruments. How do you explain that? Do you claim the real culprit stole your client's scalpel in advance because he was planning the murder and wanted to shift the blame onto Aono? That just won't work! How could the murderer know the professor would decide to tell us about his discovery immediately after dinner? And Sweetchild himself had only just guessed the secret of the shawl. Remember the state he was in when he came running into the salon!"

"Nothing could be easier for me than to explain the missing scalpel. It is not even a matter of supposition, but of hard fact. Do you remember how things began disappearing from people's cabins after Port Said? The mysterious spate of thefts ended as suddenly as it had begun. And do you remember when? It was after our black stowaway was killed. I have given a lot of thought to the question of why he was on board the *Leviathan,* and this is my explanation. The Negro was probably brought here from darkest Africa by Arab slave traders, and naturally he arrived in Port Said by sea. Why do I think that? Because when he escaped from his masters, the Negro didn't simply run away; he boarded a ship. He evidently believed that since a ship had taken him away from his home, another ship could take him back."

"What has all this got to do with our case?" Gauche interrupted impatiently. "This Negro of yours died on the fifth of April, and Sweetchild was killed yesterday! To hell with you and your fairy tales! Jackson, take the prisoner away!"

The commissioner set off decisively toward the door, but the diplomat grabbed his elbow in a viselike grip and said in a repulsively obsequious voice: "My dear M. Gauche, I would like to follow my arguments through to their conclusion. Please be patient for just a little longer."

Gauche tried to break free, but this young whippersnapper had fingers of steel. After his second attempt failed, the commissioner decided not to make himself look even more foolish. He turned to face Fandorin.

"Very well, five more minutes," he hissed, glaring into the insolent youth's serene blue eyes.

"Thank you. Five minutes will be more than enough to shatter your final piece of hard evidence. I knew that the runaway slave must have a lair somewhere on the ship, so I looked for it. But while you were searching the holds and the coal bins, Captain, I started with the upper deck. The black man had only been seen by first-class passengers, so it was reasonable to assume he was hiding somewhere close by. I found what I was looking for in the third lifeboat from the bow on the starboard side: the remains of his food and a bundle of his belongings. There were several pieces of colored cloth, a string of beads, and all sorts of shiny objects, including a small mirror, a sextant, a pince-nez, and a large scalpel."

"Why should I believe you?" roared Gauche. His case was crumbling to dust before his very eyes.

"Because I am a disinterested party who is prepared to confirm his testimony under oath. May I continue?" The Russian smiled his sickening little smile. "Thank you. Our poor Negro was evidently a practical individual who did not intend to return home empty-handed."

"Stop, stop!" cried Renier, with a frown. "M. Fandorin, why did you not report your discovery to the captain and me? What right did you have to conceal it?"

"I did not conceal it. I left the bundle where it was. But when I came back to the lifeboat a few hours later, after the search, the bundle was gone. I was sure it must have been found by your sailors. But now it seems that the professor's murderer got there before you and claimed all the Negro's trophies, including M. Aono's scalpel. The c-criminal could have foreseen that he might need to take . . . extreme measures and carried the scalpel around with him as a precaution. It might help put the police off the scent. Tell me, M. Aono, was the scalpel stolen from you?"

The Japanese hesitated for a moment before reluctantly nodding.

"And you did not mention it because an officer of the Imperial Army could not possibly possess a scalpel, am I right?"

"The sextant was mine!" declared the redheaded baronet. "I thought . . . but that doesn't matter. So it turns out that savage stole it. Gentlemen, if someone's head is smashed in with my sextant, please bear in mind that it has nothing to do with me."

Bewildered by this final and absolute disaster, Gauche squinted inquiringly at Jackson.

"I'm very sorry, Commissioner, but it seems you will have to continue your voyage," the inspector said in French, twisting his thin lips into a smile of sympathy. "My apologies, M. Aono. If you would just hold out your hands . . . Thank you."

The handcuffs clinked mournfully as they were removed.

The silence that ensued was broken by Renate Kleber's frightened voice: "I beg your pardon, gentlemen, but then who is the murderer?"

PART THREE

BOMBAY TO
PALK STRAIT

Gintaro Aono

⸺◦◦◦⸺

The eighteenth day of the fourth month,
in view of the southern tip of the Indian peninsula

It is now three days since we left Bombay, and I have not opened my diary even once since then. It is the first time such a thing has happened to me since I made it a firm rule to write every day. But I decided upon the break deliberately. I had to come to terms with an overwhelming torrent of thoughts and feelings.

The essential significance of what has happened to me is best conveyed by a haiku that was born spontaneously the very moment the inspector of police removed the iron shackles from my wrists.

> *Lonely is the flight*
> *Of the nocturnal firefly,*
> *But stars throng the sky.*

I realized immediately that it was a very good poem, the best I have ever written, but its meaning is not obvious and requires elucidation. I have meditated for three days on the changes within my being, until I think I have finally discovered the truth.

I have been visited by the great miracle of which every man dreams—I have experienced satori, or catharsis, as the ancient Greeks called it. How many times has my Mentor told me that if satori comes, it comes when it will and on its own terms; it cannot be induced or impeded! A man may be righteous and wise, he may sit in the za-zen pose for many hours each day and read mountains of sacred texts, but still die unenlightened. And yet the radiant majesty of satori may be revealed to some idler who wanders aimlessly and foolishly through life, transforming his worthless existence in an instant! I am that idler. I have been lucky. At the age of twenty-seven I have been born again.

Illumination and purification did not come to me in a moment of spiritual and physical concentration, but when I was wretched, crushed, and empty, when I was reduced to no more than the wrinkled skin of a burst balloon. But the dull clanking of those irons signaled my transformation. Suddenly I knew with a clarity beyond words that I am not I, but . . . No, that is not it. That I am *not only I*, but also an infinite multitude of other lives. That I am not some Gintaro Aono, third son of the senior counselor to his Serene Highness Prince Shimazu: I am a small and yet precious particle of the One. I am in all that exists, and all that exists is in me. How many times I have heard those words, but I only understood them . . . no, I only experienced their truth on the fifteenth day of the fourth month of the eleventh year of Meiji, in the city of Bombay, on board an immense European steamship. The will of the Supreme is truly capricious.

What is the meaning of this tercet that was born of my inner intuition? Man is a solitary firefly in the gloom of boundless night. His light is so weak that it illuminates only a minute segment of space; beyond that lies cold, darkness, and fear. But if you turn your frightened gaze away from the dark earth below and look upward (you need only turn your head!), you see that the sky is covered with stars, shining with a calm, bright, eternal light. You are not alone in the darkness. The stars are your friends; they will help you. They will not abandon you in your distress. And a little while later one understands something else, something equally important: A firefly is also a star like all the others. Those in the sky above see your light, and it helps them endure the cold darkness of the Universe.

My life will probably not change. I shall be the same as I was before—trivial and absurd, at the mercy of my passions. But this certain knowledge will always dwell in the depths of my soul, my salvation and comfort in times of difficulty. I am no longer a shallow puddle that any strong gust of wind can spread across the ground. I am the ocean, and the storm that drives the all-destroying tsunami across my surface can never touch my inmost depths.

When my spirit was flooded with joy at this realization, I recalled that the greatest of virtues is gratitude. The first star I glimpsed glowing in the blackness around me was Fandorin-san. Thanks to him I know that the World is not indifferent to me, Gintaro Aono, that the Great Beyond will never abandon me in misfortune.

But how can I explain to a man from a different culture that he is my *onjin* for all time? The European languages do not have such a word. Today I plucked up my courage and tried to speak with him about this, but I feel that the conversation came to nothing.

I waited for Fandorin-san on the boat deck, knowing that he would come there with his weights at precisely eight.

When he appeared, wearing his striped tricot (I must inform him that loose clothes, not close-fitting ones, are best suited for physical exercise), I approached him and bowed low in obeisance. "Why, M. Aono, what's wrong?" he asked in surprise. "Why do you stay bent over and not straighten up?" Since it was impossible to make conversation in such a posture, I drew myself erect, although in such a situation I knew that I ought to maintain my bow for longer. "I am expressing my eternal gratitude to you," I said, greatly agitated. "Oh, forget it," he said, with a careless wave of his hand. This gesture pleased me greatly—Fandorin-san wished to belittle the significance of the boon he had bestowed on me and spare his debtor excessive feelings of gratitude. In his place any nobly raised Japanese would have done the same. But the effect was the reverse—my spirit was inspired with even greater gratitude. I told him that henceforth I was irredeemably in his debt. "Nothing irredeemable about it," he said with a shrug. "I simply wished to take that smug turkey down a peg or two." (A turkey is an ugly American bird whose pompous, strutting gait seems to express a risible sense of self-importance: figuratively speaking—a conceited and foolish person.) Once again I was struck by Fandorin-san's sensitivity and tact, but I had to make him understand how much I owed to him. "I thank you for saving my worthless life," I said and bowed again. "I thank you three times over for saving my honor. And I thank you an infinite number of times for opening my third eye, with which I see what I could not see before." Fandorin-san glanced (with some trepidation, it seemed to me) at my forehead, as if he were expecting another eye to open up and wink at him.

I told him that he is my *onjin*, that henceforth my life belongs to him, and that seemed to frighten him even more. "Oh, how I dream you might find yourself in mortal danger so that I can save your life, as you have saved mine!" I exclaimed. He crossed himself and said: "I think I would rather avoid that. If it is not too much trouble, please dream of something else."

The conversation was going badly. In despair I cried out: "Know that I will do anything for you!" And then I qualified my oath to avoid any subsequent misunderstanding: "If it is not injurious to my emperor, my country, or the honor of my family."

My words provoked a strange reaction from Fandorin-san. He laughed! I am certain I shall never understand the redheads. "All right, then," he said, shaking me by the hand. "If you insist, then by all means. I expect we shall be traveling together from Calcutta to Japan. You may repay your debt by giving me Japanese lessons."

Alas, this man does not take me seriously. I wished to be his friend, but Fandorin-san is far more interested in Senior Navigator Fox, a common man lacking in wisdom, than in me. My benefactor spends much time in the company of this windbag, listening attentively while he brags about his nautical adventures and amorous escapades. He even goes on watch with Fox! I must confess I feel hurt by this. Today I heard Fox's lurid description of his love affair with an "aristocratic Japanese lady" from Nagasaki. He talked about her small breasts and her scarlet mouth and all the other charms of this "dainty little doll." It must have been some cheap slut from the sailors' quarter. A girl from a decent family would not even have exchanged words with this foreign barbarian! The most hurtful thing of all was that Fandorin-san was clearly interested in these ravings. I was about to intervene, but just at that moment Captain Renier approached them and sent Fox off on some errand.

Oh yes! I have not mentioned a most important event that has taken place in the life of the ship! A firefly's feeble glow blinds his own eyes so that he cannot see his surroundings in their true proportions.

On the eve of our departure from Bombay, a genuine tragedy occurred, a calamity beside which my own sufferings pale into insignificance.

At half past eight in the morning, when the steamer had already weighed anchor and was preparing to cast off, a telegram was delivered from ashore to Captain Cliff. I was standing on the deck, looking at Bombay, the scene of such a crucial event in my life. I wanted that view to remain engraved on my heart forever. That was how I came to witness what happened.

The captain read the telegram, and his face underwent a startling transformation. I have never seen anything like it. It was as if an actor of the No theater had suddenly cast off the mask of the Fearsome Warrior and donned the mask of Insane Grief. The old sea dog's rough, weather-beaten face began to tremble. Then the captain uttered a groan that was also a sob and began pacing frantically around the deck. "Oh, God," he cried out in a hoarse voice. "My poor girl!" He dashed down the steps from the bridge and went to his cabin—as we discovered later.

The preparations for sailing were interrupted. Breakfast began as usual, but Lieutenant Renier was late. No one spoke of anything but the captain's strange behavior, and all tried to guess what could have been in the telegram. Renier-san looked into the salon as the meal was coming to an end. The first mate appeared distraught. He informed us that Cliff-san's only daughter (I have mentioned earlier that the captain doted on her) had been badly burned in a fire at her boarding school. The doctors feared for her life. The lieutenant said that Mr. Cliff was beside himself. He had decided to leave the *Leviathan* and return to England on the first available packet boat. He kept saying that he must be with his little daughter. The lieutenant repeated over and over again: "What is going to happen now? What an unlucky voyage!" We did our best to comfort him.

I must admit that I strongly disapproved of the captain's decision. I could understand his grief, but a man who has been entrusted with a task has no right to allow personal feelings to govern his actions. Especially if he is a captain in charge of a ship. What would become of society if the emperor or the president or the prime minister were to set personal concerns above their duty? There would be chaos. The very meaning and purpose of authority is to fight against chaos and maintain harmony.

I went back out on deck to see Mr. Cliff leave the ship that had been entrusted to him. And the Most High taught me a new lesson, the lesson of compassion.

Stooping low, the captain half walked and half ran across the gangway. He was carrying a travel bag in one hand and there was a sailor following him with a single suitcase. When the captain halted on the quayside and turned to face the *Leviathan,* I saw that his broad face was wet with tears. The next moment he began to sway and collapsed forward onto his face.

I rushed across to him. From his fitful breathing and the convulsive twitching of his limbs, I deduced that he had suffered a severe haemorrhagic stroke. When Dr. Truffo arrived he confirmed my diagnosis.

It often happens that the strident discord between the voice of the heart and the call of duty is too much for a man's brain to bear. I had wronged Captain Cliff.

After the sick man was taken away to a hospital, the *Leviathan* was detained at its mooring for a long time. Renier-san, ashen-faced with shock, drove to the telegraph office to conduct negotiations with the shipping company in London. It was dusk before he returned. He brought the news that Cliff-san had not recovered consciousness: Renier-san was to assume temporary command of the ship and a new captain would come aboard in Calcutta.

We sailed from Bombay after a delay of ten hours.

For days now I do not walk, I fly. I am delighted by the sunshine and the landscapes of the Indian coastline and the leisurely regularity of life on this great ship. Even the Windsor salon, which I used to enter with such a heavy heart, has now become almost like home to me. My companions at table behave quite differently toward me now—the antagonism and suspicion have disappeared. Everyone is very kind and considerate, and I also feel differently about them. Even Kleber-san, whom I was prepared to throttle with my bare hands (the poor woman!) no longer seems repulsive. She is just a young woman preparing to become a mother for the first time and entirely absorbed in the naïve egotism of her new condition. Having learned that I am a doctor, she plagues me with medical questions about all manner of minor complaints. Formerly her only victim was Dr. Truffo, but now we share the burden. And, almost unbelievably, I do not find it oppressive. On the contrary, I now possess a higher status than when I was taken for a military officer. It is astounding!

I hold a privileged position in the Windsor salon. Not only am I a doctor and an "innocent victim," as Mrs. Truffo puts it, of police brutality. I am—more important—"definitely not the murderer." It has been proved and officially confirmed. In this way I have been elevated to Windsor's highest caste—together with the commissioner of police and our new captain (whom we almost never see—he is very busy and a steward takes his food up to the bridge on a tray). We three are above suspicion and no one casts stealthy, frightened glances in our direction.

I feel sorry for the Windsor group, I really do. With my recently acquired spiritual vision, I can see clearly what none of them can see, even the sagacious Fandorin-san.

There is no murderer among my companions. None of them is suited to the role of a scoundrel. When I examine these people closely, I see that they have faults and weaknesses, but there is no black-hearted villain who could have killed eleven innocent victims, including two children, in cold blood. I would have detected the vile odor of that person's breath. I do not know whose hand felled Sweetchild-sensei, but I am sure it must have been someone else. The commissioner's assumptions are not entirely correct: The criminal is on board the steamship, but not in the Windsor salon. Perhaps he was listening at the door when the professor began telling us about his discovery.

If Gauche-san were not so stubborn and took a more impartial view of the Windsor group, he would realize he is wasting his time.

Let me run through all the members of our company.

Fandorin-san. It is obvious that he is innocent. Otherwise why would he have diverted suspicion from me when no one doubted I was guilty?

Mr. and Mrs. Truffo. The doctor is rather comical, but he is a very kind man. He would not harm a grasshopper. His wife is the very embodiment of English propriety. She could not have killed anyone, because that would simply be indecent.

M.S.-san. He is a strange man, always muttering to himself, and his manner can be sharp, but there is profound and genuine suffering in his eyes. People with eyes like that do not commit cold-blooded murders.

Kleber-san. Nothing could be clearer. First, it would be inhuman for a woman preparing to bring a new life into the world to snuff out other lives so casually. Pregnancy is a mystery that teaches us to cherish human life. Second, at the time of the murder Kleber-san was with the police commissioner.

And finally, Stamp-san. She has no alibi, but it is impossible to imagine her creeping up behind someone she knows, covering his mouth with one slim, weak hand, and raising my scalpel in the other . . . The idea is utter nonsense. Quite impossible.

Open your eyes, Commissioner-san. This path is a dead end.

Suddenly I find it hard to catch my breath. Could there be a storm approaching?

Commissioner Gauche

⌇⌇⌇

HIS DAMNED INSOMNIA was really getting out of hand now. Five nights of sheer misery, and it was getting worse all the time. And the Lord protect him if he did drop off just before the dawn; his dreams were so appalling that he woke up a broken man, his mind so numbed by his nocturnal visions that it invented all sorts of nonsense. Maybe it really was time to retire and just forget about everything. But he couldn't—nothing on earth was worse than a squalid old age spent in poverty. Someone here was all set to nab a treasure worth a billion and a half francs, and this old *flic* would have to live out the pitiful remainder of his days on a miserly hundred and twenty-five francs a month!

All night long the sheet lightning had flashed across the sky, the wind had howled in the masts, and the *Leviathan* had pitched ponderously to and fro on the heaving black rollers. Gauche lay in his bed, staring up at the ceiling, which was alternately dark and stark white—when it was lit up by lightning. The lashing rain drummed on the deck, and the glass that held his forgotten liver medicine skidded backward and forward across the table, the spoon tinkling inside it.

It was Gauche's first storm at sea, but he wasn't afraid—a sea monster like this couldn't possibly sink. It might get rattled and shaken about a bit, but certainly nothing more than that. His only problem was he couldn't get to sleep with the thunder booming away like that. The moment he started nodding off, there it went again—crash, boom!

But he must have fallen asleep somehow, because he suddenly jerked upright in bed, wondering what was happening. The cabin was echoing with the heavy, labored beating of his heart.

No, it wasn't his heart. It was someone pounding on the door.

"Commissioner!" (Bang-bang-bang.) "Commissioner!" (Bang-bang-bang-bang.) "Open up! Quickly!"

Whose voice was that? No, it couldn't be Fandorin!

"Who's there? What do you want?" cried Gauche, pressing his hand to the left side of his chest. "Have you gone out of your mind?"

"Open up, damn you!"

Oho! What kind of way was that for a diplomat to talk? Something really serious must have happened.

"Just a moment!"

Gauche pulled off his nightcap with the tassel (his old Blanche had knitted it for him), stuck his arms into the sleeves of his dressing gown, and slipped on his bedroom slippers.

When he peeped through the crack of the half-open door, he saw it really was Fandorin. In a frock coat and tie, holding a walking cane with an ivory knob. His eyes were blazing.

"What is it?" Gauche asked suspiciously, certain his nocturnal visitor could only have brought bad news.

The diplomat began speaking in an untypical jerky manner, but without stammering.

"Get dressed. Bring a gun. We have to arrest Captain Renier. Urgently. He's steering the ship onto the rocks."

Gauche shook his head—maybe it was just another of those awful dreams he'd been having?

"Monsieur le Russe, have you been smoking hashish?"

"I did not come alone," replied Fandorin.

The commissioner stuck his head out into the corridor and saw two other men standing beside the Russian. One was the half-mad baronet. But who was the other? The senior navigator, that's right. What was his name now . . . Fox.

"Pull yourself together!" said the diplomat, launching a new staccato assault. "There's not much time. I was reading in my cabin. There was a knock. Sir Reginald. He measured our position at one in the morning.

With his sextant. The course was wrong. We should go left of the Isle of Manar. We're going to the right. I woke the navigator. Fox, tell him."

The navigator stepped forward. He looked badly shaken. "There are shoals there, monsieur," he said in broken French. "And rocks. Sixteen thousand tons, monsieur. If it runs aground it will break in half like a French loaf. A baguette, you understand? Another half hour on this course and it will be too late to turn back!"

Wonderful news! Now old Gustave had to be a master mariner and lift the curse of the Isle of Manar!

"Why don't you just tell the captain that . . . that he's following the wrong course?"

The navigator glanced at the Russian.

"Mr. Fandorin says we shouldn't."

"Renier must have decided on one last desperate gamble." The Russian began jabbering away again. "He's capable of anything. He could have the navigator arrested. For disobeying orders. He could even use a gun. He's the captain. His word is law on board the ship. Only the three of us know what's happening. We need a representative of authority. You, commissioner. Let's get up there!"

"Wait, wait!" Gauche pressed his hands to his forehead. "You're making my head spin. Has Renier gone insane, then?"

"No. But he's determined to destroy the ship. And everyone on board."

"What for? What's the point?"

No, no, this couldn't really be happening. It was all a dream, a nightmare.

Realizing the commissioner wasn't going to be lured out of his lair so easily, Fandorin began speaking more slowly and clearly.

"I have only a hunch to go on. An appalling suspicion. Renier wants to destroy the ship and everyone on it to conceal his crime and cover his tracks. Hide all the evidence on the bottom of the ocean. If you find it hard to believe anyone could snuff out thousands of lives so callously, then think of the Rue de Grenelle and remember Sweetchild. In the hunt for the Brahmapur treasure, human life is cheap."

Gauche gulped.

"In the hunt for the treasure?"

"Yes," said Fandorin, controlling himself with an effort. "Renier is Rajah Bagdassar's son. I'd guessed, but I wasn't sure. Now there can be no doubt."

"What do you mean, his son? Rubbish! The rajah was Indian, and Renier is a pure-blooded Frenchman."

"Have you noticed he doesn't eat beef or pork? Do you realize why? It's a habit from his childhood. In India the cow is regarded as a sacred animal, and Moslems do not eat pork. The rajah was an Indian, but he was a Moslem by religion."

"That proves nothing!" Gauche said with a shrug. "Renier said he was on a diet."

"What about his dark complexion?"

"A suntan from sailing the southern seas."

"Renier has spent the last two years sailing the London–New York and London–Stockholm routes. Renier is half Indian, Gauche. Think! Rajah Bagdassar's wife was French, and at the time of the Sepoy Mutiny their son was being educated in Europe. Most probably in France, his mother's homeland. Have you ever been in Renier's cabin?"

"Yes, he asked me in. He asked everybody in."

"Did you see the photograph on the table? 'Seven feet under the keel . . . Françoise B.'?"

"Yes, I saw it. It's his mother."

"If it's his mother, then why 'B' instead of 'R'? A son and his mother should have the same surname."

"Perhaps she married a second time."

"Possibly. I haven't had time to check that. But what if 'Françoise B.' means 'Françoise Bagdassar'? In the European manner, since Indian rajahs don't have surnames."

"Then where did the name Renier come from?"

"I don't know. Let's suppose he took his mother's maiden name when he was naturalized."

"Conjecture," Gauche retorted. "Not a single hard fact. Nothing but 'what if' and 'let's suppose.'"

"I agree. But surely Renier's behavior at the time of Sweetchild's murder was suspicious? Remember how the lieutenant offered to fetch Mme. Kleber's shawl? And he asked the professor not to start without him. I think the few minutes Renier was away were enough for him to set fire to the litter bin and pick up the scalpel from his cabin."

"And why do you think he was the one who had the scalpel?"

"I told you, the Negro's bundle disappeared from the boat after the search. And who was in charge of the search? Renier!"

Gauche shook his head skeptically. The steamer swung over hard and he struck his shoulder painfully against the doorpost, which didn't help improve his mood.

"Do you remember how Sweetchild began?" Fandorin continued. He took a watch out of his pocket, glanced at it, and began speaking faster. " 'Suddenly it hit me! Everything fell into place—about the shawl, and about the son! It's a matter of clerical work pure and simple. Dig around in the registers at the École Maritime and you'll find him!' Not only had he guessed the secret of the shawl; he had discovered something about the rajah's son as well. For instance, that he studied at the École Maritime in Marseille. A training school for sailors. Which our Renier also happens to have attended. Sweetchild mentioned a telegram he sent to an acquaintance of his in the French Ministry of the Interior. Perhaps he was trying to find out what became of the child. And he obviously did find out something, but he didn't guess that Renier is the rajah's son. Otherwise he would have been more careful."

"And what did he dig up about the shawl?" Gauche asked eagerly.

"I think I can answer that question as well. But not now—later. We're running out of time!"

"So you think Renier himself set the fire and took advantage of the panic to shut the professor's mouth?" Gauche mused.

"Yes, damn it! Use your brains! I know there's not much hard evidence, but we have only twenty minutes left before *Leviathan* enters the strait!"

But the commissioner still wasn't convinced.

"The arrest of a ship's captain on the high seas is mutiny. Why did you believe what this gentleman told you?" He jerked his chin in the direction of the crazy baronet. "He's always talking nonsense."

The redheaded Englishman laughed disdainfully and looked at Gauche as if he were some kind of pill bug or flea. He didn't dignify his comment with a reply.

"Because I have suspected Renier for a long time," the Russian said rapidly. "And because I thought what happened to Captain Cliff was strange. Why did the lieutenant need to negotiate for so long with the shipping company over the telegraph? It means they did not know that Cliff's daughter had been injured in a fire. Then who sent the telegram to Bombay? The directors of the boarding school? How would they know the *Leviathan*'s route in such detail? Perhaps Renier himself sent the message? My guidebook says Bombay has at least a dozen telegraph offices. Sending a telegram from one to another would be very simple."

"And why in damnation's name would he want to send such a telegram?"

"To gain control of the ship. He knew that if Cliff received news like that he would not be able to continue the voyage. The real question is, why did Renier take such a risk? Not out of idle vanity—so that he could command the ship for a week and then to hell with everything! There is only one possible explanation: He did it so he could send the *Leviathan* to the bottom with all the passengers and crew on board. The investigation was getting too close for comfort; he could feel the noose tightening around his neck. He must know the police will carry on hounding all the suspects. But if there's a shipwreck with all hands lost, the case is closed. And then there's nothing to stop him picking up the casket at his leisure."

"But he'll be killed along with the rest of us!"

"No he won't. We've just checked the captain's launch, and it is ready to put to sea. It's a small craft, but sturdy. It can easily weather a storm. It has a supply of water and a basket of provisions and something else rather touching—a travel bag all packed and ready to go. Renier must be planning to abandon ship as soon as the *Leviathan* has entered the narrow channel and can no longer turn back. The ship will be unable to swing around; even if the engines are stopped the current will still carry it onto the rocks. A few people might be saved, since we are not far from the shore, but everyone who disappears will be listed as lost at sea."

"Don't be such a stupid ass, monsieur policeman!" the navigator butted in. "We've wasted far too much time already. Mr. Fandorin woke me up and said the ship was on the wrong course. I wanted to sleep and I told Mr. Fandorin to go to hell. He offered me a bet—a hundred pounds to one that the captain was off course. I thought, *The Russian's gone crazy, everyone knows how eccentric the Russians are, this will be easy money.* I went up to the bridge. Everything was in order. The captain was on watch, the pilot was at the helm. But for the sake of a hundred pounds I checked the course anyway and then I started sweating, I can tell you! But I didn't say a word to the captain. Mr. Fandorin had warned me not to say anything. And that"—the navigator looked at his watch—"was twenty-five minutes ago."

Then he added something in English that was obviously uncomplimentary about the French in general and French policemen in particular. The only word Gauche could understand was "frog."

The sleuth hesitated for one final moment before making up his mind. Immediately he was transformed; he began getting dressed with swift, precise movements. Papa Gauche might be slow off the mark, but once on the move he needed no further urging.

As he pulled on his jacket and trousers, he said to the navigator: "Fox, bring two sailors up on to the top deck, with carbines. The captain's mate should come, too. No, better not, there's no time to explain everything all over again."

He put his trusty Lefaucheux in his pocket and offered the diplomat a four-cylinder Marietta.

"Do you know how to use this?"

"I have my own, a Herstal-Agent," replied Fandorin, showing him a handsome, compact revolver unlike any Gauche had ever seen before. "And this as well."

With a single rapid movement he drew a slim, pliable sword out of his cane.

"Then let's go."

Gauche decided not to give the baronet a gun—who could tell what the lunatic might do with it?

The three of them strode rapidly down the long corridor. The door of one of the cabins opened slightly and Renate Kleber glanced out, a shawl over her brown dress.

"Gentlemen, why are you stamping about like a herd of elephants?" she exclaimed angrily. "I can't get any sleep as it is with this awful storm."

"Close the door and don't go anywhere," Gauche told her sternly, shoving her back into the cabin without even slowing his stride. This was no time to stand on ceremony.

The commissioner thought he saw the door of cabin number twenty-four, which belonged to Mlle. Stamp, tremble and open a crack, but he had no time now to worry about minor details.

On deck the wind drove the rain into their faces. They had to shout in order to hear one another.

There were the steps leading to the wheelhouse and the bridge. Fox was already waiting at the bottom with two sailors from the watch.

"I told you to bring carbines!" shouted Gauche.

"They're in the armory!" the navigator yelled in his ear. "And the captain has the key!"

"Never mind, let's go up," Fandorin communicated with a gesture. Raindrops glistened on his face.

Gauche looked around and shuddered: In the flickering lightning the rain glittered like steel threads in the night sky and the waves frothed and foamed white in the darkness. It was an awesome sight.

Their heels clattered as they climbed the iron steps, their eyes half-closed against the lashing rain. Gauche went first. At this moment he was the most important person on the whole *Leviathan*, this colossal two-hundred-meter monster drifting unsuspectingly toward disaster. The detective's foot slipped on the top step and he grabbed hold of the banister only just in time. He straightened up and caught his breath.

They were up. There was nothing above them now but the funnels spitting out occasional sparks and the masts, almost invisible in the darkness.

There was the metal door with its steel rivets. Gauche raised his finger in warning: Quiet! The precaution was not really necessary—the sea was so loud that no one in the wheelhouse could have heard a thing.

"This is the door to the captain's bridge and the wheelhouse!" shouted Fox. "No one enters without the captain's permission!"

Gauche took his revolver out of his pocket and cocked it. Fandorin did the same.

"You keep quiet!" the detective warned the overenterprising diplomat. "I'll do the talking! Oh, I should never have listened to you!" He gave the door a determined shove.

But of course the damned thing didn't budge.

"He's locked himself in," said Fandorin. "Say something, Fox."

The navigator knocked loudly and shouted in English: "Captain, it's me, Jeremy Fox! Please open up! It's an emergency!"

They heard Renier's muffled voice from behind the door: "What's happened, Jeremy?"

The door remained closed.

The navigator glanced at Fandorin in consternation. Fandorin pointed at the commissioner, then put a finger to his own temple and mimed pressing the trigger. Gauche didn't understand what the pantomime meant, but Fox nodded and roared at the top of his voice: "The French cop's shot himself!"

The door immediately swung open and Gauche presented his wet but living face to Renier. He trained the barrel of his Lefaucheux on the captain.

Renier screamed and leapt backward as if he had been struck. Now that was real hard evidence for you: A man with a clear conscience wouldn't shy away from a policeman like that. Gauche grabbed hold of the sailor's tarpaulin collar.

"I'm glad you were so distressed by the news of my death, my dear rajah," the commissioner purred, then barked out the words known and feared by every criminal in Paris. "Get your hands up in the air! You're under arrest."

The most notorious cutthroats in the city had been known to faint at the sound of those words.

The helmsman froze at his wheel, with his face half turned toward them.

"Keep hold of the wheel, you idiot!" Gauche shouted at him. "Hey you!"—he prodded one of the sailors from the watch with his finger—

"bring the captain's mate here immediately so he can take command. In the meantime, you give the orders, Fox. And look lively about it! Give the command 'halt all engines' or 'full astern' or whatever; don't just stand there like a dummy!"

"Let me take a look," said the navigator, leaning over a map. "Maybe it's not too late to just swing hard to port."

Renier's guilt was obvious. The fellow didn't even pretend to be outraged; he just stood there hanging his head, with his hands raised in the air and his fingers trembling.

"Right, then, let's go and have a little talk, shall we?" Gauche said to him. "Ah, what a lovely little talk we'll have."

Renate Kleber

⟋⟍⟋⟍⟋⟍

RENATE ARRIVED FOR breakfast later than everyone else, so she was the last to hear about the events of the previous night. Everyone threw themselves on her, desperate to tell her the incredible, nightmarish news.

Apparently Captain Renier was no longer captain.

Apparently Renier was not even Renier.

Apparently he was the son of that rajah.

Apparently he was the one who had killed everybody.

Apparently the ship had almost run aground in the night.

"We were all sound asleep in our cabins," whispered Clarissa Stamp, her eyes wide with terror, "and meanwhile that *man* was sailing the ship straight onto the rocks. Can you imagine what would have happened? The sickening scraping sound, the impact, the crunching as the metal plating ripped away! The shock throws you out of bed onto the floor and for a moment you can't understand what's happening. Then the shouting, the running feet. The floor heeling over farther and farther. And the terrible realization that the ship isn't moving, it has stopped! Everyone runs out on deck, half dressed . . ."

"Not me!" the doctor's wife declared resolutely.

"The sailors try to lower the lifeboats," Clarissa continued in the same hushed, mystical voice, ignoring Mrs. Truffo's comment, "but the crowds of passengers milling around on the deck get in their way. Every new wave throws the ship farther over on to its side. Now we are struggling to stay on our feet, we have to hold on to something. The night is pitch-black, the sea is roaring, the thunder rumbles in the sky . . . One lifeboat is finally lowered, but so many people crazed by fear have packed into it that it capsizes. The little children . . ."

Fandorin interrupted the word artist gently but firmly. "P-please, no more."

"You should write novels about the sea, madam," the doctor remarked with a frown.

But Renate had frozen motionless with one hand over her heart. She was already pale from lack of sleep and now she had turned quite green at all the news.

"Oh!" she said, and then repeated it: "Oh!"

Then she rebuked Clarissa with a stern face. "Why are you saying such awful things? Surely you know I mustn't listen to them, in my condition?"

The Watchdog was not at the table. It was unlike him to miss breakfast.

"But where is M. Gauche?" Renate asked.

"Still interrogating his prisoner," the Japanese told her. In the last few days he had stopped being so surly and given up glaring at Renate like a wild thing.

"Has M. Renier really confessed to all these appalling crimes?" she gasped. "He is slandering himself! He must be confused in his mind. You know, I noticed some time ago that he was not quite himself. Did he himself say he is the rajah's son? Well, I suppose it's better than being Napoleon's son. It's obvious the poor man has simply gone mad."

"Yes, that, too, madam, that, too," Commissioner Gauche's weary voice said behind her.

Renate had not heard him come in. But that was only natural—the storm was over, but the sea was still running high, the ship was rolling on the choppy waves, and every moment something squeaked, clanged, or cracked. Big Ben's pendulum had stopped working since the clock had been hit by a bullet, but the clock itself was swaying to and fro—sooner or later the oaken monstrosity was bound to keel over, Renate thought in passing, then concentrated her attention on the Watchdog.

"What's going on? Tell me!" she demanded.

The policeman walked unhurriedly across to his chair and sat down. He gestured to the steward to pour him some coffee.

"Oof, I am absolutely exhausted," the commissioner complained. "What about the passengers? Do they know?"

"The whole ship is buzzing with the news, but so far not many know the details," the doctor replied. "Mr. Fox told me everything, and I considered it my duty to inform everyone here."

The Watchdog looked at Fandorin and the Ginger Lunatic, then shook his head in surprise.

"I see that you gentlemen, however, are not inclined to gossip."

Renate didn't understand the meaning of his remark, but it was irrelevant to the matter in hand.

"What about Renier?" she asked. "Has he really confessed to all these atrocities?"

The Watchdog took a sip from his cup, relishing it. There was something different about him today. He no longer looked like an old dog that barks but doesn't bite. This dog looked as though it would go for you. And if you weren't careful, it would even take a bite out of you. Renate decided to rechristen the commissioner "the Bulldog."

"A nice drop of coffee," the Bulldog said appreciatively. "Yes, he confessed, of course he did. What else could he do? It took a bit of coaxing, but old Gauche has plenty of experience in such matters. Your Renier is sitting writing out his confession as we speak. He's got into the flow of it; there's just no stopping him. I left him there to finish the job."

"Why is he my Renier?" Renate asked in alarm. "Don't be ridiculous. He's just a considerate man who gave a pregnant woman a helping hand. And I don't believe that he is such a monster."

"When he's finished his confession, I'll let you read it," the Bulldog promised. "For old times' sake. All those hours we've spent sitting at the same table. And now it's all over, the investigation's concluded. I trust you won't be acting for my client this time, M. Fandorin? There's no way this one can avoid the guillotine."

"The insane asylum, more likely," said Renate.

The Russian was also on the point of saying something, but he held back. Renate looked at him curiously. He looked as fresh and fragrant as if he had spent the whole night dreaming sweetly in his own bed. And, as always, he was dressed impeccably: a white jacket and a silk waistcoat with a pattern of small stars. He was a very unusual character; Renate had never met anyone like him before.

The door burst open so violently that it almost came off its hinges, and a sailor with wildly staring eyes appeared on the threshold. When he spotted Gauche, he ran over and whispered something to him, waving his arms about despairingly.

Renate listened, but she could only make out the words "bastard" and "by my mother's grave."

"Now what's happened?"

"Doctor, please come out into the corridor." The Bulldog pushed away the plate with his omelette on it with a gesture of annoyance. "I'd like you to translate what this lad is muttering about for me."

The three of them went out.

"WHAT!" THE COMMISSIONER'S voice roared in the corridor. "Where were you looking, you numskull?"

There was a sound of hasty footsteps retreating into the distance, then silence.

"I'm not going to set foot outside this room until M. Gauche comes back," Renate declared firmly.

The others seemed to feel much the same.

The silence that descended in the Windsor salon was tense and uncomfortable.

THE COMMISSIONER AND Truffo came back half an hour later. Both looked grim.

"What we ought to have expected has happened," the diminutive doctor announced, without waiting for questions. "This tragic story has been concluded. And the final word was written by the criminal himself."

"Is he dead?" exclaimed Renate, jumping abruptly to her feet.

"He has killed himself?" asked Fandorin. "But how? Surely you took precautions?"

"In a case like this, of course I took precautions," Gauche said in a dispirited voice. "The only furniture in the cell where I interrogated him is a table, two chairs, and a bed. All are bolted to the floor. But if a man has really made up his mind to die, there's nothing you can do to stop him. Renier crushed his forehead in against the corner of the wall. There's a place in the cell where it juts out. And he was so cunning about it that the sentry didn't hear a thing. They opened the door to take in his breakfast, and he was lying there in a pool of blood. I ordered him not to be touched. Let him stay there for a while."

"May I take a look?" asked Fandorin.

"Go ahead. Gawk at him as long as you like; I'm going to finish my breakfast." And the Bulldog calmly pulled his cold omelette toward himself.

Four of them went to look at the suicide: Fandorin, Renate, the Japanese, and, strangely enough, the doctor's wife. Who'd have thought the prim old nanny goat would be so curious?

Renate's teeth chattered as she glanced into the cell over Fandorin's shoulder. She saw the familiar body with it broad shoulders stretched out diagonally across the floor of the cell, its dark head toward the projecting corner of the wall. Renier was lying facedown, his right arm twisted into an unnatural position.

Renate did not enter the cell; she could see well enough without that. The others went in and squatted down beside the corpse.

The Japanese raised the dead man's head and touched the bloodied forehead with his finger. Oh, yes, he was a doctor, wasn't he?

"O Lord, have mercy on this sinful creature," Mme. Truffo intoned piously in English.

"Amen," said Renate, turning her eyes away from the distressing sight.

Nobody spoke as they walked back to the salon.

They got back just in time to see the Bulldog finish eating, wipe his greasy lips with a napkin, and pull over his black file.

"I promised to show you the testimony of our former dining companion," he said impassively, setting out three pieces of paper on the table: two full sheets and a half sheet, all covered with writing. "It turns out it is his letter of farewell as well as his confession. But that doesn't really make any difference. Would you like to hear it?"

There was no need to repeat the invitation—they all gathered round the commissioner and waited with bated breath. The Bulldog picked up the first sheet, held it away from his eyes, and began reading.

To Commissioner Gustave Gauche
Representative of the French police

19 April 1878, 6.15 A.M.
On board the *Leviathan*

I, Charles Renier, do hereby make the following confession of my own free will and without duress, solely and exclusively out of a desire to unburden my conscience and clarify the motives that have led me to commit heinous criminal acts.

Fate has always treated me cruelly . . .

"Well, that's a song I've heard a thousand times," remarked the commissioner. "No murderer, thief, or corrupter of juveniles has ever told a court fate had showered its gifts on him but he had squandered them all, the son of a bitch. All right, then, let us continue."

Fate has always treated me cruelly, and if it pampered me at the dawn of my life, it was only in order to torment me all the more painfully later on. I was the only son and heir of a fabulously rich rajah, a very good man who was steeped in the wisdom of the East and the West. Until the age of nine I did not know the meaning of anger, fear, resentment, or frustrated desire. My mother, who was homesick for her own country, spent all her time with me, telling me about *la belle France* and gay Paris, where she grew up. My father fell head over heels in love the first time he saw her at the Bagatelle Club, where she was the lead dancer. Françoise Renier (that was my mother's surname, which I took for my own when I became a French citizen) could not resist the temptation of everything that marriage to an oriental sovereign seemed to promise, and she became his wife. But the marriage did not bring her happiness, although she genuinely respected my father and has remained faithful to him to this day.

When India was engulfed by a wave of bloody rebellion, my father sensed danger and sent his wife and son to France. The rajah had known for a long time that the English coveted his cherished casket of jewels and would not hesitate to resort to some underhanded trick in order to obtain the treasure of Brahmapur.

At first my mother and I were rich—we lived in our own mansion in Paris, surrounded by servants. I studied at a privileged lycée, together with the children of crowned monarchs and millionaires. But then everything changed and I came to know the very depths of poverty and humiliation.

I shall never forget the black day when my mother wept as she told me I no longer had a father, or a title, or a homeland. A year later, the only inheritance my father had left me was finally delivered via the British embassy in Paris. It was a small Koran. By that time my mother had already had me christened and I attended Mass, but I swore to myself that I would learn Arabic so I could read the notes made in the margins of the Holy Book by my father's hand. Many years later I fulfilled my intention, but I shall write about that below.

"Patience, patience," said Gauche with a cunning smile. "We'll get to that later. This part is just the lyrical preamble."

We moved out of the mansion as soon as we received the terrible news. At first to an expensive hotel. Then to a cheaper hotel. Then to furnished apartments. The number of servants grew less and less until finally the two of us were left alone. My mother had never been a practical person, either during the wild days of her youth or later. The jewels she had brought with her to Europe were enough for us to live on for two or three years, and then we fell into genuine poverty. I attended an ordinary school, where I was beaten and called "darky." That life taught me to be secretive and vengeful. I kept a secret diary in which I noted the names of everyone who offended me, in order to take my revenge on every one of them. And, sooner or later, the opportunity always came. I met one of the enemies of my unhappy adolescence many years later. He did not recognize me—by that time I had changed my name and no longer resembled the skinny, persecuted "hindoo" (the name they used to taunt me with in school). One evening I lay in wait for my old acquaintance as he was on his way home from a tavern. I introduced myself by my former name and then cut short his cry of amazement with a blow of my penknife to his right eye, a trick I picked up in the drinking dens of Alexandria. I confess to this murder because it can hardly make my position any more desperate.

"Well, he's quite right there," the Bulldog agreed. "One corpse more or less doesn't make much difference now."

When I was thirteen years old, we moved from Paris to Marseille because it was cheaper to live there and my mother had relatives in the city. At sixteen, after an escapade I do not wish to recall, I ran away from home and enlisted as a cabin boy on a schooner. For two years I sailed the Mediterranean. It was a hard life, but it was useful experience. I became strong, supple, and ruthless, and later this helped me become the best cadet at the École Maritime in Marseille. I graduated from the college with distinction and ever since I have sailed on the finest ships of the French merchant fleet. When applications were requested for the post of first lieutenant on the super-steamship *Leviathan* at the end of last year, my service record and excellent references guaranteed me success. But by that time I had already acquired a Goal.

As he picked up the second sheet of paper, Gauche warned his listeners: "This is the point where it starts to get interesting."

I was taught Arabic as a child, but my tutors had been too indulgent with the heir apparent and I did not learn much. Later, when my mother and I were in France, the lessons stopped altogether and I rapidly forgot the little that I knew. For many years the Koran with my father's notes in it seemed to me like an enchanted book written in a magical script no mere mortal could ever decipher. How glad I was later that I never asked anyone who knew Arabic to read the jottings in the margins! I had decided that I must fathom this mystery for myself, no matter what it cost me. I took up Arabic again while I was sailing to Maghreb and the Levant, and gradually the Koran began speaking to me in my father's voice. But many years went by before the handwritten notes—ornate aphorisms by Eastern sages, extracts from poems, and worldly advice from a loving father to his son—began hinting to me that they made up a kind of code. If the notes were read in a certain order, they acquired the sense of precise and detailed instructions, but that could only be understood by someone who had committed the notes to memory and engraved them on his heart. I struggled longest of all with a line from a poem that I did not know:

> *Death's emissary shall deliver unto you*
> *The shawl dyed crimson with your father's blood.*

One year ago, as I was reading the memoirs of a certain English general who boasted of his "feats of courage" during the Great Mutiny (the reason for my interest in the subject should be clear), I read about the gift the rajah of Brahmapur had sent to his son before he died. The Koran had been wrapped in a shawl! The scales seemed to fall from my eyes. Several months later, Lord Littleby exhibited his collection in the Louvre. I was the most assiduous of all the visitors to that exhibition. When I finally saw my father's shawl, the meaning of the following lines was revealed to me:

> *Its tapering and pointed form*
> *Is like a drawing, or a mountain.*

And:

> *The blind eye of the bird of paradise*
> *Sees straight into the secret heart of mystery.*

What else could I dream of during all those years of exile if not the clay casket that held all the wealth in the world? How many times in my dreams had I seen that coarse earthen lid swing open to reveal, once again, as in my distant childhood, the unearthly glow that filled the entire universe?

The treasure was mine by right; I was the legitimate heir! The English had robbed me, but they had gained nothing by their treachery. That repulsive vulture Littleby, who prided himself on his plundered "rarities," was really no better than a common dealer in stolen goods. I felt not the slightest doubt that I was in the right, and the only thing I feared was that I might fail at the task I had set myself.

But I made several terrible, unforgivable blunders. The first was the death of the servants, and especially of the poor children. Of course I did not wish to kill those people, who were entirely innocent. As you have guessed, I pretended to be a doctor and injected them with tincture of morphine. I only wished to put them to sleep, but due to my inexperience and fear that the soporific would not work, I miscalculated the dose.

A shock awaited me upstairs. When I broke the glass of the display case and pressed my father's shawl to my face with fingers trembling in reverential awe, one of the doors into the room suddenly opened and the master of the house came limping in. According to my information, his lordship was supposed to be away from home, but suddenly there he was in front of me with a pistol in his hand! I had no choice. I grabbed a statuette of Shiva and struck the English lord on the head with all my might. Instead of falling backward, he slumped forward, clutching me in his arms and splashing blood on my clothes. Under my white doctor's coat I was wearing my dress uniform—the dark-blue sailor's trousers with red piping are very similar to the trousers worn by the municipal medical service. I was very proud of my cunning, but in the end it was to prove my undoing. In his death throes, my victim tore the *Leviathan* emblem off the breast of my jacket under the open white coat. I noticed that it was gone when I returned to the steamship. I managed to obtain a replacement, but I had left behind a fatal clue.

I do not remember how I left the house. I know I did not dare go out through the door, and I recall climbing the garden fence. When I recovered my wits, I was standing beside the Seine. In one bloody hand I was holding the statuette, and in the other the pistol—I have no idea why I took it. Shuddering with revulsion, I threw them both into the water. The shawl lay in the breast pocket of my uniform jacket, where it warmed my heart.

The following day I learned from the newspapers that I had murdered nine other people as well as Lord Littleby. I will not describe here how I suffered because of that.

"I should think not," the commissioner said with a nod. "This stuff is a bit too sentimental already. Anybody would think he was addressing the jury: I ask you, gentlemen, how could I have acted in any other way? In my place, you would have done the same. Phooey." He carried on reading.

The shawl drove me insane. That magical bird with a hole instead of an eye acquired a strange power over me. It was as if I were not in control of my actions, as if I were obeying a quiet voice that would henceforth guide me in all I did.

"There he goes, building toward a plea of insanity," the Bulldog said, laughing. "It's an old trick; we've heard that one before."

The shawl disappeared from my writing desk when we were sailing through the Suez Canal. I felt as if it had abandoned me to the whim of fate. It never even occurred to me that the shawl had been stolen. By that time I was already so deeply in thrall to its mystical influence that I thought of the shawl as a living being with a soul of its own. I was absolutely devastated. The only thing that prevented me from taking my own life was the hope that the shawl would take pity on me and come back. The effort required to conceal my despair from you and my colleagues was almost more than I could manage.

And then, on the eve of our arrival in Aden, a miracle happened! When I heard Mme. Kleber's frightened cry and ran into her cabin, I saw a Negro who had appeared out of nowhere, wearing my lost shawl round his neck. Now I realize the Negro must have taken the bright-colored piece of cloth from my cabin a few days before, but at the time I experienced a genuine holy terror, as if the Angel of Darkness in person had appeared from the underworld to return my treasure to me!

In the tussle that followed, I killed the black man, and while Mme. Kleber was still in a faint I surreptitiously removed the shawl from the body. Since then I have always worn it on my chest, never parting with it for a moment.

I murdered Professor Sweetchild in cold blood, with a calculated deliberation that exhilarated me. I attribute my supernatural foresight and rapid reaction entirely to the magical influence of the shawl. I realized from Sweetchild's first enigmatic words that he had solved the mystery of the shawl and picked up the trail of the rajah's son—my trail. I had to stop the professor from talking, and I did. The silk shawl was pleased with me—I could tell from the way its warmth soothed my poor, tormented heart.

But by eliminating Sweetchild I had done no more than postpone the inevitable. You had me hemmed in on all sides, Commissioner. Before we reached Calcutta you, and especially your astute assistant, Fandorin . . .

Gauche chuckled grimly and squinted at the Russian.

"My congratulations, monsieur, on earning a compliment from a murderer. I suppose I must be grateful he has at least made you my assistant, and not the other way around."

The Bulldog would obviously have been only too happy to cross out that line so his superiors in Paris would not see it. But a song isn't a song without the words. Renate glanced at the Russian. He tugged on the pointed end of his mustache and gestured for the policeman to continue.

. . . assistant, Fandorin, would undoubtedly have eliminated all the suspects one by one until I was the only one left. A telegram to the naturalization department of the Ministry of the Interior would have been enough to discover the name now used by the son of Rajah Bagdassar.

And the student records of the École Maritime would have shown that I joined the college under one name and graduated under another.

I realized that the road through the blank eye of the bird of paradise did not lead to earthly bliss, but to the eternal Abyss. I decided I would not depart this world as an abject failure, but as a great rajah. My noble ancestors had never died alone. They were followed onto the funeral pyre by their servants, wives, and concubines. I had not lived as a ruler, but I would die as a true sovereign should—as I had decided. And I would take with me on my final journey not slaves and handmaidens, but the flower of European society. My funeral carriage would be a gigantic ship, a miracle of European technical progress! I was enthralled by the scale and grandeur of this plan. It is a prospect even more vertiginous than limitless wealth!

"He's lying here," Gauche interjected sharply. "He was going to drown us, but he had the boat all ready for himself."

The commissioner picked up the final sheet, or rather half sheet.

I admit that the trick I played on Captain Cliff was vile. I can only offer the partial excuse that I did not anticipate such a tragic outcome. I regard Cliff with genuine admiration. Although I wished to seize control of the *Leviathan,* I also wished to save the grand old man's life. I knew that his concern for his daughter would make him suffer, but I thought he would soon discover she was all right. Alas, malicious fate dogs my steps relentlessly. How could I have foreseen the captain would suffer a stroke? That cursed shawl is to blame for everything!

I burned the bright-colored triangle of silk on the day the *Leviathan* sailed from Bombay. I have burned my bridges.

"He burned it!" gasped Clarissa Stamp. "Then the shawl has been destroyed?"

Renate stared hard at the Bulldog, who shrugged indifferently and said, "And thank God it's gone. To hell with the treasure, that's what I say, ladies and gentlemen. We'll all be far better off without it."

The new Seneca had pronounced judgment. Renate rubbed her chin and thought hard.

> Do you find it hard to believe? Well, then, to prove my sincerity I shall tell you the secret of the shawl. There is no point in hiding it now.

The commissioner broke off and cast a cunning glance at the Russian.

"As I recall, monsieur, last night you boasted of having guessed that secret. Share your guess with us, and we shall see if you are as astute as our dead man thought."

Fandorin was not in the least taken aback.

"It is not very c-complicated," he said casually.

He's bluffing, thought Renate, *but he does it very well. Can he really have guessed?*

"Very well, what do we know about the shawl? It is triangular, with one straight edge and two that are rather sinuous. That is one. The picture on the shawl shows a mythical bird with a hole in place of its eye. That is two. I am sure you remember the description of the Brahmapur palace, in particular its upper level: a mountain range on the horizon, reflected in a mirror image on the wall. That is th-three."

"We remember, but what of it?" asked the Ginger Lunatic.

"Oh, come now, Sir Reginald," the Russian exclaimed in mock surprise. "You and I both saw Sweetchild's little sketch. It contained all the clues required to guess the truth: the triangular shawl, the zigzag line, the word 'palace.' "

He took a handkerchief out of his pocket and folded it along a diagonal to make a triangle.

"The shawl is the key that indicates where the treasure is hidden. The shape of the shawl corresponds to the outline of one of the mountains depicted in the frescoes. All that is required is to position the upper corner of the shawl on the peak of that mountain—thus." He put the triangle on the table and ran his finger round its edge. "And then the eye of the bird Kalavinka will indicate the spot where one must search. Not on the painted mountain, of course, but on the real one. There must be a cave or something of the kind there. Have I got it right, Commissioner, or am I mistaken?"

Everyone turned toward Gauche, who thrust out his thick lips and knitted his bushy eyebrows so that he looked exactly like a gruff old bulldog.

"I don't know how you pull these things off," he grumbled. "I read the letter back there in the cell and I haven't let it out of my hands for a second . . . All right then, listen to this."

In my father's palace are four halls that were used for official ceremonies: Winter ceremonies were held in the North Hall, summer ceremonies in the South Hall, spring ceremonies in the East Hall, and autumn ceremonies in the West Hall. You may remember the deceased Professor Sweetchild speaking about this. The murals in these halls do indeed portray the mountainous landscape that can be seen through the tall windows stretching from the floor to the ceiling. Even after all these years, if I close my eyes I can still see that landscape before me. I have traveled far and seen many things, but nowhere in the world is there any sight more beautiful! My father buried the casket under a large brown rock on one of the mountains. To discover which mountain peak it is, you must set the shawl against each of the mountains depicted on the walls in turn. The treasure is on the mountain with the outline that perfectly matches the form of the shawl. The place where the rock should be sought is indicated by the empty eye of the bird of paradise. Of course, even if someone knew in which general area to look, it would still take him many hours, or even days, to find the stone—the search would have to cover many square meters of ground. But there can be no possibility of confusion. There are many brown boulders on the mountains, but there is only one in that particular area of the mountainside. "A mote lies in the single eye, A lone brown rock among the gray," says the note in the Koran. How many times I have pictured myself pitching my tent on that mountainside and searching for that mote? But it is not to be.

The emeralds, sapphires, rubies, and diamonds are fated to lie there until an earthquake sends the boulder tumbling down the mountain. It may not happen for a hundred thousand years, but the precious stones can wait—they are eternal.

But my time is ended. That cursed shawl has drained all my strength and addled my wits. I am crushed; I have lost my reason.

"Well, he's quite right about that," the commissioner concluded, laying the half sheet of paper on the table. "That's all—the letter breaks off at that point."

"I must say that Renier-san has acted correctly," said the Japanese. "He lived an unworthy life, but he died a worthy death. Much can be forgiven him for that, and in his next birth he will be given a new chance to atone for his sins."

"I don't know about his next birth," said the Bulldog, carefully gathering the sheets of paper together and putting them into his black file, "but this time around my investigation is concluded, thank God. I shall take a little rest in Calcutta and then go back to Paris. The case is closed."

But then the Russian diplomat presented Renate with a surprise.

"The case is certainly not closed," he said loudly. "You are being too hasty again, Commissioner." He turned to face Renate and trained the twin barrels of his cold blue eyes on her. "Surely Mme. Kleber has something to say to us?"

Clarissa Stamp

THIS QUESTION CAUGHT everyone by surprise. But no, not everyone—Clarissa was astonished to realize the mother-to-be was not at all disconcerted. She turned a little paler and bit her plump lower lip for a moment, but she replied in a loud, confident voice with barely any hesitation.

"You are right, monsieur, I do have something to tell. But not to you; only to a representative of the law."

She glanced helplessly at the commissioner and implored him: "In God's name, sir, I should like to make my confession in private."

Gauche did not seem to have anticipated this turn of events. The sleuth blinked and cast a suspicious glance at Fandorin. Then he thrust out his double chin pompously and growled.

"Very well—we can go to my cabin, if it's so important to you."

Clarissa had the impression that the policeman had no idea what Mme. Kleber intended to confess to him.

But then the commissioner could hardly be blamed for that—Clarissa herself had been struggling to keep up with the rapid pace of events.

The moment the door closed behind Gauche and his companion, Clarissa glanced inquiringly at Fandorin, who seemed to be the only one who really knew what was going on. It had been a whole day since she had dared to look at him so directly, instead of stealing furtive glances or peering at him from under lowered eyelids.

She had never before seen Erast (oh, yes, she could call him that to herself) looking so dismayed. There were wrinkles on his forehead and alarm in his eyes; his fingers were drumming nervously on the table. Could it be that even this confident man, with his lightning-fast reactions, was no longer in control of the situation? Clarissa had seen him unsettled the previous night, but only for the briefest of moments, and then he had rapidly recovered his self-control.

It was after the Bombay catastrophe.

She had not appeared in public for three whole days. She told the maid she was not well, took her meals in her cabin, and went out walking only under cover of darkness, like a thief in the night.

There was nothing wrong with her health, but how could she show herself to these people who had witnessed her shame, and especially *him?* That scoundrel Gauche had made her a general laughingstock, humiliated her, destroyed her reputation. And the worst thing was that she couldn't even accuse him of lying—it was all true, every last word of it. Yes, as soon as she came into possession of her inheritance, she had gone dashing off to Paris, the city she had heard and read so much about. Like a moth to a flame. And she had singed her wings. Surely it was enough that the shameful affair had deprived her of her final shred of self-respect—why did everyone else have to know that Miss Stamp was a loose woman and gullible fool, the contemptible victim of a professional gigolo?

Mrs. Truffo had visited her twice to inquire about her health. Of course, she wanted to gloat over Clarissa's humiliation. She gasped affectedly and complained about the heat, but there was a gleam of triumph in her beady, colorless eyes: *Well, my darling, which of us is the lady now?*

The Japanese called in and said it was the custom in his country to pay a visit of condolence when someone was unwell. He offered his services as a doctor and looked at her with sympathy.

Finally Fandorin had come knocking. Clarissa had spoken to him sharply and not opened the door—she told him she had a migraine.

Never mind, she said to herself as she sat there all alone, picking listlessly at her beefsteak. Only nine days until Calcutta. Nine days was no great time to spend behind closed doors. It was child's play if you had been imprisoned for almost a quarter of a century. And it was better here than in her aunt's house. Alone in her comfortable cabin with good books for company. And once she reached Calcutta, she would quietly slip ashore and turn over a brand-new leaf.

But in the evening of the third day she began having very different thoughts. Oh, how right the Bard had been when he penned those immortal lines:

> *Such sweet release new freedom does beget,*
> *When cherished bonds are shed without regret.*

Now she really did have nothing to lose. Late that night (it was already after twelve), Clarissa had resolutely arranged her hair, powdered her face lightly, put on the ivory-colored Parisian dress that suited her so well, and stepped out into the corridor. The ship's motions tossed her from one wall to the other.

Clarissa halted outside the door of cabin number eighteen, trying not to think about anything. When she raised her hand, it faltered—but only for a moment, just a single brief moment. She knocked on the door.

Erast opened it almost immediately. He was wearing a blue Hungarian robe with cord fastenings and his white shirt showed through the wide gap in the front.

"G-good evening, Miss Stamp," he said, speaking quickly. "Has something happened?"

Then, without waiting for a reply, he added: "Please wait for a moment and I'll get changed."

When he let her in, he was already dressed in a frock coat with an impeccably knotted tie. He gestured for her to take a seat.

Clarissa sat down, looked him in the eyes, and began.

"Please do not interrupt me. If I lose the thread, it will be even worse . . . I know I am a lot older than you. How old are you? Twenty-five? Less? It doesn't matter. I am not asking you to marry me. But I like you. I am in love with you. My entire upbringing was designed to ensure that I would never under any circumstances say those words to any man, but at this moment I do not care. I do not want to lose any more time. I have already wasted the best years of my life. I am fading away without ever having blossomed. If you like me even a little, tell me so. If not, then tell me that also. Nothing could be more bitter than the shame I have already endured. And you should know that my . . . adventure in Paris was a nightmare, but I do not regret it. Better a nightmare than the stupor in which I have spent my entire life. Well, then, answer me—don't just sit there!"

My God, how could she have said those things aloud? It was something she could feel proud about.

For an instant Fandorin was taken aback; he even blinked those long lashes in a most unromantic fashion. Then he began to speak, stammering more than usual.

"Miss Stamp . . . C-Clarissa . . . I do like you. I like you very much. I admire you. And I envy you."

"You envy me? For what?" she asked, amazed.

"For your courage. For the fact that you are not afraid to b-be refused and appear ridiculous. You see, I am b-basically very timid and uncertain of myself."

"You, timid?" Clarissa asked, even more astounded.

"Yes. There are two things I am really afraid of: appearing foolish or ridiculous and . . . dropping my guard."

No, she couldn't understand this at all.

"Your guard?"

"You see, I learned very early what it means to lose someone, and it frightened me badly—probably for the rest of my life. While I am alone, my defenses against fate are strong, and I fear nothing and nobody. For a man like me, it is best to be alone."

"I have already told you, Mr. Fandorin, that I am not laying claim to a place in your life, or even a place in your heart. Let alone attempting to penetrate your defenses."

She said no more, because everything had already been said.

And just at that very moment, of course, someone started hammering on the door. She heard Milford-Stokes's agitated voice in the corridor.

"Mr. Fandorin, sir! Are you awake? Open up! Quickly! It's a conspiracy!"

"Stay here," Erast whispered. "I shall be back soon."

He went out into the corridor. Clarissa heard muffled voices, but she couldn't make out what they were saying. Five minutes later Fandorin came back. He took some small, heavy object out of a drawer and put it in his pocket, then he picked up his elegant cane and said in an anxious voice: "Wait here for a while and then go back to your cabin. Things seem to be coming to a head."

She knew now what he had meant by that. Later, when she was back in her cabin, Clarissa had heard footsteps clattering along the corridor and the sound of excited voices, but of course it had never even entered her head that death was hovering over the masts of the proud *Leviathan*.

"What is it Mme. Kleber wants to confess?" Doctor Truffo asked nervously. "M. Fandorin, please tell us what is going on. How can she be involved in all this?"

But Fandorin simply assumed an even gloomier expression and said nothing.

Rolling in time to the regular impact of the waves, *Leviathan* was sailing northward, full speed ahead, carving through the waters of the Palk Strait, which were still murky after the storm. The coastline of Ceylon was a green stripe on the distant horizon. The morning was overcast and close. From time to time a gust of hot air blew a whiff of decay in through the open windows on the windward side of the salon, but the draft could find no exit and foundered helplessly, barely even ruffling the curtains.

"I think I have made a mistake," Erast muttered, taking a step toward the door. "I'm always one step or half a step behind . . ."

When the first shot came, Clarissa did not immediately realize what the sound was—it was just a sharp crack, and any number of things could make such a sound on a ship sailing a rough sea. But then there was another.

"Those are revolver shots!" exclaimed Sir Reginald. "But where from?"

"The commissioner's cabin!" Fandorin snapped, dashing for the door.

Everybody rushed after him.

There was a third shot, and then, when they were only about twenty steps away from Gauche's cabin, a fourth.

"Stay here!" Fandorin shouted without turning around, pulling a small revolver out of his back pocket.

The others slowed down, but Clarissa was not afraid; she was determined to stay by Erast's side.

He pushed open the door of the cabin and held the revolver out in front of him. Clarissa stood on her tiptoes and peered over his shoulder.

The first thing she saw was an overturned chair. Then she saw Commissioner Gauche. He was lying on his back on the other side of the polished table that stood in the center of the room. Clarissa craned her neck to get a better look at him and shuddered: Gauche's face was hideously contorted, and there was dark blood bubbling out of the center of his forehead and dribbling onto the floor in two narrow rivulets.

Renate Kleber was in the opposite corner, huddled against the wall. She was sobbing hysterically and her teeth were chattering. There was a large black revolver with a smoking barrel in her trembling hand.

"Aaa! Ooo!" howled Mme. Kleber, pointing to the dead body. "I . . . I killed him!"

"Yes, I noticed," Fandorin said coolly.

Keeping his revolver trained on the Swiss woman, he went up to her and deftly snatched the gun out of her hands. She made no attempt to resist.

"Dr. Truffo!" Erast called, following Renate's every move closely. "In here!"

The diminutive doctor glanced into the gunsmoke-filled cabin with timid curiosity.

"Examine the body, if you please," said Fandorin.

Muttering some lamentation to himself in Italian, Truffo knelt beside the dead Gauche.

"A fatal wound to the head," he reported. "Death was instantaneous. But that's not all . . . There is a gun wound to the right elbow. And one here, to the left wrist. Three wounds in all."

"Keep looking. There were four shots."

"There are no more wounds. One of the bullets must have missed. No, wait! Here it is, in the right knee!"

"I'll tell you everything," Renate babbled, shuddering and sobbing. "Only take me out of this awful room!"

Fandorin put his little revolver in his pocket and the big one on the table.

"Very well, let us go. Doctor, inform the head of the watch what has happened here and have him put a guard on this door. And then rejoin us. There is no one but us now to conduct the investigation."

"What an ill-starred voyage!" Truffo gasped as he walked along the corridor. "Poor *Leviathan!*"

IN THE WINDSOR salon Mme. Kleber sat at the table, facing the door, and everyone else sat facing her. Fandorin was the only one who took a chair beside the murderess.

"Gentlemen, do not look at me like that," Mme. Kleber said in a pitiful voice. "I killed him, but I am the innocent victim. When I tell you what happened, you will see . . . But, for God's sake, give me some water."

The solicitous Japanese poured her some lemonade—the table had not yet been cleared after breakfast.

"So what happened?" asked Clarissa.

"Translate everything she says," Mrs. Truffo sternly instructed her husband, who had already returned. "Everything, word for word."

The doctor nodded, wiping his bald head with his handkerchief to remove the perspiration caused by walking so fast.

"Don't be afraid, madam. Just tell the truth," Sir Reginald said encouragingly to Renate. "This person is no gentleman—he has no idea how to treat a lady. But I guarantee you will be treated with respect."

These words were accompanied by a glance in Fandorin's direction—a glance filled with such fierce hatred that Clarissa Stamp was taken aback. What on earth could have happened between Erast and Milford-Stokes since the previous day to cause this hostility?

"Thank you, dear Reginald," Renate sobbed.

She drank her lemonade slowly, sniffling and moaning under her breath. Then she looked imploringly at her interrogators and began speaking.

"Gauche is no guardian of the law! He is a criminal, a madman! That loathsome shawl has driven everybody insane! Even a police commissioner!"

"You said you had something to confess to him," Clarissa reminded her in a cold, unfriendly voice. "What was it?"

"Yes, there was something I was hiding . . . something important. I was going to confess everything, but first I wanted to expose the commissioner!"

"Expose him? As what?" Sir Reginald asked sympathetically.

Mme. Kleber stopped crying and solemnly declared: "A murderer. Renier did not kill himself. Commissioner Gauche killed him!"

Seeing how astounded her listeners were by this claim, she continued rapidly. "It's obvious! You try smashing your skull by running at the wall in a room only six square meters! It can't be done. If Charles had decided to kill himself, he would have taken off his tie, tied it to the ventilation grill, and jumped off a chair. No, Gauche killed him! He struck him on the head with some heavy object and then made it look like suicide by smashing the dead man's head against the wall."

"But why would the commissioner want to kill Renier?" Clarissa asked with a skeptical shake of her head. Mme. Kleber was obviously talking nonsense.

"I told you—greed had driven him completely insane! That shawl is to blame for everything. Either Gauche was angry with Charles for burning the shawl, or he didn't believe him—I don't know which. But anyway, it's quite clear that Gauche killed him. And when I told him so to his face, he didn't try to deny it. He took out his pistol and started waving it about and threatening me. He said that if I didn't keep my mouth shut, I'd go the same way as Renier . . ." Renate began sniffling again and then—miracle of miracles—the baronet offered her his handkerchief.

What mysterious transformation was this? He had always shunned Renate like the plague.

"Then he put the pistol on the table and started shaking me by the shoulders. I was so afraid, so afraid! I don't know how I managed to push him away and grab the gun from the table. It was terrible! I ran away from him and he started chasing me round the table. I turned and pressed the trigger. I kept pressing it until he fell . . . and then M. Fandorin came in."

Renate began sobbing loudly. Milford-Stokes patted her shoulder tentatively, as if he were touching a rattlesnake.

Clarissa started when the silence was suddenly broken by the sound of loud clapping.

"Bravo!" said Fandorin with a mocking smile, still clapping his hands. "Bravo, Mme. Kleber. You are a great actress."

"How dare you!" exclaimed Sir Reginald, choking with indignation, but Erast cut him short with a wave of his hand.

"Sit down and listen. I shall tell you what really happened." Fandorin was absolutely calm and seemed quite certain he was right. "Mme. Kleber is not only a superb actress; she is quite exceptionally talented in every respect. She possesses true brilliance and breadth of imagination. Unfortunately, her greatest talent lies in the criminal sphere. You are an accomplice to a whole series of murders, madam. Or rather, not an accomplice, but the instigator, the leading lady. It was Renier who was *your* accomplice."

"Look," Renate appealed plaintively to Sir Reginald. "Now he's gone crazy, too. And he was so calm and quiet."

"The most amazing thing about you is the superhuman speed with which you react to a situation," Erast continued, as though she hadn't even spoken. "You never defend yourself—you always strike first, Mlle. Sanfon. You don't mind if I call you by your real name, do you?"

"Sanfon! Marie Sanfon? Her?" Dr. Truffo exclaimed.

Clarissa realized she was sitting there with her mouth open. Milford-Stokes jerked his hand away from Renate's shoulder. Renate herself looked at Fandorin pityingly.

Fandorin said: "Yes, you see before you the legendary, brilliant, ruthless international adventuress Marie Sanfon. Her style is breathtakingly daring and inventive. She leaves no clues or witnesses. And, last but not least, she cares nothing for human life. The testimony of Charles Renier, which we shall come to later, is a mixture of truth and lies. I do not know, my lady, when you met him or under what circumstances, but two things are beyond all doubt. First, Renier genuinely loved you and tried to divert suspicion from you until his very last moment. And second: It was you who persuaded the son of the Emerald Rajah to go in search of his inheritance— otherwise why would he have waited for so many years? You made Lord Littleby's acquaintance, acquired all the information you required, and worked out a p-plan. Obviously at first you had counted on obtaining the shawl by cunning and flattery—after all, his lordship had no idea of the significance of that scrap of cloth. But you soon became convinced it would never work: Littleby was absolutely fanatical about his collection and he would never have agreed to part with any of his pieces. It was not possible to obtain the shawl by stealth, either—there were armed guards constantly on duty beside the display case. So you decided to keep the risk to a minimum and leave no traces, the way you always prefer to do things. Tell me, did you know Lord Littleby had not gone away, that he was at home on that fateful evening? I am sure you did. You needed to bind Renier to you with blood. It was not he who killed the servants—you did."

"Impossible!" said Dr. Truffo, throwing his hand in the air. "Without medical training and practice, no woman could give nine injections in three minutes! It's quite out of the question."

"First, she could have prepared nine loaded syringes in advance. And second . . ." Erast took an apple from a dish and cut a piece off it with an elegant flourish. "M. Renier may have had no experience in using a syringe, but Marie Sanfon does. Do not forget that she was raised in a convent of the Gray Sisters of St. Vincent, an order founded to provide medical assistance to the poor, and their novices are trained from an early age to work in hospitals, leper colonies, and hospices. These nuns are highly qualified nurses—and, as I recall, young Marie was one of the best."

"But of course. I forgot. You're right," the doctor said, lowering his head penitently. "Please continue. I shall not interrupt you again."

"Well then, Paris, the Rue de Grenelle, the evening of the fifteenth of March. T-two people arrive at the mansion of Lord Littleby: a young doctor with a dark complexion and a nurse with the cowl of her gray nun's habit pulled down over her eyes. The doctor presents a piece of p-paper with a seal from the mayor's office and asks for everyone in the house to gather together. He probably says it is getting late and they still have a lot of work to do. The inoculations are given by the nun—deftly, quickly, painlessly. Afterward the pathologist will not discover any sign of bruising at the sites of the injections. Marie Sanfon has not forgotten what she learned in her charitable youth. What happened after that is clear, so I shall omit the details: The servants fall asleep, the criminals climb the stairs to the second floor, Renier has a brief tussle with the master of the house. The murderer fails to notice that his gold *Leviathan* badge has been left behind in Lord Littleby's hand. Which meant that afterward, my lady, you had to give him yours—it would be easier for you to avoid suspicion than the captain's first mate. And I expect you had more confidence in yourself than in him."

Up to this point Clarissa had been gazing spellbound at Erast, but now she glanced briefly at Renate. She was listening carefully, an expression of offended amazement on her face. If she was Marie Sanfon, she had not given herself away yet.

"I began to suspect both of you from the day that poor African supposedly fell on top of you," Fandorin said to Renate. He bit off a piece of the apple with his even white teeth. "That was Renier's fault, of course— he panicked and got carried away. You would have invented something more cunning. Let me try to reconstruct the sequence of events, and you can correct me if I get any of the details wrong. All right?"

Renate shook her head mournfully and propped her plump cheek on her hand.

"Renier saw you to your cabin—you certainly had things to discuss, since your accomplice states in his confession that the shawl had mysteriously disappeared only a short while before. You went into your cabin, saw the huge Negro rifling through your things, and for a moment you must have been frightened—if you are acquainted at all with the feeling of fear. But a second later your heart leapt when you saw the precious shawl on the Negro's neck. That explained everything: When the runaway slave was searching Renier's cabin, the colorful piece of material had caught his eye and he decided to wear it round his massive neck. When you cried out, Renier came running in, saw the shawl, and, unable to control himself, pulled out his dirk. You had to invent the story about the mythical attack—to lie down on the floor and hoist the Negro's hot, heavy body onto yourself. I expect that was not very pleasant, was it?"

"I protest, this is all pure invention!" Sir Reginald exclaimed heatedly. "Of course the Negro attacked Mme. Kleber, it is obvious! You are fantasizing again, mister Russian diplomat!"

"Not in the least," Erast said mildly, casting a look of either sorrow or pity at the baronet. "I told you I had seen slaves from the Ndanga people before, when I was a prisoner of the Turks. Do you know why they are valued so highly? Because, for all their great strength and stamina, they are exceptionally gentle; they have absolutely no aggressive instinct. They are a tribe of farmers, not hunters; they have never fought a war against anyone. The Ndanga could not possibly have attacked Mme. Kleber, not even if he was frightened to death. M. Aono was surprised, at the time, that the savage's fingers had left no bruises on the delicate skin of your neck. Surely that is strange?"

Renate bowed her head thoughtfully, as though she herself were amazed at the oversight.

"Now let us recall the murder of Professor Sweetchild. The moment it became clear that the Indologist was close to solving the mystery, you, my lady, asked him not to hurry, but to tell the whole story in detail from the beginning, and meanwhile you sent your accomplice out, supposedly to fetch your shawl, but in actual fact to make preparations for the murder. Your partner understood what he had to do without being told."

"It's not true!" Renate protested. "Gentlemen, you are my witnesses! Renier volunteered of his own accord! Don't you remember? M. Milford-Stokes, I swear I'm telling the truth. I asked you first, do you remember?"

"That's right," confirmed Sir Reginald. "That was what happened."

"A t-trick for simpletons," said Fandorin, with a flourish of the fruit knife. "You knew perfectly well, my lady, that the baronet could not stand you and never indulged your caprices. Your little operation was carried through very deftly—but on this occasion, alas, not quite neatly enough. You failed to shift the blame onto M. Aono, although you came very close to succeeding." At this point Erast lowered his eyes modestly to allow his listeners to recall precisely who had demolished the chain of evidence against the Japanese.

He is not entirely without vanity, thought Clarissa, but to her eyes this characteristic appeared quite charming and only seemed to make the young man even more attractive. As usual, it was poetry that provided the resolution of the paradox:

> *For even the beloved's limitation*
> *Is worthy, in love's eyes, of adoration.*

Ah, mister diplomat, how little you know of Englishwomen. I believe you will be making a protracted stay in Calcutta.

Fandorin maintained his pause, as yet quite unaware that his faults were worthy of adoration, or that he would arrive at his new post later than planned, and then continued.

"Now your situation has become genuinely perilous. Renier described it quite eloquently in his letter. And so you take a terrible decision that is nonetheless, in its own way, a stroke of genius: to sink the ship together with the punctilious commissioner of police, the witnesses, and a thousand others. What do the lives of a thousand people mean to you, if they are preventing you from becoming the richest woman in the world? Or, even worse, if they pose a threat to your life and liberty?"

Clarissa looked at Renate with horrified fascination. Could this young woman, who was rather bitchy but otherwise seemed perfectly ordinary, really be so utterly wicked? It couldn't be true! But not to believe Erast was also impossible. He was so eloquent and so handsome!

A huge tear the size of a bean slithered down Renate's cheek. Her eyes were filled with mute appeal: *Why are you tormenting me like this? What did I ever do to you?* The martyr's hand slipped down to her belly and her face contorted in misery.

"Fainting won't help," Fandorin advised her calmly. "The best way to bring someone around is to massage the face with a slap. And don't pretend to be weak and helpless. Dr. Truffo and Dr. Aono consider you as strong as an ox. Sit down, Sir Reginald!" There was a steely ring to Erast's voice. "You will have your chance to intervene on behalf of your damsel in distress—afterward, when I am finished. Meanwhile, ladies and gentlemen, you should know that we have Sir Reginald to thank for saving all our lives. If not for his . . . unusual habit of taking the ship's position every three hours, we would have been breakfasting on the b-bottom of the sea today. Or rather others would have been breakfasting on us."

"Where's Polonius?" the baronet blurted out with a laugh. "At supper. Not where he eats, but where he is eaten." Very funny.

Clarissa shuddered. A larger wave than usual had struck the side of the ship, clinking the dishes against one another on the table and setting Big Ben swaying ponderously to and fro.

"Other people are no more than extras in your play, my lady, and the extras have never really meant anything to you. Especially in a matter of some fifty million pounds. A sum like that is hard to resist. It led poor Gauche astray, for instance. But how clumsy our master detective was as a murderer! You are right, of course—the unfortunate Renier did not commit suicide. I would have realized that for myself if your assault tactics had not thrown me off-balance. What force does a letter of f-farewell carry on its own? From the tone of the letter, it is clearly not a final testament—Renier is still playing for time, hoping to plead insanity. Above all, he is relying on you, Mlle. Sanfon; he has grown used to trusting you implicitly. Gauche calmly tore off a third of a page at the point he thought was best suited for an ending. How clumsy! The prospect of the treasure of Brahmapur had driven our commissioner completely insane. After all, it was his salary for three hundred thousand years!" Fandorin gave a sad chuckle. "Do you remember how enviously Gauche told us the story of the gardener who sold his stainless reputation to a banker for such a good price?"

"But why kill M. Renier?" asked the Japanese. "The shawr had been burned."

"Renier very much wanted the commissioner to believe that; to make his story more convincing, he even gave away the shawl's secret. But Gauche did not believe him," said Fandorin. He paused for a moment and said: "And he was right not to."

You could have heard a pin drop in the salon. Clarissa had just breathed in, but she forgot to breathe out. She wondered why her chest felt so tight; then she realized and released her breath.

"Then the shawl is safe?" the doctor asked tentatively, as though afraid of startling a rare bird. "But where is it?"

"That scrap of fine material has changed hands three times this morning. At first Renier had it. The commissioner did not believe what was in the letter, so he searched his prisoner and f-found the shawl on him. The thought of the riches that were almost in his grasp deranged him, and he committed murder. The temptation was too great. Everything fitted together so neatly: It said in the letter that the shawl had been burned; the murderer had confessed to everything; and the steamer was heading for Calcutta, which is only a stone's throw from Brahmapur. So Gauche went for broke. He struck his unsuspecting prisoner on the head with some heavy object, rigged things to look like a suicide, and came back here to wait for the sentry to discover the body. But then Mlle. Sanfon played her hand and outsmarted both of us—the commissioner and myself. You are a most remarkable woman, my lady," said Erast, turning toward Renate. "I had expected you to start making excuses and blaming your accomplice for everything now that he is dead. It would have been very simple, after all. But no, that is not your way. You guessed from the way the commissioner was behaving that he had the shawl, and your first thought was not to defend, but to attack. You wanted to get back the key to the treasure, and you did!"

"Why must I listen to this nonsense?" Renate exclaimed in a tearful voice. "You, monsieur, are nobody and nothing. A mere foreigner! I demand that my case be handled by one of the ship's senior officers!"

The little doctor suddenly straightened his shoulders, stroked a strand of hair forward across his olive-skinned bald patch, and declared: "There is a senior ship's officer present, madam. You may regard this interrogation as sanctioned by the ship's command. Continue, M. Fandorin. You say this woman managed to get the shawl away from the commissioner?"

"I am certain of it. I do not know how she managed to get hold of Gauche's revolver. The poor fool was probably not afraid of her at all. But somehow she managed to and demanded the shawl. When the old man wouldn't give it to her, she shot him, first in one arm, then in the other, then in the knee. She tortured him! Where did you learn to shoot like that, madam? Four shots, all perfectly placed. I'm afraid it is rather hard to believe that Gauche chased you round the table with a wounded leg and two useless arms. After the third shot he couldn't stand any more pain and he gave you the shawl. Then you finished your victim off with a shot to the center of his forehead."

"Oh, God!" Mrs. Truffo exclaimed unnecessarily.

But Clarissa was more concerned about something else.

"Then she has the shawl?"

"Yes," said Erast with a nod.

"Nonsense! Rubbish! You're all crazy!" Renate (or Marie Sanfon?) laughed hysterically. "Lord, this is such grotesque nonsense!"

"This is easy to check," said the Japanese. "We must search Mme. Kleber. If she does not have the shawr, then M. Fandorin is mistaken. In such cases in Japan, we cut our berries open."

"No man's hands shall ever search a lady in my presence!" declared Sir Reginald, rising menacingly to his feet.

"What about a woman's hands?" asked Clarissa. "Mrs. Truffo and I will search this person."

"Oh, yes, it would take no time at all," the doctor's wife agreed eagerly.

"Do as you like with me," said Renate, pressing her hands together like a sacrificial victim. "But afterward you will be ashamed."

The men went out and Mrs. Truffo searched the prisoner with quite remarkable dexterity. She glanced at Clarissa and shook her head.

Clarissa suddenly felt afraid for poor Erast. Could he really have made a mistake?

"The shawl is very light," she said. "Let me have a look."

It was strange to feel her hands on the body of another woman, but Clarissa bit her lip and carefully examined every seam, every fold, and every gather in the underwear. The shawl was not there.

"You will have to get entirely undressed," she said resolutely. It was terrible, but it was even more terrible to think that the shawl wouldn't be found. What a blow for Erast! How could he bear it?

Renate raised her arms submissively to make it easier to remove her dress and said timidly: "In the name of all that is holy, Mlle. Stamp, do not harm my child."

Gritting her teeth, Clarissa set about unfastening Renate's dress. When she reached the third button, there was a knock at the door and Erast's cheerful voice called out: "Ladies, stop the search! May we come in?"

"Yes, yes, come in!" Clarissa shouted, quickly fastening the buttons.

The men had a mysterious air about them. They took up a position by the table without saying a word. Then, with a magician's flourish, Erast spread out on the tablecloth a triangular piece of fabric that shimmered with all the colors of the rainbow.

"The shawl!" Renate screeched.

"Where did you find it?" asked Clarissa, feeling totally confused.

"While you were searching Mlle. Sanfon, we were busy, too," Fandorin explained, looking smug. "It occurred to me that this prudent individual could have hidden the incriminating clue in the commissioner's cabin. But she only had a few seconds, so she could not have hidden it too well. It did not take long to find the crumpled shawl where she had thrust it under the edge of the carpet. So now we can all admire the famous bird of paradise, Kalavinka."

Clarissa joined the others at the table and they all gazed spellbound at the scrap of cloth for which so many people had died.

The shawl was shaped like an isosceles triangle, with sides no longer than about twenty inches. The colors of the painting were brilliant and intense: a strange creature with pointed breasts, half woman and half bird like the sirens of ancient times, stood with its wings unfurled against a background of brightly colored trees and fruit. Her face was turned in profile, and instead of an eye the long curving lashes framed a small hole that had been painstakingly trimmed with stitching of gold thread. Clarissa thought she had never seen anything more beautiful in her life.

"Yes, it's the shawl, all right," said Sir Reginald. "But how does your find prove Mme. Kleber's guilt?"

"What about the travel bag?" Fandorin asked in a low voice. "Do you remember the travel bag we found in the captain's launch yesterday? One of the things I saw in it was a cloak we have often seen on the shoulders of Mme. Kleber. The travel bag is now part of the material evidence in the case. No doubt other items belonging to our good friend here will also be found in it."

"What reply can you make to that, madam?" the doctor asked Renate.

"The truth," she replied, and in that instant her face changed beyond all recognition.

Reginald Milford-Stokes

. . . THEN SUDDENLY HER face was transformed beyond all recognition, as though someone had waved a magic wand and the weak, helpless little lamb crushed by a cruel fate was instantly changed into a ravening she-wolf. She straightened her shoulders and lifted her chin, her eyes suddenly ablaze and her nostrils flaring as if the woman before us had turned into a deadly predator—no, not a she-wolf, one of the big cats, a panther or lioness who has scented fresh blood. I recoiled; I could not help it. My protection was certainly no longer required here!

The transformed Mme. Kleber cast Fandorin a glance of searing hatred that pierced even that imperturbable gentleman's defenses. He shuddered.

I could sympathize entirely with this strange woman's feelings. My own attitude to the contemptible Russian has also changed completely. He is a terrible man, a dangerous lunatic with a fantastic, monstrously depraved imagination. How could I ever have respected and trusted him? I can hardly even believe it now!

I simply do not know how to tell you this, my sweet Emily. My hand is trembling with indignation as it holds the pen. At first I intended to conceal it from you, but I have decided to tell you after all. Otherwise it will be hard for you to understand the reason for the metamorphosis in my feelings toward Fandorin.

Yesterday night, after all the shocks and upheavals I have described above, Fandorin and I had an extremely strange conversation that left me feeling both perplexed and furious. The Russian approached me and thanked me for saving the ship, and then, positively oozing sympathy and stammering over every word, he began talking the most unimaginable, monstrous drivel. What he said was literally this—I remember it word for word: "I know of your grief, Sir Reginald. Commissioner Gauche told me everything a long time ago. Of course, it is none of my business, and I have thought long and hard before deciding to speak to you about it, but when I see how greatly you are suffering, I cannot remain indifferent. The only reason I dare say all this is that I have suffered a similar grievous loss, and my reason was also undermined by the shock. I have managed to preserve my reason, and even hone its edge to greater sharpness, but the price I had to pay for survival was a large piece of my heart. But, believe me, in your situation there is no other way. Do not hide from the truth, no matter how terrible it might be; do not seek refuge in illusion. And, above all, do not blame yourself. It is not your fault that the horses bolted, or that your pregnant wife was thrown out of the carriage and killed. This is a trial, a test ordained for you by fate. I cannot understand what need there could possibly be to subject a man to such cruelty, but one thing I do know: If you do not pass this test, it means the end, the death of your very soul."

At first I simply could not understand what the scoundrel was getting at. Then I realized! He imagined that you, my precious Emily, were dead! That you were the pregnant lady who was thrown from a carriage and killed! If I had not been so outraged, I should have laughed in the crazy diplomat's face! How dare he say such a thing, when I know that you are waiting there for me beneath the azure skies of the islands of paradise! Every hour brings me closer to you, my darling Emily. And now there is nobody and nothing that can stop me.

Only—it is very strange—I cannot for the life of me remember how you came to be in Tahiti, alone without me. There certainly must have been some important reason for it. No matter. When we meet, my dear friend, you will explain everything to me.

But let me return to my story.

Mme. Kleber straightened up, suddenly seeming taller (it is amazing how much the impression of height depends on posture and the set of the head), and began speaking, for the most part addressing Fandorin.

"All these stories you have hatched up here are absolute nonsense. There is not a single piece of proof or hard evidence. Nothing but assump-

tions and unfounded speculation. Yes, my real name in Marie Sanfon, but
no court in the world has ever been able to charge me with any crime. Yes,
my enemies have often slandered me and intrigued against me, but I am
strong. Marie Sanfon's nerve is not so easily broken. I am guilty of only
one thing—of loving a criminal and a madman to distraction. Charles and
I were secretly married, and it is his child that I am carrying under my
heart. It was Charles who insisted on keeping our marriage secret. If this
misdemeanor is a crime, then I am willing to face a judge and jury—but
you may be sure, mister homegrown detective, that an experienced lawyer
will scatter your chimerical accusations like smoke. What charges can you
actually bring against me? That in my youth I lived in a convent with the
Gray Sisters and eased the suffering of the poor? Yes, I used to give myself
injections, but what of that? The moral suffering caused by a life of secrecy
and a difficult pregnancy led me to become addicted to morphine, but now
I have found the strength to break free of that pernicious habit. My secret
but entirely legitimate husband insisted I should embark on this voyage
under an assumed name. That was how the mythical Swiss banker Kleber
came to be invented. The deception caused me suffering, but how could I
refuse the man I loved? I had absolutely no idea about his other life and his
fatal passion, or his insane plans!

"Charles told me it was not appropriate for the captain's first mate
to take his wife with him on a cruise, but he was concerned for the health
of our dear child and could not bear to be parted from me. He said it would
be best if I sailed under a false name. What kind of crime is that, I ask
you?

"I could see that Charles was not himself, that he was in the grip of
strange passions I did not understand, but never in my worst nightmare
could I have dreamed he committed that terrible crime in the Rue de
Grenelle! And I had no idea he was the son of an Indian rajah. It comes as
a shock to me that my child will be a quarter Indian. The poor little mite,
with a madman for a father. I have no doubt at all that Charles has been
completely out of his mind for the last few days. How could anyone sane
attempt to sink a ship? It is obviously the act of a sick mind. Of course I
knew nothing at all about that insane plan!"

At this point Fandorin interrupted her and asked with a hideous little grin: "And what about your cloak, packed so thoughtfully in the travel bag?"

Mme. Kleber—Miss Sanfon—that is, Mme. Renier . . . or Mme. Bagdassar? I do not know what I ought to call her. Very well, let her remain Mme. Kleber, since that is what I am used to. Mme. Kleber replied to her inquisitor with great dignity: "My husband evidently packed everything ready for our escape and was intending to wake me at the last minute."

But Fandorin was unrelenting. "But you were not asleep," he said with a haughty expression on his face. "We saw you when we were walking along the corridor. You were fully clothed and even had a shawl on your shoulders."

"I could not sleep because I felt strangely alarmed," replied Mme. Kleber. "I must have felt in my heart that something was wrong . . . I was shivering and I felt cold, so I put on my shawl. Is that a crime?"

I was glad to see that the amateur prosecutor was stumped. The accused continued with calm self-assurance: "The idea that I supposedly tortured that other madman, M. Gauche, is absolutely incredible. I told you the truth. The old blockhead went insane with greed and he threatened to kill me. I have no idea how I managed to hit him with all four bullets. But it is pure coincidence. Providence itself must have guided my hand. No, sir, you cannot make anything of that, either!"

Fandorin's smug self-assurance had been shattered. "I beg your pardon!" he cried excitedly. "But we found the shawl! You hid it under the carpet!"

"Yet another unfounded assertion!" retorted Mme. Kleber. "Of course the shawl was hidden by Gauche, who had taken it from my poor husband. And despite all your vile insinuations, I am grateful to you, sir, for returning my property."

And so saying, she calmly stood up, walked over to the table, and took the shawl!

"I am the legitimate wife of the legitimate heir of the Diamond Rajah," declared this astonishing woman. "I have a marriage certificate. I am carrying Bagdassar's grandson in my womb. It is true that my deceased husband committed a number of serious crimes, but what has that to do with me and our inheritance?"

Miss Stamp jumped to her feet and tried to grab the shawl from Mme. Kleber.

"The lands and property of the rajah of Brahmapur were confiscated by the British government," my fellow countrywoman declared resolutely. "That means the treasure belongs to her majesty Queen Victoria!"—and there was no denying that she was right.

"Just a moment!" our good Dr. Truffo put in. "Although I am Italian by birth, I am a citizen of France and I represent her interests here. The rajah's treasure was the personal property of his family and did not belong to the principality of Brahmapur, which means its confiscation was illegal! Charles Renier became a French citizen of his own free will. He committed a most heinous crime on the territory of his adopted country. Under the laws of the French Republic, the punishment for such crimes, especially when committed out of purely venal motives, includes the expropriation of the criminal's property by the state. Give back the shawl, madam! It belongs to France." And he also took a defiant grip on the edge of the shawl.

The situation was a stalemate, and the crafty Fandorin took advantage of it. With the Byzantine cunning typical of his nation, he said loudly: "This is a serious dispute that requires arbitration. Permit me, as the representative of a neutral power, to take temporary possession of the shawl so that you do not tear it to pieces. I shall place it over here, a little distance away from the contending parties."

And so saying, he took the shawl and carried it across to the side table on the leeward side of the salon, where the windows were closed. You will see later, my beloved Emily, why I mention these details.

And so the bone of contention, the shawl, was lying there on the side table, a bright triangle of shimmering color sparkling with gold. Fandorin was standing with his back to the shawl in the pose of a guard of honor. The rest of us were bunched together at the dining table. Add to this the rustling of the curtains on the windward side of the room, the dim light of an overcast afternoon, and the irregular swaying of the floor beneath our feet, and the stage was set for the final scene.

"No one will dare to take from the rajah's grandson what is his by right!" Mme. Kleber declared, her hands set on her hips. "I am a Belgian subject and the court hearing will take place in Brussels. All I need to do for the jury to decide in my favor is promise that a quarter of the inheritance will be donated to charitable work in Belgium . . . A quarter of the inheritance is eleven billion Belgian francs, five times the annual income of the entire kingdom of Belgium!"

Miss Stamp laughed in her face: "You underestimate Britannia, my dear. Do you really think your pitiful Belgium will be allowed to decide the fate of fifty million pounds? With that money we shall build hundreds of mighty battleships and triple the size of our fleet, which is already the greatest in the world! We shall bring order to the entire planet!"

Miss Stamp is an intelligent woman. Indeed, civilization could only benefit if our treasury were enriched by such a fantastic sum. Britain is the most progressive and freest country in the world. All the peoples of the earth would benefit if their lives were arranged after the British example.

But Mr. Truffo was of a different opinion entirely. "This sum of a billion and a half French francs will not only finance France's recovery from the tragic consequences of the war with Germany, but will allow her to create the most modern and well-equipped army in the whole of Europe. You English have never been Europeans. You are islanders! You do not share in the interests of Europe. M. de Perier, who until recently was the captain's second mate and is now in temporary command of the *Leviathan,* will not allow the shawl to go to the English. I shall bring M. de Perier here immediately, and he will place the shawl in the captain's safe!"

Then everyone began talking at once, all trying to shout one another down. The doctor became so belligerent that he even dared push me in the chest, and Mme. Kleber kicked Miss Stamp on the ankle.

Then Fandorin took a plate from the table and smashed it on the floor with a loud crash. As everyone gazed at him in amazement, the cunning Byzantine said: "We shall not solve our problem in this way. You are getting too heated, ladies and gentlemen. Why don't we let a bit of fresh air into the salon? It has become rather stuffy in here."

He went over to the windows on the leeward side and began opening them one by one. When Fandorin opened the window above the side table on which the shawl was lying, something startling happened: The draft immediately snatched at the feathery material, which trembled and fluttered and suddenly flew up into the air. Everyone gasped in horror as the silk triangle went flying away across the deck, swayed twice over the handrails—as if it were waving good-bye to us—and sailed off into the distance, gradually sinking lower and lower. We all stood there, dumbfounded, following its leisurely flight until it ended at some distant point among the lazy white-capped waves.

"How very clumsy I am," said Fandorin, breaking the deadly silence. "All that money lost at sea! Now neither Britain nor France will be able to impose its will on the world. What a terrible misfortune for civilization. And it was half a billion rubles. Enough for Russia to repay its entire foreign debt."

That was when things really started moving.

With a war cry, halfway between a whistle and a hiss, that made my skin crawl, Mme. Kleber grabbed a fruit knife from the table and made a mad dash at the Russian. The sudden attack caught him by surprise. The blunt silver blade swung through the air and stabbed Fandorin just below his collarbone, but I do not think it went very deep. The diplomat's white shirt was stained red with blood. My first thought was: God does exist, and he punishes scoundrels. As he staggered backward, the villainous Byzantine dodged to one side, but the enraged Fury was not satisfied with the damage she had inflicted, and, taking a firmer grip on the handle, she raised her hand to strike again.

And then our Japanese colleague, who had so far taken no part in the discussion and remained almost unnoticed, astonished us all. With a piercing cry like the call of an eagle, he leapt up almost as high as the ceiling and struck Mme. Kleber on the wrist with the toe of his shoe! Not even in the Italian circus have I ever seen a trick to match it!

The fruit knife went flying into the air, the Japanese landed in a squatting position, and Mme. Kleber staggered backward with her face contorted, clutching her injured wrist.

But still she would not abandon her bloodthirsty intent! When she felt her back strike the grandfather clock (I have already written to you about that monster), she suddenly bent down and lifted up the hem of her dress. I was already dazed by the speed of events, but this was too much! I caught a glimpse (forgive me, my sweet Emily, for mentioning this) of a slim ankle clad in a silk stocking and the frills of a pair of pink pantaloons, and a second later, when Mme. Kleber straightened up, a pistol had appeared out of nowhere in her left hand. It was very small and double-barreled, finished in mother-of-pearl.

I do not dare repeat to you word for word exactly what this creature said to Fandorin—you probably do not know the meaning of such expressions, anyway. The general sense of her speech, which was most forceful and expressive, was that the "rotten pervert" (I employ euphemisms, for Mme. Kleber expressed herself rather more crudely) would pay for his lousy trick with his life. "But first I shall neutralize this venomous yellow snake!" cried the mother-to-be: She took a step forward and fired at Mr. Aono, who fell on his back with a dull groan.

Mme. Kleber took another step and pointed her pistol straight at Fandorin's face. "I really do never miss," she hissed. "And I'm going to put a bullet right between those pretty blue eyes of yours."

The Russian stood there, pressing his hand to the red patch spreading across his shirt. He was not exactly quaking in fear, but he was definitely pale.

The *Leviathan* heeled over harder than usual—a large wave had struck it amidships—and I saw that ugly monstrosity, Big Ben, lean farther and farther over, and then . . . it collapsed—right onto Mme. Kleber! There was a dull thud as the hard wood struck the back of her head and the irrepressible woman fell flat on her face, pinned down by the heavy oak tower.

Everyone dashed across to Mr. Aono, who was still lying on the floor with a bullet in his chest. The wounded man was conscious and kept trying to get up, but Dr. Truffo squatted down beside him and pressed on his shoulders to make him lie back. The doctor cut open his clothes to examine the entry wound and frowned.

"It is nothing," the Japanese said in a low voice through clenched teeth. "The rung is barery grazed."

"And the bullet," Truffo asked in alarm. "Can you feel it, my dear colleague? Where is it?"

"I think the burret is stuck in the right shoulder brade," replied Mr. Aono, adding with astonishing composure, "The rower reft quadrant. You will have to section the bone from the back. That is very difficult. Please forgive me for causing you such inconvenience."

Then Fandorin did something very mysterious. He leaned over the wounded man and said in a quiet voice: "Well, now, Aono-san, your dream has come true—now you are my *onjin*. I am afraid the free Japanese lessons will have to be canceled."

Mr. Aono, however, seemed to understand this gibberish perfectly well and he even managed a feeble smile.

When the Japanese gentleman had been bandaged up and carried away on a stretcher by sailors, the doctor turned his attention to Mme. Kleber.

We were really surprised to discover that the solid oak had not smashed her skull in; it had only given her a substantial bump on the head. We pulled the stunned criminal out from under London's finest sight and moved her to an armchair.

"I'm afraid the baby will not survive the shock," sighed Mrs. Truffo. "The poor little thing is not to blame for his mother's sins."

"The baby will be all right," her husband assured her. "This . . . lady possesses such tremendous vitality that she will certainly have a healthy child, with an easy birth at full term."

Fandorin added, with a cynicism that I found offensive: "There is reason to hope that the birth will take place in a prison hospital."

"It is terrible to think what will be born from that womb," Miss Stamp said with a shudder.

"In any case, the pregnancy will save her from the guillotine," remarked the doctor.

"Or from the gallows," laughed Miss Stamp, reminding us of the bitter wrangling between Commissioner Gauche and Inspector Jackson.

"The most serious threat she faces is a short prison sentence for the attempted murder of Mr. Aono," Fandorin remarked with a sour face. "And extenuating circumstances will be found for that: temporary insanity, shock, the pregnancy. As she herself demonstrated quite brilliantly, it will be absolutely impossible to prove anything else. I assure you, Marie Sanfon will be at liberty again very soon."

It is strange, but none of us mentioned the shawl, as if it had never even existed, as if the scrap of silk that had carried off into oblivion a hundred British battleships and the French *revanche* had also taken with it the feverish stupor that had shrouded our minds and souls.

Fandorin stopped beside his fallen Big Ben, which was now fit for nothing but the rubbish dump: The glass was broken, the mechanism was smashed, and the oak panel was cracked from top to bottom.

"A magnificent clock," said the Russian, confirming yet again the well-known fact that the Slavs have no artistic taste whatever. "I shall certainly have it repaired and take it with me."

The *Leviathan* gave a mighty hoot on its whistle, no doubt in greeting to some passing vessel, and I began thinking that soon, very soon, in just two or three weeks, I shall arrive in Tahiti and we shall meet again, my adored little wife. Everything else is mere fog and vapor, an insubstantial fantasy.

We shall be together and we shall be happy in our island paradise, where the sun always shines.

In anticipation of that joyful day,
I remain your tenderly loving

Reginald Milford-Stokes

About the Author

Boris Akunin is the pen name of Grigory Chkhartishvili, who was born in the republic of Georgia in 1956; he is a philologist, critic, essayist, and translator of Japanese. He published his first detective stories in 1998 and in a very short time has become one of the most widely read authors in Russia. He has written ten Erast Fandorin novels to date, and is the author of two other series as well. Akunin enjoys almost legendary popularity in Russia. He lives in Moscow.

About the Translator

Andrew Bromfield was born in Hull in Yorkshire, England. He has lived in Moscow for long periods, where he cofounded the literary journal *Glas,* and now lives and works in rural Surrey. He is best known for his acclaimed translations of the series and novels of Victor Pelevin, including *The Life of Insects, Buddha's Little Finger,* and *Homo Zapiens.*

About the Type

This book is set in Fournier, a typeface named for
Pierre Simon Fournier, the youngest son of a
French printing family. He started out engraving
woodblocks and large capitals, then moved on to
fonts of type. In 1736 he began his own foundry and
made several important contributions in the field of
type design; he is said to have cut 147 alphabets of
his own creation. Fournier is probably best
remembered as the designer of St. Augustine
Ordinaire, a face that served as the model for
Monotype's Fournier, which was released in 1925.